FEB 1 2 2020

HUDSON
PUBLIC LIBRARY COLLECTION

FIC
KARDON

Kardon, R.D.

Flygirl

HUDSON PUBLIC LIBRARY
3 WASHINGTON STREET
HUDSON, MA 01749
ADULT: 978-568-9644
CHILDREN: 978-568-9645
www.hudsonpubliclibrary.com

FLYGIRL

a novel

by

R. D. KARDON

FBI Anti-Piracy Warning: The unauthorized reproduction or distribution of a copyrighted work is illegal. Criminal copyright infringement, including infringement without monetary gain, is investigated by the FBI and is punishable by up to five years in federal prison and a fine of $250,000.

Flygirl
First Edition
Copyright © 2019 R. D. Kardon
All rights reserved. Printed in the United States of America.
For information, address Acorn Publishing, LLC,
3943 Irvine Blvd. Ste. 218, Irvine, CA 92602.

No part of this book may be used or reproduced in any manner whatsoever, including Internet usage, without written permission from the author.

This story is a work of fiction. References to real people, events, establishments, organizations, or locales are intended only to provide a sense of authenticity and are used fictitiously. All other characters, and all incidents and dialogue are drawn from the author's imagination and are not to be construed as real.

Cover design by Damonza
Damonza.com

ISBN—Hardcover 978-1-947392-22-9
ISBN—Paperback 978-1-947392-21-2
Library of Congress Control Number: 2018050645

To the women and men who flew the Blue Ridge J32,
collectively, the '32 Guys.'

To my family, for better or worse.

"The pilot-in-command of an aircraft is directly responsible for, and is the final authority as to, the operation of that aircraft."

Federal Aviation Regulations Part 91, §91.3(a)

PART I:
THE JOB
August 1997

One

TRIS LOST ALL visibility as the airplane pierced a thick slab of fog. She slid her focus from the miasma outside the cockpit window to the flight instruments in front of her. They were her eyesight now. She trusted them. They told the truth.

She scanned the gauges and smiled. Tris heard their silent language; woman and machine entwined in the exceptional conversation of flight.

"Clear Sky Two-Five-One, cleared for the approach," the Columbus, Ohio approach controller announced over a scratchy connection. Tris nodded to Captain Danny Terry, sitting two feet away in the left seat. His jaw clenched as he worked the radios on their last flight of the day.

"Gear down," Tris commanded.

The landing gear groaned and clicked as they lowered into position. Locked on final approach, the turboprop glided toward the runway, a concrete strip somewhere below them. Its twin engines spun in sync on the airplane's wings. Tris monitored every bump and twitch of the plane. She answered each with a tap of the controls. *Flying is a series of small corrections.*

Tris nudged the yoke to bank the airplane left, the plastic coated steering column cool beneath her hands. She thought of all the ways pilots measure movement: degrees of heading, feet of altitude, ticks of the clock. Always counting up, down, until the next critical moment. As Clear Sky 251 slid toward the ground, Tris counted down.

Then she saw the flash. Just for a second, an amber warning light flickered.

"Danny, check the gauges. We had a caution."

"Five hundred," the airplane's synthesized altitude alert announced. Tris checked the altimeter. So close to the ground and they still had zero visibility through the late-summer glare.

"I don't know," Danny said as he scanned the gauges. "Wait. It's the oil pressure on number one. The needle's going crazy. It could be nothing, just a blip."

Or the number one engine could be about to fail.

"Ok." She'd need full power on both engines to climb if they couldn't land—and she might not have it.

"Nothing in sight." Danny squirmed forward in his seat to catch the first glimpse of runway lights. His breath grew more labored with every foot of altitude they lost. He wouldn't see the runway until the very last second, if at all—right when Tris would decide to land the plane or thrust it back up into the soup.

"Roger." Tris stayed focused and in control. As seconds passed, the plane slid lower, lower, in a stable descent. The only sounds were the whir of spinning dials, the click of needles, the white noise of flight. Tris eyed the altimeter, her hands soft but firm on the power levers.

Danny's hand twitched behind hers; a backup. He strained to see the runway. Decision time loomed a few feet away.

The caution light blinked again. Tris had to keep her eyes on the navigation gauges. The closer the airplane got to the ground, the more sensitive those indicators became. If she strayed off course, even a little, she'd lose all guidance and have to climb, or else there was no telling where they'd hit the ground. She felt Danny's hands move closer to the controls, protecting them in case she faltered.

She didn't. Tris saw the runway, dead ahead.

"I've got it," Danny said quickly as he keyed the mike. "Columbus Tower, Clear Sky Two-Five-One, runway in sight."

"Roger, Clear Sky Two-Five-One, Runway Two-Four, cleared to land, wind two-five-zero at three knots."

"Landing," Tris said. She looked outside, blinked to focus, and kept the plane moving straight along the runway centerline, edging toward the earth. The altimeter registered field elevation just as the plane's rear wheels softly touched the ground. Tris pulled the power levers to idle and drew the control wheel back toward her chest. As airspeed bled off, the airplane's nose wheel tapped the runway. She pressed the brakes and they slowed to taxi speed.

"I have the airplane," Danny's hand briefly touched hers as she reluctantly ceded control of the aircraft to the captain.

"That was close. Nice job, again," Danny said as his scan moved slowly from side to side, careful to steer the aircraft clear of obstacles in the path of the wings. The hint of crow's feet around his eyes creased as his smile broadened.

"Thank you, *master*."

Danny snorted in reply. One of their many lingering private jokes, the impetus long forgotten.

Once Flight 251 taxied off the runway, Tris returned to her typical duties as first officer, moving handles and flipping switches. Her job was important—critical, in fact. The plane couldn't fly without two pilots, but she longed for command.

"Tough day. Damn glad I had you with me. Still can't believe you'd ever want to leave all this glamour behind."

"You mean you're not gonna at least wait until we get to the gate to talk about this?" Last week, Tris received a call to interview for a pilot job with a corporate flight department. She and Danny had talked about little else all day.

"How is anyone at this airline gonna get through a schedule like we had today without you?" He was only half joking. It was the casual way the captains at this small commuter airline let Tris know they wanted her as their first officer. Especially in weather like this, when quick decisions had to be made.

She accepted Danny's backhanded compliment gladly and with pride, but it wasn't enough. At thirty-four, she was only three years into her flying career. Most of the captains she flew with at Clear Sky were way younger and had been flying much longer. They started their aviation careers in college, long before Tris ever touched the controls of an airplane. While they built flight time, Tris was teaching English to middle school kids. She needed to catch up.

"Second-in-command is only a stepping stone, Danny. You know that better than anyone." Danny made captain at Clear Sky two years ago. He commanded an airliner, albeit a small, slow one.

Danny guided the plane into the gate, set the brake, and called for the shutdown checklists. The crew ran them expertly and then relaxed a bit as the aircraft door squeaked open and ground handlers deplaned the passengers.

He moved his slender, six-foot-one frame across the cockpit's center console, edging closer to the right seat. Danny looked into Tris's eyes with gravity befitting an in-flight emergency.

"Upgrade to captain here at Clear Sky. Come on, stick around, Flygirl." He used Bron's nickname for her, but it didn't help his cause. Bron believed that every pilot should be a captain, the sooner, the better.

"It'll take way longer for me to upgrade here. I can move up faster in a corporate flight department *and* fly a jet."

"I hear you. But aren't you going to miss being mistaken for a flight attendant?"

"Who says it'll stop?" she shot back.

Passengers constantly asked Tris about the drinks menu and whether they were serving peanuts or pretzels. On the outside, she took it as a joke. After all, it gave her the opportunity to use one of her favorite lines: "Sorry. I wasn't pretty enough to be a flight attendant, so they made me a pilot instead." She'd bat her eyelashes, flip her stick-straight brown hair and thrust her slim hips to the side in her best glamour pose. It always got a nervous laugh and ended the discussion.

Tris considered the consequences of leaving as she ran through final checklist items, readying the plane for the next crew. She'd miss flying with Danny and her other friends at Clear Sky, probably more than she realized. *If* she got the job.

"It's that, sure, but not *just* that," she said more to herself than to him. Danny understood why she wanted the job, but only in part. Ambition, yes, but her need for the left seat went way beyond proving that she was qualified to be a captain.

After what she did to Bron...she owed him.

Two

DANNY LEANED AGAINST a lamppost as he and Tris waited for the van to their hotel, absent-mindedly pushing a pair of Ray-Bans up on his nose. His dark blonde hair was dented from wearing headsets all day.

He inhaled the cool evening air, the clouds now a welcome relief from the hot summer sky, and stole a long glance at Tris. Her hair looked curly in the hotel lobby earlier this morning. Now it hung straight. That was the only toll this long, intense workday took on her. She still looked fresh, unrumpled, as if their crew duty day had just begun. He shrugged. Maybe that's just how he saw her.

Danny checked his pager, then started right back where they left off before the tense approach into Columbus.

"So, what do they fly again?" He asked, referring to the corporate flight department at Tetrix, Inc., the Fortune 100 company where Tris would interview next week.

"An Astral and a Gulfstream."

"Gulfstream? Wow, you'd really be movin' on up in the world."

Danny hummed the theme song from that old TV sitcom. To go from flying a nineteen-seat turboprop to a state-of-the-art business jet was a mammoth professional step.

"Yeah, I wish. Maybe someday. This position is for the Astral. Smaller. But still faster than what we're flying now."

"What isn't?"

"Ha! Right."

He argued that Tris should spend more time at the commuter, gain more experience, and ensure an easy upgrade.

"Why leave now? Upgrade here. With all the time you'll have in the airplane, training will be a breeze this time." He looked down and shook his head. He knew he'd gone too far.

"I'm sorry," he added a moment later.

"It's ok."

Danny rubbed his chin and continued. "Yeah, so anyway, you'd skate through training, then build your time in the left seat as pilot-in-command while you have a schedule. Then, when a job comes up with a larger airline, grab it. The PIC time will make you more competitive."

Tris nodded but said nothing. She stared off into the distance, a look Danny knew all too well from their days together in the simulator at Clear Sky; Tris a new-hire first officer and Danny an upgrading captain. She had listened but didn't agree.

Danny knew her as well as anyone at Clear Sky, including Bron. She'd walked away from a ten-year teaching career to become a pilot. Tris left a whole life behind. And then she lost Bron.

It surprised them both that she'd gotten this interview. Danny just assumed that Tris would hang around Clear Sky longer, and warm to him over time. That he'd be right there when she was ready to date again.

"I hear you," she said, probably for the fifth time that day. "But

I have at least four years before upgrading here at my seniority." Clear Sky was a union shop, and date of hire determined upgrade, period.

"Well, but those corporate jobs, Tris, they're so political. There's no union, no protection. Managers can do whatever they want, advance whoever they want. And anyway, what's the rush?" He'd waited patiently to upgrade at Clear Sky when his seniority number came up.

"If I can upgrade faster, why not? I'll fly a new, complex luxury jet. I'll see the world, first class, on someone else's dime," she said, referring to the upscale travel arrangements corporate pilots enjoyed as they flew their passengers to exotic international locations.

Danny pressed on. "You know Tris, the transition to jets from turboprops, it's a challenge. You've never flown anything like what they have. And upgrade to captain…well, you know the old saying. You'll have to 'know everything about the airplane no matter how trivial or worthless and fly it like God!'"

They both snickered, but their levity had an edge to it. While she was certainly a kickass pilot, learning to fly that jet would be an enormous challenge—probably the biggest she'd face in her short career. She almost flunked out of training at Clear Sky. It had to weigh on her mind.

"Look, I don't even have the job yet. This is just an interview. If nothing else, it'll be good practice."

"Suit yourself, Flygirl. But don't those corporate flying jobs usually go to the department manager's buddies? Any idea who you're competing against?"

"Negative. A friend told me about the opening, gave me the name of the chief pilot, and I sent a résumé." Commuter pilots were always sending out résumés, but they were rarely noticed. Something about Tris must have rung a bell with the Tetrix Chief Pilot.

The bright green hotel van approached through the cluster of cars bunched up at the curb by the airline arrival doors.

"Come on." Danny motioned to Tris. The van nosed over toward them, their pilot uniforms making them easy to recognize. Tris and Danny bounced their roller bags off the curb as the van weaved its way behind the exaggerated tails of black limos and tenuously parked cars.

Columbus was a fun overnight. The crew stayed at a decent hotel and had fourteen hours between check-in and work the next day. The last couple of nights they were on minimum crew rest and had to either grab a cold sandwich or order costly room service. Tonight, they'd be served in a restaurant. No doubt the conversation about her interview would continue over dinner.

"So, where will it be tonight?" Danny asked. "Chili's or Outback?"

"Chili's." They both loved the burgers, and it was much cheaper than steak. "But if I get that job, next time it'll be Outback!" She wiggled her eyebrows up and down rapidly like Groucho Marx.

Tris rolled her bag to the back of the van and hoisted it inside. She thumbed through a magazine on the bench seat next to him. *Would next time be different? Could she actually make it through jet training?*

Danny had his own concerns. As the van bounced toward the hotel along the streets of Columbus, he swallowed the questions he really wanted to ask her.

What will happen to me if you go? Will I ever see you again?

Three

TRIS NAVIGATED BY the sound of jet engines and the smell of hot rubber and gasoline. As each grew louder and stronger, Exeter Airport drew closer and her heart beat faster. In fitful sleep the night before, she answered interview questions posed by faceless men, inserting a smile here, a hand gesture there. When the alarm rang at 6:30 a.m., Tris popped up in bed, wide awake in seconds.

The drive took her past run-down low-rise buildings. Mobile homes, fast-food joints, dive bars, and the occasional strip club slid by the driver's side window. When she found herself at the turn for the main terminal, Tris remembered the old joke she and her fellow flight instructors would tell about driving to tiny rural airports all over the state—pointed in the right general direction, a pilot's car will always find the airport.

When she finally saw the outline of the main terminal, the train track's automatic barriers and flashing red lights forced her to a halt. She put her old Corolla in park as a line of freight cars slowly screeched by.

Tris watched a 747 on final approach above her, its four engines hanging off of the wings, massive gear assembly down. It probably moved at 160 knots, but it appeared to float toward the runway. The majesty of this enormous jet had awed Tris ever since she was a little girl.

Grandpa Ed had introduced her to flying. On Sundays, he would come over early and have breakfast with Tris and her parents. Her mother would make blueberry pancakes that had a secret ingredient Tris still didn't know.

"Let's go, Princess Patricia. Let's see the miracle of flight," he'd say as he wiped his mouth and drained his cup of black coffee. She'd jump up from the table, kiss her parents goodbye, and run out to Grandpa's truck.

They'd make the two-hour drive from the tiny town of Pittston to the big-city airport. Tris would watch the cornfields roll by, as Grandpa's old pickup bounced along with his hands locked in the ten-and-two position on the steering wheel.

When the terminal doors opened, she would run to the plate glass window looking out over the ramp, pressing her nose up against the glass and trying to rub it against the bulls-eye tip of a 747 parked at the gate. White with a red stripe, the letters "TWA" painted on the side.

"Grandpa, it's so big. How can it fly?"

He'd smile down at his only grandchild. "That's the miracle, princess."

Now, whenever Tris saw a 747 in flight, she could almost feel the calloused warmth of Grandpa's hand on hers. Those days at the airport, with her hand in his while she stood nose-to-nose with the gigantic jet, were the moments she treasured from a childhood that always seemed too short.

Tris's dad died when she was eight. Her mother was adrift after that, sometimes forgetting to cook or clean. From time to time when

Tris walked in the door after school, her mother stared at her like she was an unexpected visitor.

Grandpa died just a few years after her father. Tris felt more alone than ever after the two most important men in her life floated away like helium balloons.

The train passed, the barriers rose, and Tris moved on. She'd flown into Exeter many times at Clear Sky and knew the alignment of its crossing runways like the lines in the palms of her own hands. In her mind, she held a full-color picture of how they looked from the air, like a postage stamp glued to the middle of the city.

Her mouth went dry. She swallowed twice and shimmied in her seat to loosen the grip of the shoulder strap that locked against her chest. As she checked the street signs for her next turn, Tris daydreamed about flying the Astral for Tetrix all over the world.

"Look where I am, Grandpa," she'd say from ramps in Europe, Asia, maybe even Africa! Well-paid corporate crews slept in five-star hotels with lengthy sits in high-end vacation destinations at the ready in case the executives they flew changed their plans. And this job promised the most important benefit: the chance to become a captain without having to wait for her seniority number to come up.

Then something Danny had said popped back into her mind. Why would they interview *her*? Why not just pick a current Astral captain, maybe a pilot at a smaller operation who'd been flying it for years? Or, better yet, some poor guy whose company had gone out of business or had a run of bad financial luck and had to sell their expensive private jets? Why interview a fifteen-hundred-hour regional airline pilot flying a nineteen-seat turboprop?

She'd turned it over in her mind for days after her trip with Danny ended. Tris paid attention to current events. Headlines about affirmative action lawsuits dominated the media, and conforming hiring policies were announced through the gritted teeth of every airline's human resources department. Getting a female pilot on the team would make any company look better in the male-dominated world of aviation.

She told herself it didn't matter why she was chosen to interview, even if she had a leg up "just because." She'd rise on merit. *I'm smart. What I lack in experience I'll make up for with enthusiasm. What I don't know I can learn. I will do any job, no matter how small or undignified, with a smile. I will show them that I am the best person for this job. I will work harder than anyone else there.* She tightened her fist and pumped it in the air.

Tris headed into uncertainty but felt no fear. She imagined herself as a character from one of her favorite books, Upton Sinclair's *The Jungle*. Today, she was Jurgis Rudkus; hardworking, on the edge of survival, willing to do the impossible to succeed. Of course, ultimately, poor Jurgis could not endure.

She would.

Four

THE WEST SIDE of Exeter Airport was reserved for private jets owned by celebrities, the uber-wealthy, and corporations. As she drove closer, Tris saw the outline of two Gulfstreams and a Citation Jet, preening in the morning sun. She glanced down at the clock on her car's dashboard. Twenty-five minutes until the interview.

As she turned into a parking area just a few yards from runway One-Four Left, the ground rumbled from the force of a full power takeoff. She rose from the car and centered her skirt, which had twisted during the drive. Her pumps clicked on the asphalt pavement between her car and the secured entry door with the number "5026" on it.

The woman who set up her interview had given her a quick rundown of the department. Tetrix currently employed five pilots, and a group of mechanics, cleaners and dispatchers, all supervised by Chief Pilot Brian Zorn and his boss, the department head David Willett.

Tris had on her very best suit, a grey herringbone. She wore the same one for her interview at Clear Sky. Her airline buddies teased her that she couldn't call it a "lucky" suit, since it wasn't navy blue. Another silly airline superstition. She smoothed her skirt again and tucked in the white cotton blouse she'd ironed with extra starch to make sure the buttons didn't gap. She didn't want to look like a balloon at the end of a Popsicle stick.

Security cameras pointed in all different directions at the front entrance. Tris rang the doorbell, and a female voice responded, probably the same person whom she talked to before. A buzzer sounded, followed by a click as the door moved slightly open.

Tris walked straight toward the woman at the front desk—definitely the one who had let her in. A nameplate said "Ann-Marie Markham."

"Hi. I'm Tris Miles." Tris extended her hand over the reception desk. A petite slender woman stood to grasp it. Ann-Marie had long blonde hair that fell to her waist. She was dressed in business clothes—blue pinstripe slacks and a light pink shell. Her appearance made Tris glad she'd chosen a suit for the interview.

"Hi, Patricia. Ann-Marie," she said in an officious and formal tone, her facial expression neutral.

Tris nodded. "Nice to meet you. It's Tris," she repeated as Ann-Marie directed her to a row of chairs. The reception area looked more like the entrance to a business office than a place where pilots flew airplanes. She'd expected a disorganized assembly of worn couches, folding chairs, and tables covered with crumbs like those in the Clear Sky crew room just across the airport. Instead, Tris saw two doors labeled "Conference" and several glass-walled offices. She smiled at Ann-Marie, who nodded before picking up the telephone to make a call.

Tris sat calmly, eyes straight ahead. She didn't want to be seen craning her neck to check out the surroundings, so she investigated only to the limits of her peripheral vision. She'd gotten great interview advice when she looked for teaching jobs right out of graduate school: the interview begins the moment an employee of the company you're meeting with can see you.

She noticed a piece of lint on her skirt. She tried to brush it off. When she couldn't, Tris realized the fabric had pilled from years of machine washing. *If I get this job, the first thing I'll do is buy a new one.*

A critical moment in her brief flying career—maybe a life-altering one—ticked closer. Yet she didn't wring her hands, rhythmically tuck her hair behind her ears, or feel the slightest racing pulse. Tris expected nerves, almost *wanted* to feel them. She folded her hands impatiently and glanced up at a clock hung on the wall behind Ann-Marie's chair.

How much longer until she had to face her past?

Five

"RIGHT. OK."

Zorn hung up with Ann-Marie and primed himself to meet Patricia Frances Miles. First, he smoothed his salt-and-pepper hair and straightened his tie. He wore the only clean white shirt he could find in his closet this morning. He hated when that happened. He avoided wearing this particular shirt because it strained against his gut, though not long ago it had fit him perfectly. But he had stopped running, ate the same rich food on the road, and still downed a couple of beers each night after dinner, all while nearing fifty.

He rapped twice on the glass in between his office and Willett's, and soon both of them were sitting at a small conference table near Zorn's desk. He wanted to start the interview right on time.

"Ok, let me get her," Zorn said on the tick of 9:30 a.m.

As Tris rose from her chair to greet him, Zorn sized her up—a habit he'd picked up years ago. Straight brown hair fell below her shoulders, longer than his wife's, but not as long as Ann-Marie's. The FAA medical certificate she'd sent along with a copy of her pilot's license listed her as five-foot-seven and 145 pounds. That looked right—at least the height did. Guessing women's weight remained a mystery to him, and his wife strongly discouraged it.

He noticed she carried most of her weight in her chest, and he couldn't help but wonder how she would fill out her uniform. He shook that image off.

As he worked his gaze down from grey-brown eyes to pale, unadorned lips, he was drawn to her wrists and hands. They were larger than he expected. He saw short, stout fingers poking out of wide chutes. An incongruous male attribute on someone who was otherwise all *girl*.

"Hi, Patricia. I'm Brian Zorn, the chief pilot." Zorn put his hand out in a noncommittal fashion, the way his father had taught him to shake hands with a woman.

"Tris Miles." Her hand grasped his with power and shook it for the maximum acceptable amount of time. This surprised him, although he kept a gruff expression. Zorn believed that a firm handshake showed confidence and strength of character. Another lesson from his father.

As he led her to his office, he caught a glimpse of Willett in repose. Slumped in his chair, he doodled on his notepad, his head cocked to the side and his burgeoning bald spot dusted by barely discernable grey hairs. As Tris followed, Zorn wondered, based on her grip, whether she or Willett would win a fistfight. He'd put his money on the girl.

Tris sat opposite Zorn as Willett asked questions about her flying background.

Zorn pretended to study something in his lap. He concentrated on her voice to get a sense of how she'd sound on the radio with Air Traffic Control. Zorn could tell the difference between someone indecisive—or worse, scared—and someone who could make lifesaving decisions by the tone of their voice. So far, she sounded pretty good.

Willett wrapped up his part of the interview with a review of the Tetrix employee benefits while Zorn glanced at Tris. She looked mesmerized.

"Why would you leave behind a teaching career to become a pilot of all things?" Zorn asked, gently tossing a round glass paperweight between his hands.

Tris chuckled politely. "Yes, of course. Well, there were a lot of reasons. I grew up in Pittston, and we had a little airport there. I loved the sound of the airplanes flying over our house. Also, when I was a kid, I wanted to be an astronaut!"

This made both men smile, Zorn still twisting the paperweight around the fingers of his left hand.

"At the time, you know, there weren't any female astronauts. My friends all got jobs. I wanted to go to college, so I chose to be a teacher."

When she described her teaching career, Zorn stopped fiddling and looked her over again. She looked fit. Slim build, like a runner. Like his wife used to look. He passed his hand through thinning hair and adjusted his belt buckle, which cut into the stout round of his belly.

"I love teaching, I do, but I've been fascinated by airplanes ever since I was a little girl. Then a friend took me flying with him and let me take the controls. After that, I knew I just had to fly."

Zorn pressed her. "Well, how do we know that, if we hire you, you won't be on to the next thing in a couple of years?" Some thrust and parry were called for. It was expensive to train a pilot.

Tris took a deep breath and looked around the room. Zorn

wondered if the pause was spontaneous or rehearsed. He couldn't tell. She was good, this one.

"For me, teaching was fulfilling. I used my intellect, my book knowledge, and learned skills. But flying, well...I get to use my head *and* my hands. And it expanded my world." She raised both hands and held her arms out wide. "It's just very satisfying."

Both men glanced at each other. Willett nodded. Zorn stirred slightly in his seat. Then he sat upright and put down the paperweight.

Just then he heard a compressor whir and welcomed the cool air. The room had gotten stuffy.

Zorn took her in a bit before he spoke again. She didn't wring her hands or fiddle with her hair. Her posture was upright, but not stiff. This pilot was confident. She'd need to be.

"This is a co-pilot position," Zorn began as the air-conditioner hummed over his words. "We require 1,500 flight hours, 250 hours multi-engine time, and advanced training."

Tris's muscles contracted at the words "advanced training" but she recovered quickly. He'd hit a nerve.

"So, Tris, how did your training go at the commuter?" Her airline training records weren't available to corporate employers.

Tris looked directly into his eyes as she spoke. "I passed my initial training," she said. She paused and glanced quickly down at her feet, then back up. "That was over two years ago. I've been flying the line ever since."

Zorn suspected there was more she wasn't sharing. And at that moment he had a choice: he could probe further or move past it. She wasn't sweating and didn't fidget or look away. In fact, she almost stared him down, as if daring him to press.

Whatever she held back, he let it go. He liked her.

Zorn caught her glance and they locked eyes. They established an incorporeal connection. "I am what I say I am," was the message she sent in their unspoken dialogue. She was trying to tell him something else. His stoic expression thawed in minute increments until he finally understood. She *had* to have this job.

"Ok, so, here's one," he said.

Tris braced.

"Are you familiar with the expression 'what happens on the road stays on the road?'"

"I am," she replied.

Of course she knew it. Pilots loved to gossip, especially about the antics of other pilots on overnights. But once the trip was over, the airplane was parked at the gate and everyone headed home toward his or her real life, anything that happened was history.

She shifted in her seat but never took her eyes off Zorn. He was satisfied. He'd rattled her a little, but she hung in there. She'd keep their secrets. He was sure of it.

"So," he said after he considered the information in front of him, "before we take you out to the hangar to see the airplanes, do you have any questions for us?"

Tris nodded and leaned forward.

"If I were lucky enough to fly for you, sir, how long would it be before I'd upgrade to captain?"

"How quickly a new pilot assimilates here in the department, how fast they master the Astral, they all count," Zorn said, taken aback by her question. "We'll provide some in-house training initially and look at getting you professionally trained, you know, at FlightSafety, after about six months, if things go well. But upgrade to captain. Well." Zorn looked over at Willett again. "That, Miss Miles, will depend on you."

"Now, how about we show you the airplanes?" Willett broke the mood.

"Absolutely." She gave Zorn a slight nod and popped out of her chair, anxious like a puppy keeping pace with her master.

Six

TRIS SWALLOWED THE aftertaste of her omission and followed Zorn and Willett toward her future. She had told the truth—just not all of it.

She'd spotted copies of her license and medical certificate on Zorn's desk during the interview. Had he found a way to get her training records? Danny grilled her with every possible question they could ask about training, and she had ready answers. Yet, when it came up, Tris skipped to the happy ending. She had passed.

She shook it off and stepped behind Zorn and Willett on their way to the hangar. She'd worked so hard since then, done so well. Tris couldn't let her failures cut off her best path to the captain's seat. *It was two years ago. I'm a totally different pilot now.* Surely Bron would have understood.

Yet she'd dug her fingernails so far into her left palm she'd practically broken the skin. Thankfully Zorn stopped asking about training—otherwise, she'd probably have drawn blood. Tris rubbed the half-moon shapes with her right hand.

30

The nondescript, one-story industrial building that housed the Tetrix flight department offices opened into an enormous airplane hangar. Its exterior door was fully raised, exposing a panoramic view of Exeter Airport.

Sunshine lit up the first fifteen feet of the gleaming hangar floor. The sound of her pumps reverberated through the huge space. Step by step, the Astral took form. The museum-like setting reminded Tris of places she'd visit as a child. *Look, but don't touch.*

"Be careful, it's slippery." Zorn's voice brought her back to the moment. He pointed down, and it took her a minute to realize that the danger of slipping was due to the immaculately polished concrete surface. At the commuter, the only reason she'd take a header in a hangar was that a sloppy mechanic had spilled oil or hydraulic fluid.

A couple of guys in work shirts with the Tetrix emblem stood by the Astral. Their uniforms had the names "Brad" and "Chip" embroidered on them next to the Tetrix trademark, a crane which symbolized the sprawling construction projects the company spearheaded all over the world. The men stopped their conversation when she stepped close enough to overhear.

"Hi." She waved at them as she walked behind Zorn and Willett up the Astral's airstairs. They nodded, wide-eyed.

The sun reflected off the gold hardware on the front galley cabinets as Tris climbed into the jet. It was awkward at first, the three of them in the narrow vestibule. But Zorn and Willett squeezed out of the way and pointed Tris toward the cockpit.

Tris inhaled the sharp scent of dust and metal at the cockpit threshold as she scanned the intricate switch panels. She heard the hum of avionics; saw the red, green, and amber indicator lights. She raised her hand and let it hover above the switch panel. Heat rose from the metal plate that covered a complex web of powerful electronic cables just inches away.

"Check out the cabin." Zorn smiled like a little kid. He waved his hand toward leather recliners, a couch, and what looked like a dining table. Opening the galley cabinets, he revealed a stack of embossed bone china, sterling silver flatware, and real crystal glasses.

The three of them stood in the Astral for only a few minutes. Tris couldn't shake the feeling that she'd finally been invited to the penthouse. But just to look, not to stay. Not yet.

With the tour over, the three of them filed back into the office. Willett said goodbye first and walked away. Tris waved to Ann-Marie as Zorn escorted her to the door.

"Nice meeting you, Patricia," Zorn said formally. "We'll give you a call in about two weeks and let you know. Fly safe."

"Thanks, Mr. Zorn. This was a thrill for me," she said and nodded toward the hangar. They shook hands again. Once she turned away from him, she broke into a broad, self-satisfied grin. It went well.

She pulled out the keys to the Corolla. Just two years ago, Tris taught new flight students to fly single-engine airplanes no more powerful than her car. The summers she'd spent flying around the airport, practicing takeoffs and landings in ninety-degree heat, sitting shoulder-to-shoulder with a sweating student or her own instructor. And early winter mornings, kneeling on the ramp, checking the aircraft's landing gear in subfreezing temperatures with snow and slush all around her. Just to build flight time. Time, like an advanced degree, was the experience essential to professional ascent.

That time brought her here. She visualized the switches, buttons, and levers that made the Astral fly close to the speed of sound.

This was why.

Seven

"YOU'VE GOT THE job." Zorn called Tris three days after her interview. "It's yours if you want it."

Tris hadn't moved since she'd hung up the phone. She'd accepted his offer on the spot, but she didn't feel elation or the thrill of success.

They picked a start date, and Zorn had already assigned a training captain—an ex-military pilot, Ed something. She couldn't remember his last name.

Tris respected military pilots. Lots of the guys she flew with at Clear Sky started in the military. She'd even considered ROTC when she was in high school. Her mother had discouraged her, as usual. "Oh, Patricia, young girls don't go into the military. That's a man's work," she'd said.

Dissuasion was her mother's predictable reaction to anything vaguely outside the norm. Her slavish devotion to the known, the safe, made sense. The death of Tris's father turned her into a single mother, something she was never cut out to be. Until getting remarried, she supported the two of them on the small payment from his life insurance policy and her salary as a cashier at the local Shop-N-Go.

It was assumed that Tris would go to college, but no one in her family had money to pay for tuition. Tris worked summers stocking shelves at the same Shop-N-Go and took out loans to attend a small liberal arts university near her home. Most of her friends majored in education, so she did, too.

There were no teaching jobs available in Pittston after graduation. If she'd moved closer to Exeter she could have found work easily in an urban school. Instead, she accepted an academic scholarship to enroll in graduate school. She'd earn more teaching with a master's, she'd reasoned. It couldn't hurt.

Then a college friend received his private pilot's license and offered to take her for a ride. They toured the flat landscape of the southern tip of the state when he dared Tris to take the yoke. "Just for a few minutes," he said. At once, Tris experienced an indescribable elation as she guided the airplane around the sky.

As soon as they parked the plane, Tris went to sign up for a lesson. After her first hour at the controls of the tiny yellow and white single-engine Piper Warrior, she was hooked. Tris went directly from the airplane post-flight inspection to the head of the flight school's office to talk about training options, costs, and how much time it would take her to get her license.

Flying became the dream she'd always had, a reality so urgent it crashed through all of her 'some days' or 'maybes.' Something about flying said, "Go. Go now." She wasn't looking for a new career, but it found her anyway.

Then the doubts surfaced. Flight training was expensive. She had no savings and hadn't had a steady teaching job since she earned her degree. Then there was her master's, which was more than half finished. The real-world consequences of a career change made Tris crawl back into her head and push thoughts of flying aside. She finished her master's and moved to Exeter. A series of teaching jobs each ended in bitterness over funding and layoffs. And more time passed.

One afternoon, Tris was grading papers in the teacher's lounge. She heard the high-pitched whine of jet engines overhead. She went to the window and watched from below as an airliner descended into Exeter Airport.

It wasn't her grandfather that she thought of. Tris saw her mother, smoking a cigarette at their green Formica kitchen table after a long day on her feet at the cash register.

Tris surveyed the open room in the teacher's lounge. One colleague ate her lunch out of a Tupperware container. Another worked on a lesson plan. Tris would never be satisfied living her life in such confined spaces. She had to expand her universe, become a piece of the sky instead of someone who just looked up at it in wonder.

She would risk failure and mistake—but not regret.

For almost two years, Tris taught full-time and studied at night. She'd spend every weekend at the airport training to earn her Certified Flight Instructor rating.

Teaching people to fly was nothing like the classroom she came from. Her regular hours morphed into the extremes of the business day, first thing in the morning until long after five. Flight training was expensive—Tris knew that well. Her students were no longer high-schoolers, but busy professionals at the top of their careers who had to squeeze flight lessons in between meetings and business trips.

Tris had to fly on her students' schedules, or she wouldn't fly at all. Every day, she woke at dawn. After a cup of coffee and some breakfast, she made the forty-five-minute drive to Westin Airport, with its one runway and narrow taxiway that had grass growing out of the cracks.

A leaky trailer perched at the end of a long dirt road was home to Westin Flight School. After early training flights, Tris would wedge herself into a worn leather chair and read a book until lessons picked up again in the late afternoon. After each long, stop-start day, Tris trudged home, slowed by fatigue, sometimes long after dark.

After a year, Clear Sky hired her. She was an airline pilot! But the pay was terrible. At the end of the month, her take-home pay was less per hour than what she earned as a flight instructor, which was even less than her miserly teacher's salary. Another trade-off, as Tris leaped up the experience ladder flying Clear Sky's fleet of multi-engine turboprop aircraft.

And now she had Tetrix. It was a coup, she knew it. First, it was about getting the job. Done. But the great money, benefits, and five-star hotels came with a catch. She had to qualify in the Astral, to learn it and fly it. Until the second she hung up the phone with Zorn, she hadn't focused on the depth of the challenge—or what it would mean if she failed. Another training event like the one at Clear Sky and that would be it. Career over. She'd never make it up to him.

It was game time. She *had* to win.

Eight

DANNY STOOD ON the small concrete patio outside Tris's living room. Her vertical blinds were open and the curtains pushed to the sides of the sliding glass door. He watched Tris finger the edges of a framed photograph of Bron, one they took on a trip to Barbados. Danny remembered it well; he'd covered Bron's schedule so Bron could take that vacation with her. Danny still had the unopened bottle of rum Bron brought back to thank him.

Danny had said he'd stop by at some point today. Tris expected him to enter from the patio since it was a shorter walk from the apartment complex parking lot. Sometimes he'd find her sitting outside waiting for him.

Today she was in the living room, hunched over on that old couch staring at her ex-boyfriend's photo. Her hair wasn't combed, and she had on a faded Clear Sky T-shirt and baggy sweatpants. Those fuzzy slippers she wore, shaped like the head of a moose with antlers, were her favorites.

Just the way she sat on that couch, the way she'd surrounded it with photos of him, of them, reminded Danny of how she and Bron became a couple. It was Bron's old couch, one he posted for sale on the crew room bulletin board. Tris and Bron both marked the beginning of their relationship as the day Tris bought, and Bron delivered, this piece of secondhand furniture.

Danny started to feel like a voyeur, so he rapped on the slider.

"Oh my god," Tris exclaimed when she heard the quick taps on the glass. "Hey! Way to sneak up on someone!" She let him in.

"You looked lost in thought, Flygirl. What's up?"

She smiled. "I got Tetrix. I. Got. Tetrix. Can you believe it?"

Danny had a flash of jealousy. Oh, he could believe it. In his head, he heard that old refrain, how much easier it was for women to get flying jobs these days. But he would never say that to Tris. He knew how hard she worked just to get this far and what she'd overcome. She was a great pilot, a great person. He didn't really want a corporate job anyway.

"All right then! This calls for a special celebration. We might even have to splurge on imported beer!" They both laughed. On a commuter pilot's salary—even a captain's—whatever beer they found on sale at the local grocery store was the toast of choice.

"I have two Molson's in the fridge. I've been saving them for just such an occasion." Tris bounced toward her tiny kitchen. Danny was thrilled to see her so happy. He would miss her in the crew room and the cockpit. They enjoyed each other's company on the road without too much tension. He simply loved being around her and he'd wanted to ask her out for a long time. But she was Bron's girl.

By the time Tris brought the beers back—in frosted glasses!— he'd removed his uniform tie and undid the top two buttons of his pilot shirt. He sat on the couch and lit a cigarette. Danny offered her one and she gladly took it. A secret they shared, one only Bron knew. This was a big event, and a smoke was called for.

He inhaled and blew a series of smoke rings. "So, tell me about the interview. What's the deal with the two bosses?"

"No clue. I didn't want to ask. Brian Zorn, the chief, said almost nothing for the longest time. He just took notes and played with something on his desk. And he asked me some things toward the end, basic questions."

She entertained Danny for a while with some interview details, but he only half-listened. He wished she would just stay at Clear Sky.

"How many others did they interview? Who'd you beat out for the job?"

"No idea." She took a long drag.

"Any clue what the other pilots in the department are like?" Danny had heard all the same stories as Tris about corporate pilots. They were widely considered to be second tier to the airline guys—by the airline guys, anyway.

Clouds of smoke hung between them. "Nope. I just met the chief and the manager. And the woman behind the front desk. I know there are three other pilots. Six total now, with me." Her lips broadened into a full smile, which made her eyes close. He'd better distract himself before something started to rise.

He refocused on their conversation. "Ok. So tell me about the Astral. Did you get to see it?"

"Oh yeah. It's awesome. Really sleek wing," she began and gave Danny an animated review of what sounded like a dream machine.

"So," he said, "what's the training plan for you?" That caught her attention, as he knew it would. She frowned and looked at him out of the corner of her eye.

"I don't know, actually." She fiddled with a loose thread on her sweatpants. "I asked when I would upgrade to captain. They didn't say specifically, but I came away with the impression it would take less than a year."

"Upgrade in a year," he said. "Actual *upgrade* to captain, or just a type rating? They can get you the type, the qualification, without giving you command, right?"

It was one thing to fly the plane to the standards set for captains by the FAA. That'll earn a type rating. No pilot could fly as captain without it. But every pilot had to show the judgment required to be pilot-in-command before being given the responsibility. "We're talkin' about lives here, man," he and Bron would say to upgrade candidates at Clear Sky. Bron believed that the ability to command was the true measure of a pilot.

"Maybe six months to a type rating. Captain, pilot-in-command, they said, 'Depends, Patricia.'" She lowered her chin and deepened her voice, mimicking one of the Tetrix guys.

Danny just smiled. During their initial training, Tris was an amazing supporting player. Danny called her Radar O'Reilly, after the character from M*A*S*H who always knew what would happen before it did. She had trouble flying the airplane at first, but slowly, her skills came around, one maneuver at a time.

Yet no matter how hard she tried, she couldn't master the V1 cut—the nightmare scenario when an airplane's engine failed on takeoff. In that life-or-death moment, there was no time for thought—only motion—and it had to be right. If not, in the simulator, the airplane pretended to crash. In the real world, people died.

That maneuver ate up the most experienced pilots, not because it was physically hard; every pilot he'd ever met had the strength in their hands and feet to handle it, including Tris. He thought it might be a 'head' thing. Maybe the sheer gravity of the situation; the stakes of the moment caused some pilots to temporarily lose their minds.

Time after time as the instructor failed an engine on takeoff in the simulator, Tris froze. Danny would look over at her and grin, anything to show he was on her side and wanted her to succeed. She'd smile like she understood. And they'd try it again. But at the critical moment, she was a little too slow, a little late. The simulated runway would slide off to the side as the 'aircraft' hurtled into some building or fence. And the screen ahead would go black.

Danny had seen new hires give up and walk away over the years, go back to jobs in the simple airplanes they already knew they could fly. But not this girl. After every screwup, she'd nod and say, "Let's set it up again."

She studied and practiced the maneuver over and over again. He counted the hours she sat at a cardboard reconstruction of the cockpit, running through procedures, touching the one-dimensional pictures of flight controls and power levers, whispering appropriate commands.

Tris practiced silently, her hands and feet moving as they would in the airplane. In their crew car when they drove to dinner. In the grocery store when they stopped to pick up food. There, shopping carts became rudders, which she would thrust forward one way or the other depending on whether Danny said "right" or "left engine failure." Fresh carrots became power levers. The cheese display was the instrument panel.

Some of the other guys in the training cycle made fun of her behind her back. "Miles of shrapnel," they called her after the detritus of a crash. The airline pushed her to take a check ride, which of course she failed the first time. And the second.

Clear Sky wanted to cut her loose after the second bust. Luckily, the head of training was a friend of Danny's. He begged them to give her one more chance. And then it clicked. Tris passed her check ride and went to work as a regular line pilot.

But, she never forgot. She thought about little else before the interview. Over and over again, Danny challenged her with questions about training, things the interviewers might ask. And with each practice answer, Tris became more confident.

"Did they ask about training?"

Tris hesitated. "Yes."

"And?"

"I told them I passed."

"Really?" Danny was surprised. Tris never shied away from what happened.

"I did pass. Eventually," she said and looked up at him in a way that begged him to move on. But this was too important. The record of her check ride busts was out there.

"Do you think they know?"

"They didn't let on if they did. No, I don't think so." And then, after a few more seconds of silence, she added, "Danny, I thought about telling them. And then, there was this moment, you know, when I was sure they were going to ask. But they didn't. They just didn't. And I thought, hey, it's behind me. That's where I should leave it."

Tough call. "Good enough, good buddy." Danny wondered if he wouldn't have done exactly the same thing.

After a few minutes, the conversation lulled. They sat on opposite ends of the couch, smoking cigarettes. He wanted to touch her, to hold her. Would she return his embrace with something more than a quick, sisterly hug? He decided to chance it.

And changed his mind. What if he scared her away? No. Too risky. He might not get another chance.

He broke the silence. "Congratulations, Tris. It couldn't have happened to a nicer person or a better pilot." He was surprised when she looked away. "What's wrong?"

They'd talked it to death.

"It's too soon, Danny. I think it might be too soon." And then he realized it wasn't at all about training.

She looked wistful, then sad. "He'd be happy about this, right?

He'd want me to be a captain."

Danny hesitated. "Sure he would."

Bron was dead, but he was still present in every bend, corner, and crevice of her little apartment.

Nine

"THERE YOU ARE. Welcome. We're glad to have you here."
Willett stood by Ann-Marie's desk as Tris walked through the door.
Her first day at Tetrix: a Thursday. The whir of a compressor was
drowned out by the roaring engines of a jet taking off right outside.
Business as usual at the airport.

"Thanks! Thrilled to be here, Mr. Willett." His outstretched
hand barely closed over hers. Another wimpy handshake. Willett was
about an inch or two shorter than Tris with a round face and body.
He looked a little like Humpty Dumpty.

"David, please." He ran his hand over the few wisps of hair at
the very top of his head, eyeing her up and down with a salacious grin.
He probably meant to do it surreptitiously, but she caught him. She
smirked at the quick "check out." Tris vacillated between being slightly
annoyed and reassured that she made the right wardrobe choice.

Ann-Marie had told her to dress in business casual clothes. Tris
was embarrassed to admit she wasn't sure what that meant. She knew
her suit would be too much but didn't think jeans were appropriate.

The only other thing she had in the closet was a houndstooth skirt. She paired it with the same white cotton shirt she'd worn to the interview. Of course, she checked herself just outside the Tetrix entrance to make sure it lay smooth in front.

"Follow me. I'll show you your desk." Willett led the way to an immaculate cubicle. A rectangular piece of particleboard had cut-outs for a phone cord and electrical cables, a touch-tone phone, a stapler, and a stack of books on it. She recognized the Astral training materials right away.

Willett hastily grabbed a manual and almost toppled the pile. "Whoa," he blurted out as he tried to keep the books from falling. He handed Tris a small loose-leaf folder.

"This is our operations manual. We feel pretty strongly about the rules we follow. We're not an airline," he said with a hint of sarcasm, glancing over to make sure she'd caught it, "but we're professional and follow the rules. Make sure you read this through. And here are your books for the Astral." He pointed to the teetering stack.

With exaggerated effort Willett stuck his hand in his pocket and pulled it out slowly, revealing a small, silver key. He offered it to her in his open palm as if it were a precious heirloom. With great ceremony, he motioned for Tris to take it.

"And here is your key to the Astral. You'll be needing that." He pursed his lips together in a self-satisfied grin. "Check in with Ann-Marie up front before you go. She'll talk to you about your schedule." And then he was gone.

Tris hadn't noticed before, but once Willett walked away, she sensed, rather smelled, someone else in the room. He'd been sitting in another cube the whole time. He rose above the partition and walked over to her. As he moved closer, she recognized the scent of Old Spice. The only cologne her father ever wore.

He was tall, at least six-foot-two she guessed, and looked like he was in his early forties. His wavy dark brown hair highlighted eyes the color of oak leaves.

"Hi, Patricia. I heard you were starting today. Welcome." He wore a blue button-down shirt tucked into tan Dockers, held on his long, slender torso by a plain brown leather belt. His clear, resonant baritone reminded her of classical music.

"Tris," she corrected, standing to greet him. They shook hands, and she was relieved that finally, someone at Tetrix took hers with a firm grasp.

"This is all pretty new to me." She tried to look him in the eye, not appraise him the way Willett had just done to her. It was challenging.

"Larry Ross," he said. "Nah, it's easy. Just important to keep on top of what there is."

Don't stare. Pivot to airplanes. He was another Tetrix pilot, a colleague. "So, are you flying today?"

"Nope. Catching up on paperwork." His wide grin framed a perfectly straight set of teeth that made her think of the bleached white sand on the beach in Barbados. "You know, updating some charts, clearing off my desk. And I have to do a big expense report. Just returned from an international trip." He let his voice trail off a bit, baiting Tris to ask where he'd been.

"Where to?"

"Paris, yeah, five days." He rolled his eyes as if he'd said Detroit.

"Paris? Five days! Sounds awesome. I'd love a trip like that."

He chuckled. "You say that now. After you've done it a dozen times, you'll just want to be back home." With that, he handed her a bunch of professional publications he'd been holding, most of which Tris was familiar with. They had small pieces of white paper with a list of initials on them.

"I just cross my initials off, really, and then pass 'em on to the next desk. Don't want 'em sitting on your desk for too long or people start noticing." His voice trailed off again as he handed her the pile.

Ross held himself in the typical pilot posture: shoulders back, chest out. He had the kind of looks that made men believe they were invincible. Her commuter buddies would call him "stud boy," their moniker for any guy who could effortlessly attract women, or at least more easily than they could. Tris noticed the wedding band on his left hand and wondered who the lucky girl was.

Neither spoke for several seconds. "Ok, then," Ross finally said. "Welcome again! Let me know if you have any questions." He headed off toward reception.

Tris was sure she was alone in the pilot area. Ever since she learned to fly on instruments, Tris needed to get the big picture. She taught her students to always be a step or two ahead of the airplane, anticipating what might happen next. Over the years, Tris began to order her world in the same way.

To orient herself to her new surroundings, Tris walked slowly around the room. The Tetrix pilot area was a large space dissected by eight cubicles, each separated by dividers. It had an antiseptic feel, as though the desks, the chairs, the rug sprang directly out of shrink wrap. Harsh overhead fluorescent bulbs provided the only interior light.

Other than a blown-up sectional chart outlining the city of Exeter from the air at night, the walls were blank. Tris didn't see any labels on file drawers hinting at what might be inside. She opened one, then another. They were empty.

There was an exterior door, an employee entrance accessible directly from the parking lot. Soon, she'd be using it herself. Tris smiled at this minor conceit. In some small way, it made her part of this group. An insider in a place she wanted to belong.

The partitions between cubicles were only around five feet high, easy to see over while standing. As she circled, she noticed only three desks had personal items on them: family pictures, thumbtacked notes, favorite cartoons. She moved slowly, pausing at each desk to get some sense of the man who sat there.

One boasted a navy squadron patch thumbtacked to its cloth-covered wall. The same desk had a framed picture of a bald man on a speedboat with his arm wrapped around the waist of a middle-aged woman. Tris figured it was her training captain, Ed, in the picture. The cubicle next to his had multiple pictures of three small children of various ages. Probably the other captain's desk. *What was his name again?*

As Tris walked by the cube where Ross had been sitting, she saw a framed photograph of a man standing on a pool deck next to a stunning blonde in a string bikini with a small boy in tow. At first glance, it looked like the stock photo of models that came with the frame. But the man in the picture was Ross. Naturally, someone who looked like him would have a gorgeous wife and a beautiful child.

Tris finished her tour at her own desk, sat down, and ran her fingers over the blue plastic cover of the Astral's systems manual, checklist, and Quick Reference Guide. The trifecta of training books. The outline of an Astral was sketched on the cover of each, along with its manufacturer's name and the aircraft series number—AsL1000.

Tetrix used the Astral for domestic flights to points east along with international flights crossing the Atlantic to Europe. The company's Gulfstream IV typically went west and over the Pacific.

Tetrix hired her because they needed a pilot. That meant the sooner she was trained on the Astral, the sooner she could contribute. The quality of her training would be critical. She'd hoped to meet the man who'd guide her to success in the Astral. But he was nowhere around.

Ten

"YES," ANN-MARIE said in a clipped, professional tone when she saw Tris approach. It was more statement than question. Tris had heard laughter coming from reception and wanted to join in.

Ross and Ann-Marie stood by a large whiteboard. Tris nodded quickly at Ross and addressed Ann-Marie.

"I just came up to say hi. Is that the schedule?" Tris motioned to the whiteboard.

"It is."

"So, how does it work?"

Ann-Marie rolled a chair out of the way to create some space for Tris to come closer. Ross didn't move, and Tris found herself standing close enough to smell his cologne again. She involuntarily leaned away from him, slightly embarrassed by his proximity. Pilots generally avoided cologne and perfume in the cockpit in case their crewmates had allergies. He said he wasn't flying today, but why wear Old Spice to work at an airplane hangar?

"You're already on a trip. Did you see it?" Ann-Marie pointed to the Astral schedule for Thursday of the following week.

"You'll be observing. Sitting in the jump seat watching Ed Deter, your training captain, and this guy." She pointed her thumb at Ross. "Brian Zorn, you know, the Chief Pilot, right? Well, he's mapped out your training and wanted to make sure you flew along on some trips right away."

"Great. Can't wait. The trip is going to Asheville?"

"Yes, Roger has family down there." Roger. *Who was Roger?*

Ann-Marie shot a glance over at Ross and then at Tris. Ross raised his eyebrows and smiled. He stuck his hand in his pocket and pulled out a money clip. Ann-Marie had her wallet ready.

Then Tris remembered. "Roger Emerson. The Chairman. I guess we do a lot of overnights down there then?"

Ross shook his head, defeated, and Ann-Marie laughed as he handed her five dollars. "See! I knew she'd get it," Ann-Marie grabbed the bill from Ross, and then turned to Tris. "No, not often. If he goes down there, it's usually just for dinner with his mother and he flies home the same night. When he goes on extended vacation there, we park the aircraft and airline the crew home, especially if it's over the holidays."

Tris nodded. From the schedule entry, it looked like this trip started later in the day.

"So this is a 4 p.m. show?"

Ann-Marie laughed. "4 *a.m.* This isn't a dinner trip. He has an early meeting, then lunch with mom."

"Oh-dark-thirty." Ross laughed. Tris was a bit startled when he spoke. He had been so quiet. Tris didn't smell his cologne anymore and had almost forgotten he was there.

"Got ya!" he said, amused.

"Poor girl. You've gotta fly with *this* one." Ann-Marie rolled her eyes at Ross.

"I think you're working me too hard." Ross smiled, pretending to sound angry.

"Oh right! Yeah." She flipped her long blonde hair over her right shoulder. "I guess that whole week you didn't fly last month when the Gulfstream was down for maintenance was real stressful for you. Yeah. Uh-huh." Ross laughed and threw up his palms in defeat.

"Thanks, Ann-Marie. I'm off," Ross said before turning to Tris. "It's great to meet you. See you soon."

Now alone with Ann-Marie, it seemed too abrupt to just walk away, but awkward to try and make conversation.

"Seems nice," Tris said quietly, nodding toward where Ross had been standing just seconds before.

Ann-Marie waited a beat before responding. "He is," she finally said. "Do you want to hear the rest of your schedule?"

"Sure. What do you have for me?" Tris asked in the same way she'd speak to crew scheduling at the airline, which is exactly what Ann-Marie was. The scheduler literally controlled your life. A good relationship with scheduling could make the difference between a fourteen-hour duty day in the middle of nowhere and a three day trip to the islands. Ann-Marie was someone Tris would treat very, very well.

"Ok. I see you have in-house tomorrow with Deter. That's your first day of ground training; probably company procedures, maybe a walk-around of the Astral. Ten a.m."

"Great. Ann-Marie—"

"Uh-huh?" Corporate face, no smile.

"So, is there any syllabus or training...I don't know, *plan* I guess you'd say?"

"No idea. You'll have to ask Zorn."

Tris looked toward Zorn's dark office. "Looks like he's out right now. Is he coming in today?"

"Ha! No way. He has a 5 a.m. show on the Gulfstream

tomorrow. No chance he comes in today."

"Ok, thanks. I guess Ed Deter will explain things to me tomorrow."

Ann-Marie's body stiffened and she looked away from Tris. "No doubt," she said as she picked up her phone to make a call. Tris had already opened her mouth to ask about Deter, but the conversation was over.

None of the other pilots were around. Except for Ann-Marie and the occasional ringing phone, the office was quiet. She thought of the laughter, the complaining, the buzz of people grabbing their flight bags and running to their planes she was so used to in the crew room at Clear Sky. She longed for a couch she could plop down on next to another pilot, who'd slide over to make room for her, sip coffee, and simply ask, "So, how's the weather out there?"

On the very first day of her new job, she'd had three brusque conversations, heard her schedule, and been given a stack of manuals to study. Her training captain wasn't there. The chief pilot, the man who had sounded so excited when he had offered her the job, wasn't there. Willett had already left the office.

As Tris headed back to her desk, she passed what looked like a storeroom of some kind. She opened the door and saw rows of shelves with boxes of single-serving snacks. Cookies, peanuts, mini cans of Pringles. Against one wall was every kind of soft drink imaginable. On another, she saw drink mixers and tiny liquor bottles, stock for the airplanes.

On one of the shelves, she spotted a small, loose-leaf notebook. There was a piece of masking tape on the spine with the name "Deter" written in black marker. He must have left it there.

Deter's name came up during her interview when Zorn and Willett briefly described the other pilots in the department. They only mentioned he was ex-navy, a retired commander who used to make carrier landings.

To Tris, he was the most important person at Tetrix. She couldn't wait to meet him.

Eleven

ROSS STOPPED AT a red light in front of O'Slattery's. Their tiny parking lot was empty. A cool breeze slipped through the open windows of his new '98 Cutlass as he considered his options.

How he wished he could go in and grab a beer. He checked his watch. 2:30 p.m. Not too early for one.

But he had to get home—that was the deal he and Devon had made. Someone would always be at home when their son was, and James was due back from school in forty-five minutes. Without a set flight schedule, that commitment was tricky for Ross, so the responsibility generally fell to Devon. She'd recently become a lot less forgiving about his absences from home.

Ross was a pilot when they met fifteen years ago. She had thought what he did was cool and always wanted to join him on his late night charter flights, back when he was first building flight time. Devon would throw on a pair of old blue jeans, grab a maga-zine, and sit beside Ross in the passenger seat for the long hours aloft, some-times in airplanes without heat in the dead of winter.

She never complained; they were young and in love.

His beautiful girlfriend knew what she was getting into when they walked down the aisle. But over the years, she'd lost patience with him being away from home so much, especially after their son was born. She liked the money he made at Tetrix, but that didn't stop her from reminding him that he wasn't around as much as she'd like him to be.

Today, Devon had a hairdresser's appointment. "Leaving at one, home by four," she'd told Ross that morning. Ross had no idea what she did there for three hours since she looked pretty much the same when she returned home as when she left. It was just another one of those things they didn't discuss.

Now that the new pilot was on board, he had something different to think about. There hadn't been a whole lot going on since the drama over RJ had died down. He overheard Deter complain to Zorn again the other day about hiring a girl. He'd hoped to avoid any conflict, but there he was, flying her first observation trip together with Deter next week. *She better fly like Chuck Yeager or Deter will never let it go.*

Zorn had said she was good-looking, but Ross rated her as just average. Light brown hair, brown eyes. Zorn's report on the size of her tits was right on, though. Impressive.

What really struck him, he had to admit, was the way she looked him directly in the eye. Ross didn't look anyone in the eye unless absolutely necessary. Outside of the cockpit, he didn't want anyone to know what he was thinking. She seemed straight up. Maybe she'd be direct, say what was on her mind. It would be a refreshing change from Devon, who wanted him to be a mind reader.

Ross sat in the car for a few minutes after he pulled into his custom-built driveway, which Devon designed herself. He wanted just a little bit of peace before he had to attend to his never-ending honey-do list. Other than the time he spent with his son, his life was all about doing what Devon asked, bringing money home, and watching it sail out the door. Eventually, he pulled himself into the marble entryway of his home. For a smallish three bedroom house, his wife had managed to spend a fortune refurbishing it.

First thing he did was walk to the kitchen and grab an Old Milwaukee from the fridge. He downed it while standing up, opened another, and took it to the den.

The stack of credit card bills lay exactly where he left them that morning on his desk. Saks: $3,322.00. Just two visits. Lord and Taylor: $541.93. One visit. The same day as one of the visits to Saks. Devon must not have had a hair appointment, aerobics class or any of her other usual distractions that day.

Out the window, he saw their lush garden and imagined Devon there, framed by their white roses and blue lilacs. He visualized her perfect profile. She still had the same blonde hair and dark-skinned good looks he had fallen for so long ago. In moments of total honesty, he admitted her seemingly effortless beauty was the main reason he married her.

No, no, that wasn't true. Her looks were a big part of it, of course. The two of them were also a lot alike and once wanted the same things. Each enjoyed travel and horseback riding at her daddy's Montana ranch, and spending time on Ross's father's farm. They also both grew up in traditional families where mom stayed at home and dad worked hard to support them. He and Devon dreamed of two large American cars in the garage, breakfast and dinner around a common table, and a son, daughter, and dog.

He tried to support her in style. "Happy wife, happy life," his father always said. But Ross was a pilot, not a rich rancher like her daddy. No nine-to-five. No family dinner every night. Only one child. A small house. *At least we have the dog,* Ross thought as he reached down to scratch his beagle's head. Ross made more money than he ever expected to and he really hit the jackpot for a pilot who didn't go to college and wasn't in the airlines. But it still wasn't enough for Devon.

Ross had been a pilot with Tetrix for almost eight years. And every year the money got better, the schedule easier. Every time his salary went up or he received a ten-thousand dollar bonus, Devon nagged him about a bigger house or a newer car. And Ross became less and less satisfied with his life.

Thinking about his marriage depressed him, so he re-focused on that new girl. *We'll see how long she lasts.* He had told Zorn that pairing her with Deter for training was just like putting a detonator on a pile of that powder stuff they'd use on the farm to loosen the hardpan.

Zorn had shrugged it off, but Ross wondered just how long it would take before Deter got under her skin—or she got under his, which would be far worse. He knew how mean Deter could be. Oh well. Not his problem.

Just then, he heard the refrigerator door open and close. "Hello, son," he called toward the thing he loved most in the world.

"Hi, Dad. Homework, right?"

"Right."

James was safely home. Ross returned to Devon's credit card bills. Later, he could tell by the scent of hairspray and perfume that wafted all the way to the back of their house that she was home. She popped her head in to say hello on her way to their bedroom. As he expected, her hair looked pretty much the same as it had that morning.

Twelve

TETRIX CAPTAIN ED Deter bubbled just a few degrees below his boiling point when he arrived at the hangar. He hurled the entrance door to the pilot area against the stop and blocked it with his body as it flew closed. Zorn had scheduled a training session for him with the new hire, so he had to cancel his tennis game to trudge to the airport.

Deter grumbled and shook his head when he found the pilot area empty. He threw his briefcase in his cube and stomped over to ask Ann-Marie where the Fucking New Guy was.

"She's in the hangar. In the Astral, I think. She's been here for an hour." Ann-Marie glanced over at the clock. Deter was late for the training session.

"Well, go get her, will you?" Before Ann-Marie could respond, Deter turned toward the coffee machine. He filled a Styrofoam cup and went to grab a bag of Chips Ahoy! from the stockroom.

Just two days ago, he'd arrived for an Astral flight when Willett and Zorn ushered him into a meeting. He assumed he was finally getting a training date on the Gulfstream. They'd had the aircraft a year and he was the only Tetrix pilot who didn't fly it. It was time. He deserved to captain the company's most powerful jet.

Deter squeezed his stocky frame into the tiny guest chair in Zorn's office and found himself wrapped in a taut, uncomfortable hug. He brought up the subject before either boss had a chance to speak.

"So, when am I going to school on the Gulfstream? That's what we're here to talk about, right?"

Both Willett and Zorn bested Deter in the middle-aged-man hair competition. Zorn had a full head of it, mostly gray, and Willett a few wisps on top. At 52, Deter was completely bald. He still considered himself in better shape than either younger man. At least he worked out every day.

"Well, yes, it's indirectly about the G-IV." Zorn cleared his throat before he went on. "But first, we have great news! We hired Patricia Miles as a new co-pilot on the Astral. As the lead captain on the Astral, we want you to do her in-house training."

Deter rose like lava spurting from an erupting volcano. His chair stuck to him, so he dropped back down with a thud.

"Look, Brian... Man, wait a minute. This isn't what I signed up for. No way, not even close." He grappled for composure. He quickly tried to marshal every logical argument he could think of why he should not have to train this girl. He told them not to hire her in the first place. Her flight time was too low. She'd never flown a jet. And now he was supposed to train her? *Oh hell no.*

Zorn continued as if Deter hadn't even spoken. "I need you to do it, Commander," his reference to Deter's naval rank beyond patronizing. "You'll be able to make sure she meets our standards on the Astral. No one knows that airplane better than you." Zorn made it sound like an exotic treat with a small bonus tossed his way. But it was just a shit sundae, even if it came with a cherry on top.

Then Willett made it worse. "She seems motivated. She'll be a good soldier."

Deter bristled at the image of woman as soldiers. He hadn't warmed to this concept even when the military rescinded the Risk Rule to allow women in combat. Soldiers and pilots relied on each other for their lives. He hadn't met a woman yet whose hands he'd put his life into.

A female pilot in the Astral was more than just a bad idea. It dredged up bad memories, like when he lost his first chance at the command of a squadron. "Sorry," his CO had said. "We need more women officers at the top." He never forgot his CO's words. As he played them back in his mind, the voice he heard sounded just like Zorn's.

"Why aren't you just bringing Dicky on?" Dicky Lord was an ex-army buddy of Willett's who also applied for the job. "He's a hard-working guy who needs a break. He'll be just as motivated and he's already captain-qualified on a jet." Deter wouldn't mind training Dicky.

"Ed, Dicky's flying a Crustacean," Zorn said, referring to the standard put-down of Dicky's current airplane, the slow-moving Citation Jet. "It's not a whole lot faster than that turboprop Patricia flies. Look, the next time we have a vacancy, Dicky's our number one choice. We decided to try something different this time."

Screw it. "Then I want a training date on the Gulfstream."

"Can't give you one." Willett responded this time. He had the final say. There was nothing left to discuss. It was done.

And now here Deter sat, at his desk with no trip to fly and a baby co-pilot to train.

He heard a female voice that wasn't Ann-Marie's. Within seconds, a slender girl in a loose top with brown hair stuck her hand out. "Hi. I'm Tris Miles. Nice to meet you." Tris? He thought her name was Patricia. Shouldn't her nickname be Patty or Trish or something?

"Right." Deter barely pressed her hand, then pulled a ground school outline he'd pirated from FlightSafety out of his bag. "Meet me in the conference room." He nodded toward the room with an oblong conference table and floor-to-ceiling window walls.

She brought her Astral manuals into the room with her and looked small behind the imposing stack. There was a pen and notebook on the table in front of her.

He walked in and handed her a single photocopied page. "Read this. Tell me when you're finished." Deter reclined in one of the leather conference chairs.

"Sure."

He'd barely opened the tennis magazine he'd brought to read when she said she was done.

"Ok, then. We have a flight to Asheville coming up. Come a few minutes early. I'll show you the pre-flight." He rose to leave, almost making it to the door.

"So, uh, do you have a few minutes to answer some questions? I've looked at the manuals, and maybe you can give me some details."

Deter's mouth opened, his jaw almost on his chest. How the hell did she already have questions? She hadn't even observed a flight in the Astral yet. He chuckled, sat back down in a chair by the door and slouched.

"All right, sure. What the heck."

She asked a question or two about pressurization. Why in the world would she want to talk about that right now? Who gave a shit? Ask about the trips, the overnights, the passengers, company procedures.

Deter started out marginally interested, then slid past neutral to irritated. Before long, he looked up at the clock on the wall.

"Are we done?" He was abrupt, maybe even rude. He didn't care.

She gave him a tight smile. "Yes. Thank you."

"Ok. See ya." He looked back up at the clock. Maybe he could play tennis today after all.

Thirteen

*"**WHAT TIME IS** it?" Tris giggled as she and Bron wrestled with the door to the Exeter crew room. They had just brought in the last flight of the day for Clear Sky, a maintenance trip with no passengers. She caught a glimpse of the clock on the wall. 3:15 a.m. There wasn't even a lineman out on the ramp to help them park.*

Bron grabbed her around the waist and pressed his lips against her. He could barely wait for the two of them to move clumsily through the crew room door and fall on the couch. They couldn't take their hands off one another. With the lights out, they rolled around on the well-worn furniture as one. Each tore off the other's clothes. Tris moved on top, but they finished with Bron looking down at her from above.

"Nice flight, First Officer Miles," he joked. She punched his shoulder lightly and pulled him toward her.

"Thank you, Captain," she answered, pretending to salute. "Thanks for skipping the coffee and tea, and going straight for meeeeee!" They laughed as only two exhausted pilots could. But Tris was every bit as happy as she was tired.

Tris had allowed herself to daydream. Freight and check haulers parked their planes and headed to crash pads to grab some sleep before that night's late run. Heat plumes rose from Citations, Hawkers, Falcons, and Challengers parked on the ramp, ready to take executives east for early meetings. Tris loved the airport at oh-dark-thirty, as the aviation world moved from night to light. She looked at her watch. 4:05 a.m.

"Early bird, eh?" An overnight ramper called to her as he walked out onto the tarmac.

"Yeah, I guess. Just getting ready to launch. Out and back to Asheville."

"Have fun."

She checked her watch in an exaggerated motion to emphasize how early it was.

"Yup! Livin' the dream!"

The ramper smiled. "Cool. Safe flight." He flashed her a peace sign.

She and the ramper hadn't met before, but their connection through aviation was real and immediate. It was like running into another American while traveling in a non-English-speaking country. The bond you shared was the common language, the culture. Aviation—its talk, its rituals, its traditions—wound people together whose paths might otherwise have never crossed.

The Astral shone in the hangar's overhead fluorescent light as if a detailing crew had waxed it just a few minutes before. She checked her watch again. 4:10 a.m. Still no sign of Deter nor Ross. Her eyes darted back and forth to the hangar entrance; she wanted to get started.

Her first meeting with Deter last week was, well, disappointing. Deter had shown up late, and while she hadn't been sure what to expect physically, the stocky bald man who seemed to walk sideways was not it.

Their discussion wasn't like any training session she'd ever had. It lasted only a few minutes. Deter shoved an ersatz-printed outline of ground instruction subjects at her and told her to read it. It was a fuzzy copy of a formal training syllabus he must have gotten during one of his trips to FlightSafety in Dallas. She looked it over while he read a magazine and sipped his black coffee.

Tris was so excited to talk about systems and prepared a list of questions. He answered one or two, then started to tap his fingers on his knee, which popped up and down like a jackhammer. Tris figured training was over, so she tried to be friendly.

"So, Ed, did you see *Law & Order* last night?" Popular TV shows were a tried and true conversation starter.

"Yes." *Tap-tap-tap.*

"Yeah, it was a good one."

Yawn.

"Where do you live?"

"Avon," he said, referring to the upper-middle class bedroom community on the outskirts of Exeter County only an hour from where she was raised in Pittston.

"How long is the drive to the airport?"

"Forty minutes usually. It always seems longer when I have to come in on a non-flying day."

Then Deter looked at the clock, stood up, and left.

And now, ready to observe her first flight in the Astral, here she sat right on time. Deter was late again.

With nothing else to do and no one to instruct her, Tris walked around the plane, following the diagram in the training manual. She chuckled at what she must look like: the rookie standing with the cumbersome loose-leaf book in her hand.

Her review complete, she headed up to the cockpit. Tris wanted to touch the complex system of buttons and switches arranged above the pilot seats, feel their response to her fingertips. But she knew she shouldn't. It was her airplane, yet she knew nothing more about it than what a few manual pages told her.

Tris was about to head back to her desk when she saw Deter standing at the foot of the Astral's airstairs.

"Just getting a look?" he said, amused.

"Hi! Yeah, wanted to get a jump on things."

Deter shook his head, turned around, and walked back through the mechanics' area toward the office.

"And a very good morning to you, too," Tris muttered, heard only by the moon making its daily descent below the horizon.

Fourteen

AS THE SUN finally lit the sky, Tris went looking for Ross. She found him in the pilot area feeding trip data into the flight-planning computer.

At the push of a button, a complex program would send an optimized route directly to the Astral's navigation system via satellite. When the autopilot was engaged, the aircraft could practically fly itself to their destination. "PFM," her commuter buddies would say. *Pure Fucking Magic.* Or Patricia Frances Miles, she'd remind them with a smile.

Ross heard her come in and turned around.

"Hey. First trip, eh? Excited?"

"Yes." She smiled broadly. "Anything I can do to help you?"

"No. This is pretty basic. Just relax and enjoy it."

Relax. Sure.

Tris reached deep into her purse and pulled out a wad of tissue paper. Folded inside was a set of silver Air Force wings that Diana had given to her. Tris worshipped Diana, the instructor who had taught her how to fly. When Tris earned her Flight Instructor ratings, Diana presented the wings to her.

"Just passing them on," Diana had said. Diana flew as a captain now on a 727 based in Europe for a freight carrier. Tris missed her mentor and wished Diana spent more time visiting in the US. With the time difference and the high cost of international long-distance, they barely spoke anymore.

Tris pushed the pin on the back of the wings into the fabric partition separating her cube from the one she faced. They were a prized possession. The size of a tiepin, they symbolized perseverance, dedication, and friendship.

The wings firmly in place, Tris walked over to grab the navigation chart books they needed for the trip. Ross had already pulled them and handed the stack to Tris to put in the aircraft.

"Thanks. Nice to have *something* to do," she said, and grabbed the materials. She passed Deter on her way back out to the Astral.

"I'll meet you in the aircraft," he said, walking toward the men's room.

In the cockpit as she waited, Tris took a deep breath and inhaled what she always thought of as the smell of flight: the unique mixture of hydraulic fluid and unburned fuel, with traces of exhaust from outside the airplane and cleaning fluids inside. The scent carried her to the airport whenever she caught a whiff of it. She smiled when non-aviation people wrinkled their noses. They just didn't understand.

The Astral's gear suddenly compressed and Deter appeared behind her.

"Trying to get the hang of it," she said. "Well, you know, as much as I can..."

Deter ignored her. He grunted at the switch panels over her head, stepped back to the door, and stuck out his head to talk to one of the Tetrix mechanics.

"Hey, Brad, can you tug us out to be fueled?"

"You bet. Can you clear the wing, Ed?" Brad nodded to the

right side of the aircraft. The Astral's right wing was close to the wall. The tug Brad drove was hooked up to the nose wheel. He couldn't see the wing tip from that vantage point.

Deter ignored the request and sat down in the cabin so Tris went to help the mechanic. Brad nodded his thanks as he drove the airplane out to the ramp. Tris gave him the thumbs up the whole way.

Once Brad unhooked the tug, Deter walked over to the airplane's refueling portal on the right wing. Tris followed him.

"We need eight thousand pounds of fuel. How many gallons?" Deter waited for an answer.

She knew this! Tris did the mental math to calculate approximately how many gallons of jet fuel equaled the desired number of pounds.

"Twelve thousand gallons," she said. "Six thousand per side."

As soon as she saw Deter roll his eyes, she realized her mistake.

"Single point refueling. And just twelve hundred gallons." He shook his head and walked away.

The turboprop Tris flew at the commuter was gravity-fueled in a tank on each wing. This was a jet. It had single point refueling under pressure. And she was so nervous she said thousand instead of hundred. *Damn.*

Tris was mortified. She shook her head and walked back into the cabin to focus on something else, anything else. The Astral was stocked with snacks, soft drinks, and alcohol for the Tetrix executives. The ornate decanters of liquor in the galley, crystal glasses, and china that matched the embossed napkins made Tris wonder about her own appearance.

She looked at herself in the lavatory mirror. Tris didn't think to wear any more makeup than the mascara and ChapStick she usually flew with. Yet she grimaced at the reflection of the washed-out girl that looked back at her. She released her hair from behind her ears. There wasn't time to curl it this morning, and she hoped it would have enough body to frame her face. Instead, it clung flat against her skull.

Her clothes made her feel even shabbier. Her Tetrix uniform wasn't ready yet; it was being cut to fit by a local tailor because the only off-the-rack uniform pants they had were men's. Her old pilot shirt had yellowed under the armpits, and her Clear Sky uniform pants were worn to a sheen.

"What are you doing?" Deter appeared behind her as if from nowhere.

"Uh, no, I, uh," she said. "I was just checking the lav supplies."

Deter stifled an eye roll. "Come watch me start the APU."

The Astral was the first aircraft Tris had flown with an auxiliary power unit, a small jet engine located in the rear of the plane that powered all of its systems on the ground, including the air conditioning and heating. Tris had been forced to gut it out in extreme temperatures many times without either. Thankfully, those days were over.

They sat side by side in the cockpit. Deter held the airplane's one checklist in his hand, but didn't look at it. He threw a bunch of switches, and the next thing she knew, she heard the unmistakable whir of an engine starting. Before she could ask a single question, Deter sprinted off the aircraft toward the pilot area. His bald head caught the sun and looked like it was on fire.

It surprised Tris that Deter had been so cavalier. The importance of checklists had been drummed into her. "The minute you think you've memorized a checklist," Bron had said, "you tell yourself it's ok to forget something that might either kill you or save your life." She decided to go over the checklist herself and confirm each button and switch position. Deter had gotten them all. He'd executed the procedure perfectly.

With nothing else to do, Tris pulled out a binder of aircraft performance charts from a small closet behind the cockpit. The dusty volume detailed the Astral's maximum takeoff weights based on temperature, runway lengths, presence of moisture, and altitude.

A few minutes later Ross climbed into the aircraft. "That's some pretty dry stuff," he said looking over her shoulder. "They'll give you that at the training facility in Dallas, won't they?"

Training. Dallas or bust. "I don't mind doing some reading. It's pretty interesting. And I won't be going to school right away."

Ross picked up on her disappointment.

"You'll get there," he said, looking around. "Where's Deter? He's supposed to get the flight plan in the box."

"No idea. He started the APU and ran back inside."

Ross flashed an irritated glance at the entrance to the pilot area. "Guess I'll have to do it. Hey, wanna see how it's done?"

Tris nodded and followed him into the cockpit.

"Here, watch me," he gestured for her to sit next to him. His fingers flew over the keyboard on the nav computer. Within what seemed like seconds, they had bearing and distance to the first airborne fix. The Astral's navigation was simple, yet state of the art. Tris looked from the full-color displays to Ross and then out to the ramp. She could get used to this.

Fifteen

ROSS CLICKED ON the autopilot with the Astral in stable cruise flight, pointed toward Asheville. Tris was belted into the jump seat behind and in between the two pilots. The company's Chairman of the Board read a magazine in the back.

"So, how are Gerri and the kids?" Ross asked Deter, talking past Tris.

"Fine, fine. Devon and James?"

"Good. Yeah, they're in Montana with my father-in-law."

"Oh yeah?"

Neither pilot turned his head during the exchange. Deter and Ross were partners in the delicate dance of cockpit conversation. After basic piloting skills and good judgment, a knack for superficial conversation was critical to aviation career success.

Flying forced people who had nothing in common and might not otherwise engage outside of the cockpit to sit together for hours with little to do. Disagreement was the last thing pilots wanted upfront. It was best to keep conversation light.

Tris looked outside at the contrails of a jet passing in the opposite direction on their left, and remembered how she'd learned that lesson. Once she had inadvertently brought up politics on a flight. Her captain then tuned in to Rush Limbaugh's program on the airplane radio. It was a mistake she only made once.

The descent, approach, and landing into Asheville were routine. Deter and Ross worked in rhythm as they brought the Astral to a full stop on the ramp just as Deter said, "Shutdown checklist complete."

Anxious to stand up, Tris opened the Astral's door for the CEO.

"Nice to meet you, Mr. Emerson." Tris stuck out her hand.

He did a brief double take. "Roger, please."

Deter then appeared by her side and squeezed past her, pushing her back toward the cockpit.

"Let *me* help you with that," he said. He grabbed the exec's briefcase, shot Tris a withering look, and trotted down the stairs toward the waiting limo.

Not sure what she'd done wrong this time, Tris picked up trash, brushed crumbs from the chairman's breakfast off of his seat, and crossed the belts. Later, she'd confirm the catering and make sure the aircraft had fresh ice and coffee for the trip back to Exeter.

At Clear Sky, all she had to do after a flight was walk off the airplane. But Tris enjoyed the extra responsibilities. She wasn't put off by wiping off tray tables, reorganizing snacks in the drawers pillaged by their passenger, or reassembling the newspaper Roger had tossed in sections all over the cabin. This was her space now, and she wanted it perfect.

Ross watched her straighten the cabin, but made no effort to help.

"So?" He sounded anxious to hear what she thought.

Tris had so many questions that she was afraid if she asked even one she'd just spin. Still so new, she kept it light.

"Looks like fun. Looking forward to flying it."

"Yeah, it handles great. Has a nice feel to it," Ross said.

Then Deter walked back into the aircraft. As usual, he held a Styrofoam cup in one hand. The other held some of the aviation publications that were passed around the crew room.

Deter looked past Ross and sat down opposite Tris. He turned his head to the side momentarily, then swiveled around to face her directly.

"So, how exactly did you get this job?"

Ross's head shot straight up, then bobbled like one of those dolls in the rear windshield of a car.

"I submitted a résumé. I interviewed." Caught off-guard, her response sounded sarcastic, but that's exactly how it happened.

"Yeah. We heard about that *interview*."

Ross stared at Deter like the older man had lost his mind.

But it didn't stop him. "We weren't invited, were we, Larry?" Deter turned to Ross, who looked as if speaking would cause him physical pain, his expression a mix of shock and fear.

Ross finally said something that sounded like, "Uhhhhhhh."

An alarm went off inside her, complete with a flashing red light, but she willed her body still. Tris wanted to wave her arms, alert others to the danger, but thank goodness they stayed rooted in her lap.

"Oh come on, Larry," Deter continued. "You know that one day they just told us they'd hired her and when she was starting. They promised we'd get a chance to meet all potential new hires. And then she just shows up." He paused to sip his coffee. "Nothing personal, of course," he said.

Ross searched maniacally for something in his briefcase. Deter's glare never left Tris. She looked right back at him and said, "I really wanted to meet you guys, too. I was sure I'd enjoy flying with you."

"I'll bet." Deter's exasperation was palpable. "You know, we had a lot of guys who wanted this job. Guys with military experience, jet experience, years and years of flying crap for substandard outfits waiting for a chance like this." He paused for effect, then spat, "And they chose *you*."

"Christ, Ed, come on," Ross finally said. "She's not privy to any of that. Like she said, she sent a résumé and she interviewed. They decided to hire her. They offered her the job. She'd have been crazy not to take it. Hell, you said yourself how many guys were in the running."

By the time Ross jumped to her defense, it was too late. The power of Deter's attack had energized every nerve in her body. Yet to anyone who walked past the Astral's open door, they just looked like three crewmembers sitting in the cabin chatting.

For a split second, Tris wanted to run off the Astral and never come back. *I can go to the terminal, get on an airplane, fly home, and never see these guys again.* But that was no real solution. She'd chosen to be exactly where she was. Deter, unfortunately, came with the package.

"You know," she looked past Deter and Ross and forced herself to speak. "I wanted this. I've always wanted this. All my commuter buddies told me I was crazy to take this job."

That surprised both men. Deter squinted and cocked his head for a brief moment, then his facial muscles clenched taut as rope in a tug-of-war. But that ever-so-slight flinch encouraged her to go on.

"I want to see the country. I want to travel the world. I want to fly international, not just pull up to the gate in Cleveland and head back to Exeter. I want to *see* things." She held out two open palms. "And I want to fly there *myself*. I want to pull up on the ramp in the cockpit in Beijing and London and Moscow as Captain of the Astral."

"*Captain*?" Deter's face burned red. "Are you fucking *kidding me*? You're talking about being a *captain*? You just got here, lady, and if you think—"

"Ed, shut up, will ya?" Ross said. "Tris, look, I think Ed just wants to know why you took this job. I mean, you had a pretty good airline gig, right?"

They were all quiet. Seconds passed like hours.

"I can't think of a better life," Tris said at last.

"Neither can I. I earned this life fighting for my country." Deter lifted his cup and drank his coffee. But she could hear the echo of the unasked question.

"What did *you* do?"

Time passed, but Tris had no idea how much. Her brain told her to look at her watch, but her muscles didn't respond. Deter's verbal assault left her bruised and swollen, yet she hadn't been touched. Neither man was in the cabin anymore. The Astral was silent.

They could come back at any moment. Tris thought she could get some privacy in the Executive Terminal ladies' room. She moved quickly, hoping to avoid both of her crewmates. She made it to the restroom door undetected, but when she opened it, another pilot stood by the sink.

"Oh!" Tris didn't expect company.

The woman was in uniform and wore epaulets with three bars on her shoulders. Another first officer. She smiled at Tris as she straightened her tie. Tris exhaled in relief.

"Hey," Tris said, "what airplane are you on?" Tris had seen a couple of Citations and a three-motor Falcon next to the Astral on the ramp.

"The Falcon 900," she said without turning her head. Then she subtly straightened up, moved her shoulders back, and looked past

Tris. Classic pilot body language for "my airplane's bigger and faster than yours."

"Wow. Nice ride."

The Falcon pilot gave Tris a barely perceptible nod, dried her hands, tossed a paper towel into the trash, and brushed nonexistent errant hairs back into her perfect bun.

"Hey, listen," Tris said, "You got a minute? I could really use some advice. I'm new on the Astral, and my training captain—"

"Nice meeting you," the woman said as she hurried out of the room.

Another blow. Tris steadied herself by placing a hand on the cold white tile wall. Demeaned and dismissed by her own crew, and then a perfect stranger. Tris felt unsteady, almost dizzy. She entered a stall and latched the door behind her.

Imbalance turned to fear. Could *Deter* know about her training history?

After a few deep breaths, she realized if Deter knew about what happened at Clear Sky, he'd have told Zorn, and she'd have never been hired. So, he was just another hurdle she had to jump, despite what she'd already overcome. *When does it end?*

After a few minutes, she peeked outside the room to check her surroundings. She spied Deter, a hairy hand on his hip, talking on a pay phone. She practically ran back out to the ramp so that he wouldn't see her.

Back in the Astral, Ross stood in the cabin as he removed something from his briefcase.

"Let it go," he said as soon as he saw her. "Don't mind Ed. He's like that sometimes. Seriously, it isn't personal."

"Not *personal?* Sounded pretty personal to me. I'm doing the best I can. I've been here, what, ten days?"

Tris had a legitimate gripe but didn't want anything she said to sound like whining. That's just what Deter would expect. This could be a defining moment for her. Ross seemed to be friendly, at least without Deter around. She wanted his support—anyone's support. She *needed* it. She couldn't fight Deter without someone by her side.

"He'll come around," Ross said with a smile. "Hey, don't you have a training flight coming up with him? Just wow him in the airplane!"

And just like that, Tris felt the weight of her failures.

Sixteen

DETER AND ROSS were the only two people in the Tetrix pilot area. Ross stood by his desk with the Asheville trip flight manifest in his hand. He'd filled in the details that Tetrix tracked and needed to drop it on Ann-Marie's desk, but couldn't seem to move in that direction. The few sheets of paper mesmerized him, as if the longer he held them, the closer he'd come to making sense of the day's events.

Ross heard crunching and smelled Pringles as Deter walked back to his cube from the stock room. Tris had gone home as soon as she'd finished cleaning the cabin.

Asheville to Exeter had to have been the most awkward leg Ross had ever flown. Tris sat in the jump seat and didn't say more than two words the whole flight. Deter acted like nothing had happened. And now they were back at base and Deter *still* wouldn't let it go.

"What is she doing here?"

Not this again. "Brian wanted someone entry level. She seems to fit that requirement. She's a nice girl. A hard worker."

"So what? I don't care if she's kind to small animals. Man, do you know how many years I slogged in crappy jobs before I got a gig like this? She hasn't been flying all that long, and she just walks into it. And she knows shit. Nothing. I spent an hour trying to train her last week. Longest fucking hour of my life."

"Yeah, I know." Ross tried to placate him, and hoped Deter would just talk himself out.

Tris had been a commuter pilot, a grueling, low paying flying job. A stepping stone for jobs at places like Tetrix. Deter had no idea what that kind of flying was like, or how she struggled to get that experience. The military had comped his flight training. Tris paid for every flight rating she earned on her own, out of pocket, on a teacher's salary. And Ross practically had to pull that information out of her. She didn't want anyone to feel sorry for her. You had to respect that, but no use pointing that out to Deter. He saw it the way he saw it.

"She's sure leading a charmed life, I'd say." Deter was on a roll. "And I'm the one who has to train her in the Astral. Man. She has no jet time at all. Christ, I hope she doesn't kill me!"

Ross held his tongue but it wasn't easy. He wondered if Deter even believed what he was saying. Every pilot, including Deter, started somewhere.

When Deter came to Tetrix, he'd been flying outdated equipment that had none of the advanced navigation and in-strumentation the Astral had. He had to learn it just like she did. Ross remembered a time or two when Deter had trouble picking up the new technology.

Could Deter have forgotten his own struggles so soon? Memory was a funny thing when you decided in advance you weren't going to like someone.

Deter tossed the empty can of chips into the wastebasket. He put his flight jacket on and grabbed his soft Eddie Bauer briefcase. "I'm outta here. You walkin' out?" he asked Ross.

"Nope. I still have some paperwork to finish."

"Ok. See ya around, Larry," Deter said as he grabbed the copy of the *Wall Street Journal* he took from the airplane, slamming the exit door against the stop.

Ross wanted to help Tris out, but he had his own doubts. Not about whether women could fly airplanes. He'd flown enough charters with superb female pilots to know that they could. He didn't judge pilots that way anymore. He'd sat next to plenty of men in the cockpit whose piloting skills scared him to death.

No, Ross was more concerned about how she would fit in with the guys in the department. And how their wives would respond when they found out she was going on overnights with them. And what if he had to fly a weeklong trip to some beach resort with her? He didn't even want to think of the conversation that would start with Devon.

Well, nothing he could do about it. She was here. And Zorn's ego was in overdrive since he hired her. He couldn't stop talking about how he had "finally integrated the flight department." Ross would help her out just to stay on the right side of Zorn. Especially after RJ got fired.

RJ had been with Tetrix for years. A real good old boy. Ross liked him. Hell, even *Deter* did. Zorn would always ask Ann-Marie to schedule the two of them together. RJ was lots of fun on the road: laid back, good stick, smart pilot. Zorn used to call RJ his best friend.

Last April, RJ and Zorn flew the trip everyone at Tetrix called the "Ball Buster." It was an annual ten-day tour of the company's European facilities. The exhausting trip sometimes required the pilots to fly to three different countries in one day.

"Zorn may not be the smartest guy in the world, but he's sure the meanest," RJ said one night after he got the ax. He and Ross shared a couple of pitchers at O'Slattery's. "Yeah, he was just lying in the weeds. Waiting for his moment. Nine years of service...dickhead. Well, best to be done with him."

"What happened?" Ross had only heard Zorn's side of the story.

"The trip went well enough. Except that every leg I flew, I made a perfect landing. And Zorn bounced it in each time. The executives in the back joked with Zorn. They wisecracked that maybe I should fly every leg. Hell, I thought it was good luck. Turns out it was the worst possible luck for me."

RJ showed up to fly a trip one day, weeks after the Ball Buster, and Willett fired him on the spot. Zorn had 'discovered' that RJ made personal calls on the company-issued portable phone while he was on the road. This was "use of company property for personal convenience," strictly prohibited by company policy. Being fired for an infraction every single pilot at Tetrix was guilty of was bad enough, but it was Zorn—his best friend—who convinced Willett he had to go. All because of a fragile ego bruised by a few hard landings.

It never mattered to Zorn if the punishment he meted out was grossly out of proportion to the crime. It was simply understood that if Zorn wanted you out for any reason or none at all, he found a way.

Now Zorn called *Ross* his best friend. Ross had wisely kept his guard up since RJ was fired. But before that, he had been careless. When he first started to sense that his marriage was in trouble a year ago, Ross got his first DUI. He paid the fine and forgot about it.

After his second DUI a few months later, his driver's license was suspended. He had to tell Zorn, to make sure they were scheduled together on Gulfstream trips. They were neighbors, so unless Zorn could drive Ross to the airport on flying days, he'd have to show up in a cab. People would ask questions.

When Ross got his license back, Zorn swore he hadn't told any-one about the DUIs, and he probably hadn't. But he'd occasionally hint at the consequences if the company (code for "Willett") or the FAA found out. At worst, Willett could fire him, which would be bad enough. The FAA, on the other hand, could pull his pilot's license for good.

During his required flight physical every six months, Ross lied on the medical questionnaire. Where it asked if he had ever been convicted of a DUI, he checked "no." It was a gamble, but Ross played the odds; the law worked on the honor system. Unless Ross was involved in an aircraft emergency or accident, the FAA would never need to check.

Devon and James left today to visit Devon's dad in Montana for a week. They flew first class. Ross had to keep his job for the sake of his family. Or soon, he feared, those tickets would be one way. If Zorn wanted this girl to succeed, Ross had to make it happen.

Seventeen

TRIS HAD CLEANED up the back of the Astral as quickly as possible to get the hell out of there and escape Deter and Ross. Still uneasy when she finally climbed into her car, Tris sped away from the Tetrix lot. She pulled over on a side street just a few blocks away.

She'd been too upset to eat in Asheville, even though they'd ordered crew meals. Now her body demanded food. Tris was just blocks from O'Slattery's. It was on her way home.

The place was empty. Only three of the dozen or so interior tables were occupied. Tris couldn't see anyone out on the patio. She walked toward the bar, which had several empty stools, and saw a couple of guys she knew from Clear Sky at one of the tables. Thank goodness, friendly faces.

"Hey, Tris. Whassup?" called Eric Estes. Tris liked Estes. His wide grin and deep dimples made him look friendly and approachable. He motioned for her to come over and sit down. Estes was always dressed in khakis and a polo shirt, the only difference was whether the shirt had short or long sleeves. Today, long. He was with a barrel-chested guy named Bill Miller. She'd never flown with him.

As Tris walked toward the table she picked a clean glass off the sideboard.

Estes stood up and hugged her. "Hey," he said, "we heard you just started a big corporate job. At Exeter?"

"Yeah. Tetrix." She pulled out the empty chair next to him, sat down and poured herself a beer from the group's pitcher. "So great to see you guys."

"Of course. So Tetrix. What do they have?"

"An Astral and a Gulfstream."

"Gulfstream! Nice!" He took a swig of beer.

"Yeah, but I'm on the Astral for now," Tris said. Estes was a typical pilot—always focused on the bigger airplane first.

"Good enough, good buddy." He patted her on the shoulder. "Don't you miss the airline world? How else ya gonna see Duluth?"

Tris laughed for the first time all day. "I miss my friends," she said. As she took a sip of beer, she realized how true that was. The bond between commuter pilots was born of mutual misery, but it was there. Yet hadn't she learned from them that flying was about bigger, faster airplanes and more money? And the importance of command?

Tris, Estes, and Miller sat around for a few minutes catching up. They ordered a second pitcher and some appetizers. Tris felt connected to these guys, and it warmed her. As time passed and the distance from the Asheville trip grew, she relaxed, becoming herself again. Deter seemed very far away.

Just as she and her two friends launched into the usual conversation about pilot career tracks, she saw Ross enter the bar. She remembered she'd seen him at O'Slattery's before. She hadn't lingered on him, even though he was good-looking. Probably because she'd been with Bron. She hardly noticed other men when she and

Bron were together. She would focus only on him, like he was the only man in the room. In the world.

"Well, hey!" Ross walked over to their table. He was dressed in an Allman Brothers T-shirt and jeans.

"Hey," she managed without looking at him.

Ross nodded to the guys with Tris: a brief head movement up and down to establish the alpha. In this group, it was obviously Ross, who assumed the stance of command, and looked at them with his eyelids lowered and chin pointed forward.

"So, Tris, what are you guys up to here?"

"Not much. We're old flying buddies." She introduced Ross to her friends in a formal but courteous manner. They all nodded again. No one rose to shake Ross's hand.

"Good to meet you. Hey guys, can I borrow this one?" He gestured toward Tris. Estes looked over at her. She nodded slightly, giving him the green light.

"Sure. Good seeing you, Tris. Way to go on that new job!"

Tris hugged the guys and slowly walked behind Ross toward the bar.

"Whiskey, neat," he said to the bartender, who glanced at Tris to see if she wanted another drink. Tris shook her head.

"Got a cigarette?" Ross turned to Tris.

"I don't, but I know where to get one. Hey, Sinead," she called over to the bartender. "Can we bum a couple of butts?"

"Sure you can," the petite, dark-haired woman answered in a thick Irish accent. Everyone who worked in the pub was from the owner's hometown in Ireland. Sinead placed Ross's drink, along with an ashtray, a book of matches, and two Marlboro Lights in front of them. Ross lit Tris's cigarette in his mouth first, took a drag, and handed it to her.

"So, that was a fun trip, eh?" He rolled his eyes and inhaled.

She wasn't sure of her footing here, but Tris needed advice. She had to try and trust someone.

"Well, the first leg was anyway. Larry, I don't know what to do about Deter. Should I tell Zorn or Willett about what he said?"

Ross didn't hesitate. "No. Don't do that. Those guys, they worship Deter. They think he's some aviation god since he used to do carrier landings in the navy."

Tris exhaled slowly. "Then I don't know what to do. I mean, I just started here. What's his problem?"

"Look, like I said to you earlier," Ross said, draining his whiskey and motioning to Sinead for another, "that's just Deter. He's kind of an asshole. But believe it or not—and I know you won't—he actually means well."

"He hates my guts. And he's my training captain!"

Ross swirled the bottom of his empty glass along the bartop. Sinead poured a shot and left the bottle next to his right hand.

"He actually doesn't hate *you*. It's more the idea..." Ross took a long pull on his cigarette and blew out the smoke. "Look, this is a guy who thinks the Tailhook Convention should be a national holiday."

"You mean like when that female pilot was attacked by naval officers? He thought that was a good thing?"

Ross ran a finger around the rim of his glass. "I remember his take on all the trouble they had that year. He thought it was all bullshit. His attitude toward you was sealed from the get."

Tris shuddered. Everyone in aviation remembered the Navy's Tailhook Convention of '91. The Gauntlet. That's all you had to say to a female pilot to raise images of physical and verbal assault by men who were supposed to be America's finest aviators. They all knew what it symbolized—women were meat. Not professionals, and definitely not pilots.

"Great. So, I never had a chance with him. Why did Tetrix even interview me if this was the deal with Deter? And why would they pair me up with him?"

Ross stubbed out his cigarette. "Zorn wanted you. End of story. And Deter will do what he's told," he said, his deep voice steady and convincing even after a couple of whiskeys.

"Anyway, he's gotta get you trained up before they'll even consider sending him to Gulfstream school." Ross looked like he was trying to stop himself from saying something he shouldn't. He took a slug of his third drink. "Zorn doesn't really want him on the Gulfstream, truthfully. He doesn't want to fly with him."

"Why not?"

Ross chuckled. "You mean you can't tell? Deter doesn't kiss Zorn's ass," he said matter-of-factly.

"So he's gonna train me, and he still might not get the Gulfstream? Does he know that?"

"I don't know. But Zorn made it clear to him he's gotta get this done and get you ready if he's gonna move into the Gulfstream." Ross poured another drink. Sinead walked over with a pack of cigarettes, two sticking out of the top.

"Need another smoke?" She asked.

Tris looked over at Ross. She'd follow his lead.

"Nah, not for me. One's my limit." He laughed at his own comment.

Tris continued the conversation as Ross stirred on the barstool beside her. "So, I'm just another excuse not to send him to Gulfstream training in Savannah?"

"Hey, I'm gonna see what's in the jukebox." Ross slid off of his seat and steadied himself against the mahogany bar.

When he moved away from Tris, the bartender leaned over.

"How do you know him?" Sinead nodded in Ross's direction.

"We fly together. He's a pilot," Tris said.

"Noooo kidding." Sinead chuckled. "Well, he's a regular."

"Really? I think I may have seen him here. Can't say for sure though."

"We call him 'Unlucky Larry,'" Sinead said.

"Yeah? Why's that?"

"Aye, hang around a bit longer and you'll see for yourself."

Sinead was right. Once Ross had downed three whiskeys, he drank on autopilot. After four or five, he switched to beer. Tris had one beer during the quick ninety minutes it took Ross to go from upright to plastered.

The crowd at O'Slattery's picked up as the afternoon wore on. Ross stumbled out of his stool and approached a pretty brunette at the bar. His lips almost touched the woman's ear as he whispered to her what a "nice guy" he was. Tris watched her lean away in disgust.

Finally, with the help of a couple of guys who tended bar with Sinead, Tris was able to steer Ross out of O'Slattery's toward his car. His big Cutlass was parked in the lot not far from her Corolla.

Tris hated drunks. They scared her, and Ross was the model for all the reasons why. Sloppy, unstable, and out of control. No way she'd let him drive. She couldn't.

She steadied him against her car, but he pushed her away. Ross had tried to walk but stumbled. As Tris forced him back against the hood, he fished his keys out of his coat pocket. He moved toward his car and dropped them on the ground.

"Oh, you're not going to drive." Tris put her hand on his chest and gently pushed him back toward her car.

"Sure I am," he said, lurching for his keys.

"Oh, hell no!" Somehow she simultaneously picked up his key ring while maneuvering him into the Corolla's passenger seat. She looked out at the heavy traffic on the highway service road. It must be close to rush hour.

"I need to call your wife. What's your number?"

"What's *yours*?" He winked at her and spit out his number. "But not there. Gone, gone, gone..."

She ran back into the bar to call his house, but Mrs. Ross didn't pick up, only the answering machine. Then she remembered his wife and son were visiting her parents in Montana.

She hurried back outside to make sure he hadn't stumbled into traffic. "I'll call you a cab," she said, running back into the bar.

"No." Ross waved his arms in the air. "Gimme my damn car keys," he yelled. He yanked on the interior handle of the Corolla's passenger door and pushed his weight against it when it wouldn't open. He hadn't thought to simply raise the button and unlock it.

"I'm fine! I'll drive!"

"No way. No way!" Tris yelled a bit louder than she'd intended. A couple just pulling up to the bar asked her if she needed help, but she took a deep breath and said no.

She had to get this situation under control. Ross could not take the wheel. She imagined him smashing into some poor unsuspecting driver, lifeless bodies being pulled from the wreckage. Loved ones picking up a phone, about to have their lives torn apart. She shivered.

No. All she had to do was buckle his seat belt and drive him home. No cab. Even if she took his keys, he might have a spare and ask the cabbie to bring him back to the parking lot.

Unlike the unalterable events of the past, she could fix this. She would save him.

"Larry, I'll take you home."

"Great!" He brightened. "I'll grill chicken!"

Tris smiled, envisioning this limp-legged, deadweight of a man trying to find his charcoal grill, much less operate it. Luckily, Ross was conscious enough to give Tris his address, and she was familiar with his neighborhood. She grabbed her Exeter street map from the back seat, harnessed him in tightly and started the car.

As she drove, Ross morphed from an angry to happy drunk. "I got the radiosh, Cap'n," he slurred, tuning to a Christian music station.

"What a friend we have in Jeeeeeeesusssss," he bellowed as they crawled along Overland Boulevard.

As the streetlights paved the way, it hit her. Her passenger was a completely bombed pilot whom she *worked* with. She tightened her grip on the steering wheel with one hand, and rubbed her forehead with the other. It would be over soon.

All of a sudden she felt his hand squeeze her shoulder. She quickly shoved him off and kept driving. About halfway to his house, Ross bolted upright in his seat and yelled "gimme your tits!" He tried to lunge toward her, but the seatbelt threw him back in his seat.

She scooched as close to the driver's door as she could, moved her seat as far forward as it would go and pressed down on the accelerator.

Finally, she saw the mailbox with Ross's house number. She pulled into the driveway and saw moths flapping around the porch light. Ross had stopped being a threat a mile back when he had passed out and began snoring. Tris shook him firmly until he grunted. Still belted in, he reached out with both arms to grab her waist and pull her towards him.

"Let go of me!" Tris wrinkled her nose in disgust. He stunk. A trail of spit had leaked down from the corner of his mouth. "We're home. Let's get you inside." She steadied him against her left side, and put her arm loosely around his waist.

His arm shot out toward her breast, but she twisted away just in time. "I don't wanna be here. I don't live here," he mumbled, falling from the car straight onto the ground.

For a second Tris wondered whether he'd given her the right address. She reached into his pocket where his wallet half stuck out and checked his driver's license. Right place.

"Larry, this is your house."

Tris helped him up by taking both of his hands, then stood behind him and gently pushed the unsteady Ross to the front door. He didn't try to touch her again. It took some doing, but she found the right key. The moment she stepped into his house, she couldn't wait to leave.

Luckily, no alarm went off. Ross tripped over the threshold and stumbled to the brown leather couch in his living room and promptly passed out. Tris could hear him snoring as she clicked the front door shut behind her.

Eighteen

THE NEXT MORNING, Tris woke up early, despite being exhausted from the night before. She padded into her tidy kitchen to start the Mr. Coffee, sluggishly searching for the filters in the pantry.

When she opened the door, something rolled off the high shelf and fell to the floor. Still bleary-eyed and a bit startled, she couldn't identify it at first and bent over to grab it.

She froze. It was Bron's tiny flashlight, the one he used to check the airplane during night flights. He'd said he'd lost it on the road, but somehow it had migrated into her kitchen. The way things tend to do in a home.

After he died, Tris thought she'd packed up all of the items he'd left at her apartment. She didn't want them popping up, bringing back painful memories.

Tris stared at the cylindrical reminder on the kitchen floor. She couldn't pick it up and instead stepped over it to finish making coffee. She didn't look at it once as the coffee brewed.

Tris hurried out of the kitchen with her steaming mug. She sat in a worn wing chair, one of the many things her mother made her take from her childhood home when she left Pittston. Exeter was only 100 miles away, but to her family, it could just as well have been on another continent.

"You'll want this chair, honey," her mother had said, "to remind you of home."

As if she needed a chair to remember. Tris was anxious to leave her mother's house and fought against taking anything with her. But, she secretly liked the chair.

Tris wished she could be like other people, warmed by memories of hearth and home. For thirteen years of her life, right up until the moment she decided to leave home and pointed her car north toward Exeter with the U-Haul attached, she'd listened to whispered conversations about the day her mother and step-father would have the tiny house in Pittston all to themselves. Tris hoped they had waited until she had gotten through the first stop sign before popping champagne.

But her mother was right about the chair, now tucked in the corner of her bedroom. She curled her feet up beneath her and realized she'd fallen asleep in the clothes she'd worn on the Asheville trip.

Tris was a mess. Slept in her clothes. Frightened by a mini-Maglite in her own kitchen. Marginalized by her training captain.

And Ross. She couldn't begin to process his behavior. She wanted—no, desperately needed—to have a real conversation with him about Deter. But he drank so much so fast. And then, in the car, he'd transformed from the helpful co-worker who came to her defense with Deter into a lecherous drunk.

Bile rose in her throat when Tris remembered how Ross tried to grope her. She'd soon have a chance to see if he held it together better on the road. A lot of guys went overboard when their families were out of town. He was probably enjoying a rare family-free night.

She just hoped she never had to shove him away again.

Deter was another problem entirely. Bottom line, Tris needed him. Her mentor Diana had told her horror stories about ex-military pilots she flew with at the freight carrier. But Diana had studied at the Air Force Academy for two years, so she was better acquainted with and equipped to handle their personalities. Tris wished Diana hadn't moved to Brussels. She'd be the perfect person to talk to right now.

If she told Danny about yesterday, beginning with Deter and ending with driving drunk Ross home, he'd probably say, "I told you so." He'd be right, too. "Corporate pilots," he'd say, "are a different breed. 'Kick the tires, light the fires.'" He'd laugh, using the old cliché to describe pilots who didn't like following procedures. Bron would say the same.

Tris looked over at a picture of her and Bron on the beach in Nassau, still in its frame on the chipped bedside table. Would he have been proud of her, glad she drove Ross home? Afraid for her, being in the car with a man who could get violent and hurt her? Just pissed that Ross drank so much in the first place when he knew he had to drive?

Her mind drifted further. Bron always called her after he completed a trip, even if he just left a message. In the car with the radio on, they'd compete over what year a song came out. He always won. And he'd smile, his grin like a string of piano keys.

Thoughts of Bron overcame her if she wasn't vigilant, and today she didn't have the energy to resist. Pictures of him were sprinkled around the bedroom in frame after frame. In some he stood by her side; in others, he was at the airport, and one was taken in the very chair where Tris sat now with her knees pulled into her chest, arms tight against her body, folded into a ball. She felt his hand smooth her limp, brown hair against the curve of her neck in a way that always made her feel like Rapunzel. She allowed herself the luxury of imagining the sound of his key in the lock, the whoosh of the opening door. Bron coming home.

Reality cracked like a slap. He'd never be home—or anywhere—again. That wasn't a problem she could ever solve.

Deter, however, had to be. He was a colossal asshole, but what else did she actually know about him? Something frustrated him, she was sure of that. She'd dismissed Ross's inebriated take that it wasn't personal, or specific to her. If not, then what *was* it?

Tris didn't realize she'd gotten up and paced over to her kitchen, careful to avoid the memory on the floor. She'd opened all the cabinets at least twice but hadn't touched anything in them. She opened the refrigerator door and stood there, cataloging the same items that had been in the exact same spot the last time she'd looked. Logically it was only a matter of time before things evened out at Tetrix, but right now the job fit like a pair of jeans she was trying to diet into.

Agitated, Tris stomped into her living room. She stood in front of her treasured book collection. Just the sight of them soothed her. They were mostly old, well-read paperbacks, yet Tris valued each volume. She'd kept every book she had ever bought, from Pulitzer Prize winners to the 'brain candy' she'd occasionally pick up to pass the time.

The first novel she remembered reading just for fun was Sidney Sheldon's *The Other Side of Midnight*. It was also the only true romance novel she'd ever read, before the genre even existed, back when *The Thorn Birds* was only considered historical fiction. Both paperbacks sat like neighbors on her shelves.

Tris settled her gaze on a couple of copies of Kate Chopin's *The Awakening*—the subject of her master's thesis. Then, on the eye-level shelf, she spotted her worn copy of *Lonesome Dove*. It was still her favorite novel from the time she bought the paperback in 1986. Some of the pages were worn, with triangles missing from the corners where Tris had marked her place.

She flipped through the pages but only saw the names Deter

and Ross as the characters. Ross would wake up with a headache. If he remembered his behavior, she hoped he'd have the grace to apologize. She could handle Deter, but luckily she had a few days off before their next scheduled training flight.

Tris reached for *The Clan of the Cave Bear*. She related to Jean Auel's heroine, a woman who also struggled to belong. Today, Tris would draw strength from Ayla's journey. She should probably study the Astral manual, but instead, she spent a few hours curled up in her mother's chair with an old friend.

All while that little piece of Bron lay on the kitchen floor.

Nineteen

"WHAT'S THAT?" DETER asked his wife Gerri, who walked toward him holding a tray filled with a chip-n-dip, glasses and a frosty pitcher. He relaxed on the loveseat in their new gazebo as the sun set.

"Margaritas!" Her wide-set blue eyes twinkled as she arranged the drinks, a basket of his favorite chips, and her delicious homemade guacamole on the patio set's glass-top table. It was late October; Indian summer in the Midwest, and the temperature was still in the high 60's at twilight.

"Thanks, hon." Deter picked up a glass and moistened the rim with his index finger before he twisted it in the salt dish. He poured a drink for Gerri and then one for himself.

"Have you heard from Steven?" Their son had just returned from his honeymoon, but they hadn't spoken to him since the wedding three weeks ago.

"He'll be here this weekend. You're not flying are you?" She tucked a strand of silver hair behind her ear.

"Nope." Deter looked up at a bird resting on the branch of a sassafras tree. The Gulfstream left for Hawaii on Saturday for a one-week sit, Zorn and Ross the crew. It was an all-expense paid vacation for those guys; just the kind of trip he'd love to be on. "I'll be home this weekend. All I have to fly this week are a couple of training flights with the new girl."

"What's her name again?"

"Patricia. Well, she goes by Tris. Kind of odd, right?"

Gerri smiled. "Well, Ed, have you asked her how she got her nickname? Is she so awful that you can't have a conversation with her?"

"Of course not." He took a long pull from his drink and munched on some chips dipped in guacamole. "She's actually very intelligent. She reads a lot, like I do. No, it's not her *personally*. It's just the way this all came about..."

Gerri sat next to him on the loveseat, her knees bent and feet pulled up underneath her. "You have to get over that, hon. You said she could fly, right?"

"Oh yeah. I mean, for her experience level, she's fine. But the Astral is a real challenge for her."

"Oh well, what about you, Ed? What's next for *you*? When is the Gulfstream coming around?"

Deter put his arm around his wife of twenty-nine years. "Not for a while yet, I guess. Damned if they'll tell me. Can't believe they put it off—again—because of..." he hesitated but simply couldn't stop himself, "...some under-qualified girl." He tensed, pulling his arm off of Gerri's shoulder. She caught it and tugged it back around her.

Deter couldn't shake how much this co-pilot hire bothered him. It was just like when he lost his first chance at command to whats-her-name...Carey? Casey? No, Cami.

Deter had few regrets about his time in the navy. But he made one huge, unrecoverable mistake: his grades in flight training. Everything about his naval aviation career came back to his grades. He wished he'd studied harder. That Cami was number one in her class and made the jet cut with ease. Deter was young, stupid; he partied more than he studied. He ended up in the C-2, delivering supplies to carriers instead of launching off of their decks to go fight.

This new girl, this Tris, even resembled Cami: slim, straight brown hair, average face. Looked him right in the eye all the time, too.

He cringed when Tris showed up for training sessions over-prepared. She always had the right answer. But she still didn't have the experience—the *gravitas*—to ask the right questions. She wanted to know what it meant when some light came on, instead of how to maximize fuel burn and passenger comfort during those longer flights. The stuff that really mattered.

Deter slapped a mosquito that had already taken a bite of his forearm and fled the scene. "So, what time will the kids be here?"

"Sunday at noon. You gonna grill?" Gerri bent her head back to rest it on her husband's chest.

"You bet." He looked around their yard at the new steam room, hot tub, and flowerbeds and considered how lucky he was. After all those years in the navy, to live like this. "Steaks for everyone," he announced as Gerri burrowed under his arm, looked up, and kissed him on the jaw.

Deter looked at his wife, his beloved Gerri. She kept up with the kids, the house, always had. Classic military wife, now reaping the rewards after all those difficult years; the constant moves, raising two kids practically alone as Deter swooped in for stretches of time between deployments. This is what Cami should have been doing—what Tris should be doing. Supporting a pilot instead of trying to be one.

Twenty

RAIN FELL LIKE machine gun fire and pelted the tin roof of the Tetrix hangar. Tris paced around the pilots' cubicles. Just six weeks into the job, it was time for her qualification flight in the Astral. Deter would be in the left seat with Zorn observing from the jump seat.

Zorn and Deter were late. Figured. Tris dumped her flight bag on the Astral and wandered up to the front desk with black coffee for herself and one with a little cream and Sweet'N Low for Ann-Marie. They were building a work friendship one cup at a time.

The two women barely had time to say hello when Zorn breezed into the reception area from the private garage only he and Willett had access to. Everyone called it "executive parking."

Zorn strode right up to Tris. "You can pre-flight when Deter gets here. I have some paperwork to do." He turned toward his office. "And we're going to Maxwell, by the way," he called to her over his shoulder.

Tris smiled at Ann-Marie. This was good luck. She knew the procedures at Exeter and Maxwell practically by heart, so she'd be able to concentrate on the airplane and her audience.

The two women looked up at the clock simultaneously. It was 10:40 a.m. Deter still hadn't arrived. Ann-Marie shook her head and grimaced. "Typical," she said.

Tris grinned, nodded, and went to check the weather forecasts for Exeter and Maxwell. The animated color radar showed rain along their route, with stronger storms spread out at least a hundred miles from both locations. The worst weather was moving east at a brisk clip and might just be out of their way by the end of the flight.

Deter threw the interior door against its stop and kept walking as it slammed shut. He ignored Tris on his way to his desk as rain dripped off the top of his head, the tip of his nose, and the hem of his coat.

Fascinated, she watched as he danced his way out of his raincoat—he slid the right sleeve completely down his arm, then grabbed his collar and swung the slicker around and pulled the left arm down and away from his body. Only when this elaborate ritual was complete did he speak.

"Where's Zorn? Is he ready?"

"In his office."

He walked in the general direction of the coffee machine.

Deter looked like he would rather swallow rusty nails than fly with her. She hoped he'd at least keep his cool in the cockpit with Zorn watching.

The door cracked open again. Ross walked in, tossed his umbrella to the side of the door, and shook off his raincoat. They hadn't seen each other since O'Slattery's almost four weeks ago. Tris had been joined at the hip with Deter for training, and Ross had been in and out flying the Gulfstream.

"Hey there," he said brightly. "I was hoping to get here before you launched. Wanted to wish you good luck. Big flight today."

Tris looked away. She hoped Ross wouldn't want to talk about that night. Frankly, she would have preferred to avoid him altogether today. But here he was: a colleague being pleasant and friendly.

"Do you have a trip today?" Tris hadn't seen anything on the schedule for the Gulfstream.

"Nope. Just came in to wish you luck."

"Really? That's nice. Thanks."

"Where are you guys going? Maxwell?"

"Yup. How'd you know?"

"Oh, that's where Zorn always likes to go for qualification flights. Lots of approaches, not that busy during the day, not that far away." Ross was right: Maxwell's air traffic consisted mostly of freight dogs— pilots who only flew in the dark.

Deter burst back into the pilot area and interrupted her conversation. "Let's go," he called and started toward the hangar. He was severely bowlegged but still moved so fast Tris had to jog to catch up. She shot a glance toward the computer and realized she hadn't printed the weather.

"I'll get the weather and bring it out to you guys," Ross said, as if reading her mind.

She smiled and caught up with Deter. He stood at the forward side of the entrance door and turned to Tris.

"Ok. Pre-flight," he ordered.

"Sure. Do you want me to tell you what I'm doing, uh, looking at?"

"You'd better. Because if you don't, I won't know if you're doing it right."

Tris began at the airplane's entrance door, as suggested in the manual. She closed and locked the door from the outside and opened it again. Check.

She worked her way toward the nose of the Astral, examining the probes poking out of the left side of the plane. They provided airspeed, altitude, and vertical speed information inside the cockpit by measuring the air pressure outside. They had to be clear. They were.

Walking a good ten feet in front of the aircraft, Tris lined up dead center with the nose, and looked at the Astral head on.

Deter didn't even wait until she planted her feet. "What are you doing? This isn't in the checklist."

Tris felt a telltale tingling in her arms and hands—her internal early warning sign that Deter might erupt. She took a breath before responding. "Checking to see if the plane is level." If the Astral sat low on one side, it could indicate a number of things, all of which were bad. She'd picked up this technique from Bron somewhere along the line.

Deter said nothing, so Tris continued along the right side of the fuselage. She saw some oil stains on the outside of the number two engine nacelle but didn't make much of it. There were no drips on the ground.

Tris was about to check the oil level on number one, but the gauge position on the inside of the nacelle next to the fuselage made it hard to read from the ground. Tris lowered the left side baggage door and climbed up to get a better look.

"Guess you're just too short for this airplane," Deter barked. One of the mechanics standing nearby started to laugh. Tris felt herself turning red and looked away for a few seconds, hiding her embarrassment. She was afraid any comeback would sound bitter or shrill. A couple of deep breaths would have to get her past this.

Her exterior inspection complete, Tris climbed into the cockpit to run the interior checks. Deter watched every move she made. "Any comments? Critique?" she asked when she finished, but he just walked back to the pilot area.

She raised her open palms to the sky and shook her head. No news must be good news. If she'd screwed up, Deter would surely have said so.

With nothing else to do, Tris checked her desk one more time to make sure she hadn't forgotten anything. Lightly, she touched the Air Force wings Diana had given her. For luck.

Deter was in Zorn's office with the door closed. They came out together, called to Tris, and headed toward the conference room where Zorn would give the briefing. Ross joined them.

"Is it ok with you if he comes along on the flight?" Zorn nodded toward Ross. Although he framed it as a question, it was clear that the only answer was "yes." *Great. Another member of the review board.* She hoped Ross would at least be a forgiving judge.

Zorn cleared his throat. "Ok, Tris, so far you've been the non-flying pilot on the Astral learning the plane. Today we're gonna see if we can release you to fly it on company trips," he said against the drumbeat of heavy rain. "We're going out to do some basic maneuvers first to give you the feel of the jet. Then we'll head over to Maxwell and do some approaches. You'll do a series of takeoffs and landings there, and we'll make an approach back in here. Sound good?"

"And I'll be in the back reading the paper," Ross joked.

Tris welcomed the chance to laugh. "Sounds good, Brian." Deter and Zorn would grade her, but surely Ross would have an opinion. It helped her to believe there might be someone on the Astral, someone at Tetrix cheering for her, even if he sat in the back with *USA Today*.

Left completely unsaid were the consequences if she didn't do well, didn't meet their standards. She pushed those thoughts aside.

Twenty-One

IT WAS ALMOST "go" time. There was a lull while Deter, Ross, and Zorn discussed something in the conference room. Tris boarded the Astral and used the time to review Maxwell's approach charts.

Deter came out first. Tris expected him to ask her about the fuel order. He did, and this time she nailed it. All pre-flight items completed, Deter took a spot in the left seat, Tris in the right. Zorn strapped himself into the jump seat just behind the two pilots. She couldn't see Ross from the pilot seat, but knew that he was in the cabin.

With all eyes on her, she turned to Deter. "Ready?"

"Let's go."

Deter pushed the power forward to get the Astral moving toward the runway in the steady rain as he and Tris did each checklist call and response. At the runway's edge, Deter set the brake and turned to Tris.

"It's your leg, your brief."

"Roger that. All right, this is a standard takeoff." Tris briskly reviewed takeoff specifics and emergency procedures. Zorn nodded along from the jump seat. "Any questions?"

Zorn and Deter both shook their heads.

"Let's go," Deter hissed.

"Exeter Tower, Astral Nine Tango X-ray, short of runway Two-Four-Left ready for takeoff."

"Astral Nine Tango X-ray, good morning. Turn right to a heading of Two-Eight-Zero, runway Two-Four-Left, cleared for takeoff." After a short pause, ATC called them back. "Astral Nine Tango X-ray, *no delay,* Boeing 737 on short final."

"We're rolling," Deter answered, nodded at Tris and pushed the power levers forward. *Showtime.*

"Airspeed alive," Deter called, followed by "Eighty knots, cross-check."

"I've got control," Tris said and took charge of the Astral. As they rumbled down the runway, her feet tapped the rudder pedals and kept the Astral moving straight ahead. As Exeter Airport rolled by outside the cockpit windows, Tris was calm and sure. *I've got this.*

"V1," called Deter. No matter what, they were flying.

"Rotate. V2," Deter called.

Tris firmly pulled the yoke toward her chest. The nose wheel of the Astral rolled off the runway in small increments as the left and right main followed. Then the aircraft hesitated for an infinitesimal beat. In that tiny, barely measurable unit of time, it seemed to hang in the air, just before it rushed away from the ground, nose pointed toward the sky, and climbed. That instant—the fraction of a second where the plane hung suspended just inches above the ground—was her favorite moment in all of flight.

After that, things happened fast.

"Positive rate," Deter announced.

"Gear up," she ordered.

"One thousand to go," Deter called as they quickly passed through three thousand feet. Tris pushed the yoke forward and the aircraft leveled off. The engine noise quieted a bit when she gently slid back the power levers to keep the Astral at the two hundred knot maximum speed required in the Exeter terminal area.

Working the radios, Deter contacted departure control.

"Astral Nine Tango X-ray, radar contact. Climb and maintain one-three-thirteen-thousand and contact center on one-three-three-point-five."

"Out of four thousand for one-three-thousand, one-three-three-point-five. Astral Nine TX."

The flight moved forward briskly, purposefully and in sync. Tris carefully stayed a few steps ahead of the airplane, ready for whatever came next. They were on their way to Maxwell, where her flying skills would be tested and assessed. The sun shone in the distance, as she piloted the Astral away from the storm.

Twenty-Two

THEY'D BEEN FLYING for over an hour as Tris configured the Astral for the final landing into Maxwell. She was fifteen knots fast, and the airplane wasn't slowing quickly enough. The cabin temperature was set to 68 degrees, yet sweat trickled down her back.

She couldn't come in fast, or the Astral wouldn't stop before the end of the runway, so she pulled a lever that raised metal airbrake panels bolted to the top of the wing. They popped straight up. The jet rumbled as it slowed.

Deter sprang. "What are you doing?" He covered Tris's hand with his and pushed the panels down. "Would you like the gear down and the before landing checklist? That would slow you down juuuuuust fine." His sarcasm bit like a mad dog.

Zorn glanced quickly at Deter but said nothing.

"Yes. Yes. Gear down before landing checklist," Tris said.

Ross popped up from his chair and stood behind Zorn. Tris flew a terrible approach and landed so hard the Astral bounced on its struts. Deter rolled his eyes in the seat next to her.

There was no denying it: Deter had rattled her. But she shook it off—she had to regain her poise to fly back to Exeter.

"Maxwell Tower, Astral Nine Tango X-ray, taxi back for departure to Exeter, and we'd like our clearance." Tris attended to tasks that pushed her back in the moment.

Takeoff was routine. As they reached cruise altitude, Zorn read something in the jump seat. She hadn't spoken to Ross the entire flight, so she figured he must be back in the cabin. The air cycle machine whirred predictably, and conversations between ATC and other aircraft on the frequency were the only other background noise.

"Exeter Approach, Astral Nine Tango X-ray, leveling four thousand. Tango," Deter announced when they were about thirty-five miles from the field.

"Astral Nine Tango X-ray, Exeter Approach. Welcome back. Expect the visual approach runway Two-Four-Left. Fly heading one-three-zero, report the field in sight."

The wind at the field blew from the northwest at nineteen knots. Tris would have a heavy right crosswind for landing. *Keep the airplane straight, right wing down, use left rudder.*

At fifteen miles out, Tris and Deter both had Exeter in sight. With visual contact, they flew straight toward the field.

Tris turned parallel to the runway and slowed the Astral.

"Gear down, before landing checklist," she called to Deter.

"*Traffic. Traffic.*"

The Astral's collision avoidance system sensed another aircraft right in front of them. It first showed up as an amber blip on the screen. Tris, Deter, and Zorn looked outside the window but couldn't see the bogey.

"*Traffic. Traffic.*" The urgency of the synthesized voice increased. The blip changed from amber to red.

Deter snapped his head from side to side. "I can't see it," Zorn cried out.

Tris keyed the mike. "Exeter Tower, Astral Nine TX needs an immediate right three-sixty. We do not have traffic in sight." She started a right turn before ATC had the chance to answer. Deter's mouth opened into a perfect 'O.'

"Astral Nine TX approved. Turn right to a heading of three-zero-zero, vectors back to the downwind. Sorry about that. We have some student traffic in the area."

After a moment, Deter confirmed the instructions. Zorn looked down, visibly relieved. Tris rolled the aircraft back on course for the airport. Deter lowered the gear and watched the three green lights illuminate. All the wheels were down and locked.

Wind buffeted the plane all the way down on final approach. Tris bumped the power levers forward and flew a little faster to counteract the crosswind. Deter's feet shadowed hers on the rudders as she kept the Astral moving straight ahead in the gusty conditions. "Get off," she wanted to shout. *My* airplane.

Tris put the Astral firmly and safely on the runway centerline. She ran required checklists as Deter taxied the airplane to the Tetrix ramp. Rain still poured over the Astral. The windshield wipers mocked her, their steady *thwap-thwap-thwap* repeating, "You blew it, you blew it, you blew it."

Judgment was only minutes away.

Deter and Zorn sprinted off the Astral without saying a word once they were parked at the gate. Ross leaned into the cockpit on his way out and whispered, "Nice job." Tris relished a few moments alone after the nerve-wracking approach into Exeter.

When she finally entered the pilot area, she expected to see Zorn and Deter waiting for her, but only Ross was there.

"Hey," she said.

"Hey. You did a nice job. Especially with that traffic. I think the guys were embarrassed that they didn't see it." He looked around to make sure he wasn't overheard.

She smiled. "Yeah. Glad we got out of there."

Ross hesitated. "Hey, you know, I didn't get to thank you for that night at O'Slattery's. You helped me out when I needed it." His smile was warm, sincere.

"No problem."

"And, you know, I really do feel bad about...well, no one has to know about, you know..."

"Thanks. Oh no. Nobody's business."

She hadn't told anyone besides Danny but couldn't shake the memory of that night. Tris could cope with Ross's lewd behavior in the car. It would be easy to keep her physical distance in the future. But she could never accept the likely consequence if she hadn't taken his keys.

Ross continued to smile at her, his eyes soft and friendly. Yet she saw him as he'd been that night, and wrapped her arms around herself at just the thought of Ross drunk at the wheel. She couldn't shake the chill, even as warm forced air pumped out of metal floor vents just feet from where she stood.

Zorn walked into the pilot area, followed by Deter.

"Well, well," Zorn said, looking them both up and down. "We're not interrupting anything are we?" His suggestive tone made Tris purse her lips like she'd just sucked on a lemon.

"Nope," said Ross, red-faced.

Tris looked at Deter, his face a mask, and then at Zorn.

"Tris, you're released to fly trips in the Astral as second-in-command, starting right away. I've told Ann-Marie to put you on the schedule."

She'd done it. Beyond relieved, she kept her elation in check, especially in front of those guys. It was just another flight to them, right?

"Wow. Thank you!" Tris stifled the impulse to raise both arms in celebration. But her cheeks lifted high as she smiled.

"And, hey, could you try and put the plane down a little softer next time?" Zorn chuckled.

"You bet," she said, as she headed up to Ann-Marie's desk to check out the schedule. Her initials appeared in the crew box for a trip on Monday and several other dates after that. She took a deep breath, moved her shoulders back, and raised her head high.

"I'm halfway there," she whispered so low that even Ann-Marie couldn't hear.

Twenty-Three

ROSS STAYED BEHIND after Tris and Deter left. With the pilot area all to himself, he mellowed to the reassuring sounds of a typical day at the airport. Office chairs rolling on plastic mats, doors opening and closing, the phone ringing at the front desk. He took a few minutes to appreciate his surroundings, temporarily free of demands.

He didn't want to go home. Devon and James were back from Montana, and the Ross family resumed its familiar routine—including a liberal dose of daily nagging from Devon on topics he'd stopped trying to predict. Ross figured he'd hang out at the airport for a while. He could catch up with Zorn, get the scoop on the training flight they just did.

He marched up to reception and saw Ann-Marie working on the schedule. He peeked over her shoulder as she erased his initials on some of Deter's Astral trips and penciled in Tris. They had all pulled extra duty on the Astral and Gulfstream since RJ was canned. *Finally, a well deserved break.*

Ross glanced at the schedule and saw the usual two- and three-day trips on the Gulfstream with him as crew. He also had a trip scheduled on the Astral with Tris in a week. She was flying with Charlie Basson in a few days, then him. Tris was mostly scheduled with Deter through the end of the year.

Ross peered over at Zorn's office. Zorn beckoned him in.

"Hey," Ross said as Zorn dug into a bag of pretzels on his desk. Ross noticed the top of Zorn's belt hinge forward; he'd really put on weight. Unconsciously, Ross patted his own flat stomach.

"Hey. Well, she flew it."

Ross gave Zorn a thumbs up. "Seemed fine to me. What did it look like from upfront?"

"Yeah, she did ok. She was a little behind. Deter yelled at her a bunch of times. Mostly for nothing, that ass. Although she pulled the air brakes on the *downwind*. Jesus. I mean, speed was hot, but she could have just put the gear down. Deter didn't even ask her if she wanted the boards retracted. He just slammed them back in." Zorn paused. "Hell, she was just getting the feel of the thing. Fucking Deter almost came out of his seat. But then she showed great situational awareness at Exeter. We had that traffic alert and none of us saw it. She got the hell outta there." He chewed on a pretzel and washed it down with his Diet Coke.

Ross edged closer to Zorn's desk from his seat in the metal office chair. "Oh yeah. Deter really lit into her when we were in Asheville about how she got the job."

"Yeah, he hasn't stopped bitching since she showed up. 'I don't know what we're going to talk about in the cockpit on trips. Baking cookies and shopping?'" Zorn grinned. "It would serve him right."

"Once he gets something in his head, he doesn't like to let it go. I see they'll be flying together a lot. You sure that's a good idea?"

Zorn squinted and cocked his head to the side. "What difference does it make to *you*?"

"Huh? What do you mean?"

"I don't know. Just a vibe I'm picking up. You two looked really, uh, *friendly* when I walked in on you earlier."

Walked in on us? "Are you kidding? What would I want with that girl?"

Zorn chuckled and changed the subject. "I want her with Deter as much as possible. It's his fucking job to train her. He took the money I gave him to be primary on the Astral. Lazy bastard. The more she flies with him, the less any of us have to deal with him."

Ross understood. And although he felt bad for Tris, he was grateful to get a break from Deter, even if they didn't crew up together very often. Ross mostly flew the Gulfstream these days.

"She's pretty anxious to be PIC, you know."

Zorn nodded while he ripped open a bag of cookies. He munched on one, then said, "Yeah, she mentioned that during the interview, too. One thing at a time. She's gotta get the hang of the airplane. Then we'll gradually move her up. She'll need about five hundred hours in the Astral before upgrade, dontcha think?"

Ross nodded and wondered if Tris knew about this plan. From his vantage point in the back, Ross thought the flight went pretty well. Her landings were rough, but everything else was right on. With all his experience flying into Exeter and Maxwell, he could visualize exactly where in relation to the airport she configured the airplane for landing, tell if she made wrong turns, or managed power poorly. Everything happened at the right time.

"Did Deter want to sign her off to fly the line?" Zorn grimaced at the suggestion. Deter had to agree, but it was Zorn who signed off company pilots.

"*I* signed her off." Pure arrogance. Never failed.

"She's fine, safe. Trainable. Deter had no real complaints. Other than the fact she's inexperienced, female, and he wouldn't have to do any training if we'd just hired Dicky or some other *guy* he knew. Blah blah blah. Typical bullshit from him. He just wants to come in, fly, and go home."

"Hey, what about that trip you and I have in a couple days. Cleveland? Man, what a drag." He fiddled with some papers on his desk.

Ross hated Cleveland trips. Exeter was in the central time zone, and if the Tetrix executives had to make a 9:00 a.m. meeting in Cleveland, takeoff was usually around 6:30 a.m. Ross didn't like getting up early; it cut into his evening recreation.

"Oh, we'll figure something out." Ross grinned. It was an overnight. Cleveland was probably the most boring location they flew to regularly, but they could always find a comfortable bar. Then it wouldn't much matter what city they were in.

"Well, we're leaving the day after tomorrow. Let me know if there are any changes. If not, I'll see you then." Zorn looked back down at his desk and started shuffling papers.

"Yup. Ok," Ross pulled himself out of the chair. "I'm outta here."

As Ross walked out of his office, Zorn called after him. "Hey, Larry?"

"Yeah?"

"About Tris. There's nothing going on with you two, right? Nothing I need to know about?"

Ross shook his head, rolled his eyes, and gave Zorn his best "you're nuts" look.

But his heartbeat increased, just a little.

PART II:
THE BALL BUSTER
March 1998

Twenty-Four

THE CREDITS HAD stopped rolling, but the lights still hadn't come on. Stepping over bits of spilled popcorn, Danny made his way in the dark behind Tris. He inhaled the lavender scent of her shampoo.

Danny barely remembered how the movie ended, even though it had finished only moments ago. Tonight was the night. He'd made up his mind to ask her.

"I'm going to find a trash can," Tris said, holding up their empty popcorn box. "I'll meet you by the door." As she moved past the concession area toward the trash bins, he watched the outline of her ass in fitted blue jeans.

It was late in the evening. Shoppers still filed by the mall's movie theatre, their heavy winter coats open as they munched on soft pretzels and Cinnabons, safe from the early March snowstorm outside. More than a foot of snow was forecast to fall overnight, but Danny had taken his pickup, so he wasn't worried about getting stuck.

Danny hung back keeping a protective eye on Tris. Even in a big shirt and no makeup, she looked beautiful. *Damn.*

When he finally caught up with her, Danny planned to have the conversation he'd rehearsed all week.

Yet he couldn't bring himself to ask her. When they were both at Clear Sky, he could say anything to her. After all, he had seniority and rank. Since she left, and he was no longer her captain, he couldn't believe how unsure of himself he'd become around her.

"What did you think of the movie?" was all he could think to say. "So, who'd you like better, Matt Damon or the other guy. What's his name?"

"I loved it. Ben Affleck? Yeah, Matt Damon is cute. And I don't think I've ever seen Robin Williams in a dramatic role before. He was terrific. Deserves an Oscar."

"Want to go get a drink?" Danny looked at his favorite ten-dollar watch. "I still have another two hours before I have to cut myself off."

Tris grimaced slightly, a signal she would say no. With the snow and early trip tomorrow, he knew he probably shouldn't be out either.

Danny's hand brushed against hers during the movie while reaching for the popcorn. She hadn't pulled away, so he gently placed his hand on top of hers. It only took a second for her to move it, slowly, gently, politely. Well, he had to start somewhere.

He wondered if he should ask to sleep on her couch tonight. Her apartment was closer to the mall than his crash pad. Nah. The last thing he wanted was to lie there looking at pictures of her and Bron displayed around her living room.

As they ambled through the thinning mall crowd, Danny caught a reflection of light off of the tiny diamond stud earrings Bron had given her for her birthday. Bron had pulled them out of his uniform jacket in the crew room to show the guys. He and Tris were paired together on a trip, and he was going to surprise her on the road.

"So, I've been thinking," Danny said. "I've got vacation coming up. I've built up a bunch of Marriott points and want to do a weekend in the Bahamas." He took a long breath and held it for a beat. He was so nervous he tried to push his sunglasses up on his nose before he realized he wasn't wearing them. "Do you have enough points to join me? I mean, you know, to come along. Hang out." He tried to make it sound like it would be two buddies in separate rooms.

Tris looked down for a few seconds before she spoke. Bad sign.

"You know, Danny, I have no idea if I even get vacation. I mean, we don't fly that much, but I'm always on the pager. Even if I'm not scheduled, theoretically a trip could pop up."

"Well, is the Astral flying with other crews? That way you'd know you're off, right?"

"Yup, that's true. But, seriously, they want me on the Astral every time its engines turn. I mean, they can't do anything else with me. I don't fly the Gulfstream."

He shoved his hands into his jean pockets. "Well, you could ask, right?" Danny knew he was sunk.

Again Tris didn't answer right away. Maybe he should just come out with it, tell her he wanted more. He'd love to call her his girl.

Bron wasn't coming back. Danny wanted to care for her; maybe fill that gap Bron left in her heart. After all, it had been almost nine months since he died.

Danny flashed back to the elegant way she pulled her hand away from his during the movie. No, it's still not time, he realized just as they'd reached the exit to the parking lot. Danny zipped his parka all the way up and tightened the strings of his hood, bracing for the cold.

Twenty-Five

BEADS OF SWEAT dotted the lines of Tetrix Captain Charlie Basson's forehead as he sipped his margarita at the Mexican joint in downtown Albuquerque. Tris had listened to Basson talk nonstop about golf during their leg together from Exeter to ABQ. As if to prove his devotion, he'd changed out of his uniform into a white Izod and red-and-blue checked shorts, reminding Tris of a billboard she once saw near the Exeter golf course: "Caution! Men in bad pants!"

But Tris couldn't get her mind off of a ten-day Europe trip she saw on the schedule for the Astral in April. Deter and Ross were on it. Why wasn't she? Maybe Basson could enlighten her. She hoped he'd loosen up over lunch before she asked him.

When the waitress finally arrived with chips and salsa, the two pilots dug in.

"So. Still liking it?" Basson asked, draining the last of his margarita.

"Yep. This is a great trip so far. Thanks, Captain!" Tris tipped her glass to Basson. He was the only Tetrix pilot so far she was completely relaxed flying with. He was reliable, affable and asked only that she do her job.

He flashed a smile at Tris, revealing yellowed teeth that criss-crossed underneath his upper lip. "Yeah? Well, I'm happy to just fly a few trips a month and spend the rest of the time at home. Unless I get a nice long trip with a great golf course nearby."

"Yeah, I get that. It's nice that you get the chance to golf on trips." Tris sipped her drink. "So, you know everyone at work pretty well. You like flying with everyone?"

Basson hesitated for a second. "Well, we all like flying with Larry Ross. He's real easy-going, a good stick. Keeps things to himself. Don't have to worry about him. And you can trust him."

"Yeah, I've done a few trips with him. I think I have one next week. Who knows? The schedule changes a lot," she said. "Mostly I've been flying with Deter."

Basson's face looked like he'd just eaten bad fish. She'd heard the rumors that Deter was always on Basson's case about one thing or another in the cockpit.

Tris shot him a knowing glance. "Guess you've had a firsthand look at him, eh?"

"Oh, I have." Basson crunched the remaining pieces of ice in his glass, then pushed his chair away from the table and sat back. According to Ann-Marie, Deter complained about Basson all the time.

Seven months into the job, she and Deter had settled into a routine. He'd make comments while she flew, which he called suggestions—but sounded more like insults and orders. If she tried to ask why, he ignored her or gave a one- or two-word answer. Deter consistently spent their overnights by himself. If Tris tried to make conversation, he'd respond curtly, if at all.

"I see we have a big Europe trip on the Astral coming up. Zorn has Deter and Ross flying it. Do you know why I'm not?"

Basson looked surprised at first, then a bit guilty.

"Well, uh, we just had a pilot meeting the other day." Now it was her turn to look surprised. Tris had not been at the meeting. She didn't even know about it.

"To talk about the Gulfstream. And Deter, well, he showed up, you know, because they told him he was gonna get trained on it soon." Basson quickly backtracked like he'd been caught doing something wrong.

He motioned to their waitress and ordered another margarita.

"Well, the guys, you know, we started talking..."

Basson struggled to make his point, which put Tris on guard. Whatever he couldn't spit out was something he either hadn't meant to or was afraid to say.

"And, yeah, well, we started talking about the Ball Buster."

"Huh? The what?"

"That ten-day trip to Europe. A real pain in the ass," he said and let out a quick self-conscious laugh. "Sorry."

Tris waved to let him know his language didn't offend her. She wanted him to keep talking. "Why do you call it the 'Ball Buster?'"

"'Cause that's what it is. It's a horrible trip. We barely get any overnight time. Maybe one night. We're away from home ten days. It sucks."

"So if it's that bad, why didn't they put *me* on it?" Tris laughed. "After all, I'm still the FNG!" The Fucking New Guy always did the crappy trips.

Basson vehemently shook his head. "Oh, you don't wanna do that one. It's a really bad trip. Deter and Ross don't want to go. I'm just glad it ain't me."

Tris didn't think Basson was telling her the whole story. "It's an awful trip and they put two captains on it? That doesn't make sense."

Basson looked away and tapped the top of his margarita glass with his finger. He looked like he both wanted to speak but knew he'd already said too much.

She pressed harder. "I wonder if they'd let me go instead of one of those guys. Or I could be relief crew. I heard that companies do that sometimes. I'm going to be flying international trips as captain eventually. I need the training."

"Look, Tris, nothing personal," he began, and she knew she wouldn't like whatever he'd say next. "It's a long trip. Guys are far from home for almost two weeks...Well, you know, the guys might have some explaining to do to their wives and all..."

Her chest constricted, disappointment tinged with genuine rage. "Nothing personal" was Tetrix shorthand for "screw you."

"What are you talking about?" She already knew, but wanted to hear it from him.

"Yeah. Well, like, I had to call my wife once we got to the hotel here and tell her where we're having lunch. And she wants me to call her again when we get back. She's not used to me flying with a woman." He added quickly, "On overnights, too."

Their lunch arrived, putting Basson out of his conversational misery. He picked up a taco and scarfed it down like he was on deadline. Errant pieces of fish and lettuce fell from the folded meal to the table, and Basson picked them up with his fingers and popped them in his mouth. No, Mrs. Basson certainly had nothing to worry about from Tris.

Tris wasn't entirely surprised by what Basson just told her. She always wondered whether wives knew what their husbands were really up to in the cockpit. Sometimes guys she flew with made oblique passes at her; sometimes the approaches were direct. It was hard to mistake 'Hey, Tris, wanna hook up at the hotel?' for anything other than what it was.

Usually, the guy started the conversation with how things were 'not good on the home front.' Problems with the wife. Either he wasn't making enough, wasn't home enough, or wasn't involved with their kids enough. And then supposedly when the wife heard he was doing a three-day trip with a female pilot, the conversation at home became even uglier. As if *his* family problems were *her* fault. And that she'd feel obligated to do something to make up for them.

With pilots like that, Tris would gently guide the conversation back to the trip. If it was an overnight, she did her best 'slam clicker' routine. She'd say goodnight at her hotel room, let the door slam behind her, and click the deadbolt shut tight.

She certainly hadn't picked up that vibe from Deter. He could barely stand being around her. Basson was apparently afraid of his wife and kept a professional distance. But Ross. She'd held off his advances. She just didn't take them seriously. But his behavior that night was always the first thing she thought about when she saw him.

Tris had to find a way to get on that trip. With international experience, she'd strengthen her credentials for upgrade. Making her pitch to Basson over tequila and triple sec gave her some useful information, but that was all. The trip wasn't scheduled until next month. She'd ask Ross the next time she saw him. He still owed her for driving him home that night.

The waitress handed Basson the check, and he stuck his company credit card on top of the receipt.

"Do you still want to walk around downtown like we talked about?" Tris hoped he'd say no. She was tired.

"Nah, I think I'll head back to the room. Maybe watch some HBO. We don't have cable at home. Gotta save money! Kids to put through college." He kept checking his watch. Mrs. Basson probably had him on a short leash.

When Tris returned to her room, she was still keyed up about the Europe trip. She often overhead the guys talking about how international experience was key to being pilot-in-command. If she proved herself on that trip, they'd have to give her the captain's seat after she nailed her training in Dallas. If it ever got scheduled.

Slow down. Slow down. One thing at a time.

Finally, the day's early morning takeoff and the lunchtime margaritas caught up with her. As she lay on top of the soft hotel bed, her thoughts drifted.

Before Bron, Tris never considered dating a pilot she flew with. Diana counseled her early on not to "dip her toe in the company pond." It was good advice. Personal drama, drama of *any* kind, was the last thing that belonged in the cockpit.

Then by some odd twist of crew scheduling at Clear Sky, she and Bron were paired together as captain and first officer three months in a row. They locked eyes on that very first trip to Philly over their dispatch release. Laughing at the ridiculously low fuel load they'd been given, they hatched elaborate plans to sweet talk the fueler into pumping with a heavy hand.

Tris was thirty-three when they met, and Bron was four years younger. And, he was her captain. A double whammy.

But he was friendly. When she told a joke, he laughed with his whole body. He treated everyone associated with the airplane with respect, from the baggage handlers to the crew schedulers. There was a calm about Bron, a way he had of defusing conflict before it ever amped up.

And he didn't come on to her, not right away. She knew she'd have trouble resisting.

She did resist—at first. By month two, she couldn't walk into the crew room without someone asking her where Bron was. During the third month they were paired together, she bought his old couch.

He delivered it on a Saturday afternoon. Soon after, it was common knowledge at Clear Sky that they were together.

Bron. Bron, who stood a true five-foot-nine—'male minimum height,' the two of them always joked—since not even the shortest pilots ever admitted to being less than five-foot-nine. Muscular torso atop skinny legs, curly black hair. And those light grey eyes that once opened like a picture window into her future.

Tris shook her head against the memory. Now, her future was the Ball Buster. Tris had to get on that trip.

Twenty-Six

"TETRIX MAINTENANCE, NINE TX. We're fifteen minutes out. Is our passenger's limo there?" Ross was surprised by the sound of Tris's voice. The Astral wasn't due back for another hour.

Brad the mechanic answered on the intercom. "Nine TX, Tetrix. Looks like you'll be right behind the Gulfstream. Pull up next to them."

"We hear you, Brad," Basson's voice shot through on the radio. "No problem. We'll walk our guy in and make sure his ride is here."

Ross and Zorn were supposed to take an executive to Jackson Hole on the Gulfstream but they had a maintenance problem and were forced to return to the hangar. Ross was disappointed at first. But now he realized he might run into Tris.

As soon as they shut down the Gulfstream's engines, Ross went to break the news to their passenger. "We have a mechanical issue with the airplane," Ross told him, "and unfortunately we can't take off until the problem is fixed." He hesitated. "Our Astral is inbound. We can continue the trip in that airplane, but it will probably take us at least an hour and a half to get it ready to go. You can spend the time in one of our spare offices in the hangar if you like."

Ross hoped the executive would cancel so he wouldn't have to rush to take the Astral back out and have some time to talk to Tris. It had been a while since he'd seen her.

"No," the executive said slowly, "you know, I think I'll just reschedule the meeting. I have a lot going on at the office." And, with that, he headed for the parking lot.

"All right then. We're terribly sorry about this," Ross called after him.

He heard the familiar sound of the Astral's engines. When he saw the plane pull onto the ramp, he couldn't help but grin.

"You look happy." Zorn tapped his shoulder, startling him.

"Well, yeah, uh, I just got three days off I wasn't planning on," he quickly responded. "Hey, there's the Astral. It's early, isn't it?"

"No idea." Zorn shrugged as he gathered his headset, jacket and charts. "If I'm not on it, I don't pay attention to the schedule."

Ross grimaced. Spoken like a true chief pilot, someone who really only cared about the size of his salary, bonus, and airplane. Ross didn't typically follow the other pilots' schedules that closely either, but he'd started looking a bit more carefully these days at where the Astral went—and with what crew.

He took his time grabbing his stuff from the cockpit, only half-listening to Zorn, who went on and on about the Gulfstream's crippled pressurization system.

Ross was the designated pilot-in-command on the aborted trip, so he took the opportunity to poke at Zorn a bit. "Hey man, you wanna take the coffee pots back in?"

For a second, Zorn looked like he'd refuse. But he grunted a little and did it anyway.

The Astral was parked outside the hangar, its engines spooling down at high frequency. Ross headed toward the plane with his fingers in his ears as the huge intake fans slowed. He opened the airplane door from the outside as soon as it was safe.

Tris was upfront finishing shutdown items. As captain, it was Basson's job to walk the passenger off of the airplane, and Ross ducked into the cockpit to let them pass by. Basson shot him a quizzical look, wondering why Ross was there and not on his scheduled flight.

"Hey, Tris," Ross said casually.

"Hey. What happened? I thought you were headed to Jackson Hole."

"Mechanical. Pressurization system."

"Bummer. I love Wyoming. That would have been a great trip."

Ross nodded. "Yeah, well, I'm happy to get some extra time off."

Tris usually wore what he thought of as the 'lady pilot' version of a tie—that thing that looked like a bow tie but crossed over itself. Today, she wore a man's tie with a caricature of a dogsled on it.

"What's that about?" Ross pointed at her tie.

"The Iditarod, of course!" She flashed a wide smile. "Hey, I have a thing about dog sleds."

Ross chuckled. She sure had her own style.

She stowed the checklist and turned around in her seat. "Hey, Larry. Can I ask you something?"

"Yeah."

"I see you and Deter have an extended Europe trip in the Astral coming up. Basson told me you guys call it the 'Ball Buster.'"

"Yeah. It sucks. We're dreading it," Ross told her. "Nine cities, ten days, two Atlantic crossings, no relief crew. A busy, multi-leg trip with only one long overnight to relax and kick back. It's a working trip, for sure. And we've both been to all of the stops, so nothing new for us."

"I'd love to do that trip, to learn international procedures," Tris said. "I'll need some international experience to upgrade to captain." Then she looked away like there was something more on her mind.

"And?" Ross asked.

"Well, do you think there would be any...uh...problem if I asked Zorn if I could go?"

"Oh. Did Basson tell you about, uh, what we discussed?" It was just as well. If anyone needed to worry, it was Ross, especially after his recent blowup with Devon. But he would love to have Tris on the trip with him and Deter. He'd just tell Devon that he didn't set the schedule. If the company put him on a trip to Europe for ten days with Tris, Devon would just have to live with it.

"Tris, I don't think they'll go for having you as a co-pilot. But *I'm* PIC on that trip. I think I might be able to talk Zorn into letting you go as an observer. Would you be ok with that, if you didn't do any flying?"

"No flying?"

Ross shook his head. "One of the passengers is Willett's boss. Zorn'll want two captains upfront. But I think he'd be ok with it as a training trip on international procedures. I can ask him. You have a valid passport, right?"

"I do."

"Ok. Let me see. Well, wait. I guess I have to ask Deter first, as a courtesy. He's the other captain on the trip, and you're his student, after all." Sarcasm slid from his words.

"Of course. I totally get it. I really appreciate it. I'd just like to go."

"All right. Let me see what I can do. I gotta go make sure the Gulfstream is buttoned up. And then head home. I better call my wife and give her the head's up." Devon wasn't expecting him back for another two days.

"Great. Thanks again. Nice to see you." She turned away to complete some chore.

Halfway down the airstairs, Ross stopped and leaned back in to catch a final glimpse of Tris. Her tie was fastened in a perfect Windsor. She'd tied one for a guy before. Or someone tied it for her.

He had to admit, the thought made him a little jealous.

Ross pulled into his driveway a little after ten. The big engine under the hood of his Cutlass popped in the cool night air, the sound overcome by some creature rustling through his hedges. A couple of patches of snow from a crazy late winter storm clung to his lawn.

Ross noticed that the lights were out in the living room. Strange. When he called from the airport, Devon had said she was watching a movie. They didn't have TVs in any of the bedrooms. Maybe the movie was over.

He knew better than to expect dinner. She wouldn't cook for him this late at night. He had stopped at Burger King and wolfed down his Whopper and fries in the car. Ross would make sure to brush his teeth before he went to kiss Devon or she'd complain he stunk of fast food.

He turned the key in the lock and stepped into a quiet house. Light peeked out from underneath the closed bedroom door. Ross turned the handle, hopefully.

"Hey," he said. Devon lay in bed under the covers reading a romance novel. Every book Devon bought at the grocery store had a picture of a half-naked woman dramatically embracing a muscular guy on the cover. Sometimes they wore leather, but mostly those old-world costumes that always made him think of damsels in distress.

"What's up? Are you sick?"

Devon pulled the covers up to her chin. "Huh? Oh, hi. No. Of course not. Just reading."

"Where's James?" There was no sign of him. Odd for a school night.

"He's sleeping over at Paul's. They're working on a school project together, so I gave him permission. His mom will drive them to school in the morning."

"Does he know my trip was canceled? I can pick him up from school tomorrow." Ross always wished he had more time to be with James anywhere, doing anything.

Devon never took her eyes off the book. "Paul's mom will bring him home tomorrow after basketball practice."

"Great, Dev. So, let me change and get washed up. I'll hop in and join you." They could take advantage of a rare kid-free night.

Devon's eyes never left her book. "I'm just going to finish this chapter and go to sleep. Good night, Larry."

That was her code for "I'll be asleep by the time you get to bed." *Shit*. He needed some release, and with James at a sleepover, this would have been a perfect opportunity.

He should have known she'd still be pissed. Some neighbor, he had no idea which one, told Devon he had come home one night "with a strange woman" when she and James were in Montana. He tried to tell her it was nothing, just a co-worker driving him home from O'Slattery's after he'd had too much to drink. Ross wasn't sure which set Devon off more—a woman driving him home, or the drinking.

He turned and walked back toward the kitchen, slowly loosening his belt. No reason to hurry and get washed up. He grabbed a beer out of the refrigerator and heard the inevitable inquiry within seconds after the tab opener snapped.

"What's that?" Devon called out.

He wished they had a bigger house, so the kitchen wouldn't be so close to the bedroom. "Just having a beer. Want one?" That would get to her.

"No, I don't *want* one, Larry, and I don't know why you do. I thought we only kept it in the fridge for company?"

"*You* stopped having a beer now and then. Not me. I still don't know what your problem is with it."

"Well, I don't like you drinking around James. It upsets him."

"James isn't here and won't be back until tomorrow, like you just said." The bedroom light clicked off. She was probably lying there in the dark seething.

He grabbed his beer and walked through the sliding glass door to their backyard. It was dark, but he kept the outside lights off. Ross imagined the list of his numerous failures his wife cataloged in her head. He unzipped his pants, stuck his right hand inside, and gave himself the welcome home he'd hoped for from Devon.

Twenty-Seven

DETER THREW THE door to the pilot area open; it banged against the stop and slammed closed. *Damn, I need to stop doing that.*

From the minute he woke in the morning, made coffee, and almost burned his toast, right up until the second he pressed the garage door opener, he was angry. Angry that he had to go to the airport four hours before his show time; angry that he had to attend yet another pilot meeting. What could it possibly be about this time?

Basson and Ross stood over the flight-planning desk laughing at computer-simulated fire evacuation training. Ross was wearing the yellow hood pilots donned to keep from inhaling smoke. Basson joked that he looked like an alien. Deter didn't see what was so funny—although Ross *did* look like an alien.

When they saw Deter, they stopped laughing. Ross pulled off the hood. His face was red and he coughed a bit while he caught his breath.

Deter inhaled. "Larry, hello." After a beat, he continued. "Ok, what's going on? You guys know what this is about?"

"Training, I think," Ross replied.

"Right. So that's why I'm here *four hours before show time*. Whose training?" he barked but got no reply. Ross and Basson had walked away.

Deter grabbed some fresh coffee and after a minute or two, headed into the stock closet with a Styrofoam cup in his hand, steam rising from the top. He looked over the snacks and began his standard internal dialogue: should he, or should he not, grab some M&M's? Seconds later, he was back at his desk, ripping the bag open.

Zorn appeared in the pilot area wearing khakis, a golf shirt, and his best *I'm-just-one-of-the-boys* grin. Like he wasn't the boss.

"Whassup, Big Ed?" Zorn asked Deter.

"Well, here I am. What can I do for you?" He was in no mood for levity.

Zorn launched right into his agenda. "I want to go over the training schedule."

Ross and Basson walked back into the pilot area. Ross munched on Pringles and Basson held a can of Coke.

"So, guys, how's she doing? For real?" Zorn nodded toward Tris's empty cubicle.

Ross and Basson looked at each other, then at him. No one spoke for several seconds.

"Look, it's just like I've been telling you in my trip reports," Deter said, referring to the three or four comments he'd jot down on every trip manifest he returned to Ann-Marie for filing. "She's *fine*. She's as good as she can be without school. My big problem is that she seems to think she's upgrading to captain when—I should say *if*—she passes her type rating check ride."

Zorn shook his head. "No, she won't be flying as captain even after she gets qualified," he said. "I want her to have at least five hundred hours in the Astral before she upgrades."

Seconds passed as Deter watched Ross, and even Basson shoot covert looks at each other. The girl probably told all of them she expected to be a captain after training. She'd certainly told him enough times.

Ross finally spoke up. "Does she know that? Does she know that she won't fly as PIC from the left seat every other leg?"

"Well, she'd better," Zorn's responded. "That's just common sense. She has, what, a hundred hours in type?"

Deter nodded. This was going his way. No need to say another word. Once Zorn had spoken, whatever topic had been on the table was closed.

"Well, now hang on a minute," Ross chimed in. "Why would you hold her back if she passes her training? Every captain has to start somewhere. We all did. And she'll always be flying with one of us. No shortage of experience here." Ross waved his hand around the room in a rainbow pattern.

Deter was truly surprised. No one questioned Zorn. Although, he had to admit, if anyone could, it was Ross. And Ross liked her. He could tell.

"Well, she needs more experience. And speaking of that," Zorn said as he looked from Ross to Deter, "you guys want me to send her to Europe with you, right?"

Deter expected him to mention this and nodded. He wanted to take a mechanic with them in case something broke, but he'd settle for her to help with the scut work.

"Yeah, let's see how she does on the Ball Buster," Zorn said. "That'll give a good indication of how far along she is dealing with the passengers anyway. I've scheduled a tentative date for her training about a week after that trip ends. That should work."

Zorn turned and started to walk back to his office. Deter couldn't believe it. Not a word about the Gulfstream.

"Hey," Deter called after Zorn, trying to catch up to him in the hallway. He tugged Zorn's arm unintentionally.

"Easy, man. What's up?" Zorn backed away a couple of steps, brushed his arm off and gave Deter an icy look.

"Sorry. Hey, can we go in your office?" Deter didn't want to get into it with Zorn out in the open. Zorn led the way into his office and closed the door.

"Ok. What?"

"So, we got her training out of the way. What about mine?"

Zorn shot him a look that would still a thundering herd of buffalo. "When she was hired, I told you we'd work on your training when she was ready to go. Isn't that what I said?" Zorn spoke slowly, enunciating his words as though Deter was a child. Deter's Adam's apple slid up and down as he swallowed hard.

"She must be 'ready to go.' You just said you were sending her to training." Deter couldn't stop himself.

"Well, she's going to need at least five hundred hours in type before she upgrades. When you move to the Gulfstream, we lose a captain on the Astral. Until she's ready to take your spot, we have to keep you on it full-time."

"That wasn't the deal, Brian. That was *not* our deal."

"But that's the way it's going to be," Zorn said and waved his hand at Deter. "Ok, I have a ton of paperwork to do. Thanks, you're doing a great job with her."

"Fuck that. I'm going to Willett." Deter looked through the glass at Willett's dark office.

"Go ahead," Zorn said without looking up. "Knock yourself out." He hesitated for a second, just long enough, before continuing. "But the chief pilot does the training schedule." He looked Deter right in the eye. "And I'm the chief pilot."

Deter stormed straight to the snack room. A few seconds later, he ripped open another bag of M&M's. The tearing sound was the only noise complementing the roar of thrust reversers and screech of brakes from aircraft landing on Exeter's runway Two-Four-Right, just yards away from the Tetrix hangar.

Twenty-Eight

WHEN TRIS OPENED the door to the pilot area, Ross, Deter, and Basson all looked at her like she'd caught them stealing. At this point, Tris had become used to having conversations halt the second she walked in. But this felt different. Before the silence, she had heard someone say "RJ," the name of their long-lost colleague.

"You're early." Deter said.

"What's going on?"

"Uh, nothing," Ross put his hands in his pockets and looked at the ground in that way children do when they have something to hide. After years in the classroom, Tris easily recognized the response.

Something was up. Ross bolted toward the reception area and Basson practically sprinted to the hangar, waving some publications and telling her to "have a good trip." Deter sat reading Michael Crichton's *Disclosure*, which Tris had coincidentally finished a couple weeks before.

"Hey, Ed. You enjoying that?" Tris pointed at the paperback.

At least she and Deter had books in common. He never asked about her master's in English Lit, but when they flew together, he was always particularly interested in what she was reading.

Deter gave her an odd look. "It's great," he said, "a real page-turner."

"Yeah, I thought so, too." *Like moving cement bricks to get this guy to talk about anything.*

Tris was just about to roll her bag out to the Astral when Zorn popped his head into the pilot area.

"Hi, Tris. Got a minute?"

"Sure. Your office?"

"Yup." She followed him and closed the door behind her.

"Ok, let me review this with you. I want to make sure we are clear on where we are and what happens next." Zorn kept it professional, superficial. He looked distracted, like he needed to get past the conversation to move on to something actually important. Tris looked behind Zorn to the parking lot; the sky had darkened since she arrived. Rain was in the forecast.

"First of all, congratulations. The guys unanimously recommended you for training. So we have a tentative date for you in Dallas." He looked down at a calendar on his desk. "You'll be gone for about two weeks. Ann-Marie will give you the details."

"One week of systems, then sim training, then a check ride, right?"

"Yes. Exactly. Thanks," Zorn said as he picked up the receiver on his desk phone and started punching in numbers. Their meeting was over. No questions, comments, or discussion expected or invited. She got the message.

Tris left Zorn's office, practically crashing into Ann-Marie.

"Oh," Ann-Marie said as she stopped short to avoid the collision. "I was looking for you." She waved Tris over to her desk and handed her the itinerary for her training in Dallas. As Tris was about to head back to the pilot area, Ann-Marie stopped her.

"Hey. Tris. Looks like you're riding the jump seat to Europe with Deter and Ross."

"Seriously? That's great!"

"It's a ten-day trip. And you're considered part of the crew." It sounded like a warning.

"Thanks, Ann-Marie. I understand."

"Don't thank me. Ross asked Zorn. That's who said yes. Thank him." Ann-Marie nodded in Zorn's direction.

Tris folded her arms on top of the reception desk and leaned toward Ann-Marie. "So, what can you tell me about the Ball Buster? Anything I should know?" Tris had quickly learned that Ann-Marie had a lot of good information and occasionally shared it.

Ann-Marie beckoned Tris toward a little-used conference room that one of the mechanics liked to smoke in. Every time Tris walked past it, she could smell the remnants of his last nicotine fix.

They walked in, but Ann-Marie didn't sit. Instead, she kept a hand on the doorknob and put her weight against the door. "I would be very, very careful if I were you." Her tone was light, unlike the message. "Deter's pissed. And, Ross, well..."

"What? Why? What's with Deter now? And Ross?"

"Look, don't tell anyone I told you," Ann-Marie looked around the room and tightened her grip on the doorknob to make sure no one could walk in. "Zorn told Deter he's not going to Gulfstream school for a while."

"What? I thought he'd go when I went to Dallas? No?"

"No. They don't have the money for it. Willett couldn't get approval for two full training events and they chose yours."

"Oh shit. Wow, he's going to be horrible on the Europe trip, isn't he? Damn." Surely Ross would be a buffer. "But what's going on with Ross?"

Ann-Marie looked surprised. "You haven't heard?"

"No. Well, maybe. I don't know. What?" Tris wasn't sure what she knew or didn't know about these guys anymore.

"Yeah, he's having some real trouble at home. Devon is making all kinds of crazy threats."

"Like what? Why?" Ross hadn't let on that anything was wrong when they talked earlier.

"Oh, the ones she usually makes, according to him. That she's gonna leave him, take their son, never come back. It's always been just talk as far as I know. But it makes him...uh...a little erratic sometimes." Ann-Marie looked embarrassed.

"In what way?" Tris asked, although she had a good idea.

The two women heard Zorn calling Ann-Marie's name from the reception area.

"Guard your six," Ann-Marie replied.

It was military slang for "watch your back."

Twenty-Nine

"HEY, FLYGIRL. I'M in town. Want a donut?" The local Dunkin' Donuts was halfway between Tris's place and the two-bedroom crash pad Danny shared with seven other guys. He still hoped scheduling would call with a trip as he waited on reserve. Bored, he didn't want to spend another night in his grimy apartment.

For years, Danny had commuted to Exeter from his home in Columbia, Missouri. Now, he was chosen to fill Bron's vacancy in the Clear Sky training department. Since he'd be in Exeter twice as much every month, he wanted something other than the crash pad's Walmart plastic furniture and bunk bed existence.

He flew his last trip with a co-pilot who had a wife and three kids. When the guy took his pilot hat off, Danny saw a picture of his family in the plastic-covered ID slot. Seeing the four smiling faces made Danny yearn for something he hadn't known he wanted. After almost twenty years in the aviation industry, he wanted a family of his own. And he wanted it with Tris.

Tris met him at the donut shop, and they walked over to a

nearby park after they got their orders. A tree with branches just beginning to fill in shaded them as they sat side-by-side on an old wooden bench. The afternoon sun was high and bright, but not warm. They sat outside to make the most of the early spring day.

"Yeah, I was supposed to go to Minneapolis," she said, biting into her toasted coconut donut. "But it canceled. That's a day off I wasn't planning on. But hey, Zorn just gave me a training date. He said, 'This is when you're going,' and then, like 'Buh-bye!'"

Danny licked frosting from his finger. "Ok, so let me see if I got this. You get your type and you're a captain? Pay bump?" His eyebrows moved up and down suggestively.

"Pretty sure," Tris said. "Yeah, I'm psyched. I guess putting up with Deter has its payoffs."

Tris broke off a piece of the donut and held it between her fingers as she spoke. She looked fantastic in her jeans, black T-shirt, and scuffed tennis shoes. She'd worn her hair loose, instead of clipped behind her head or in a ponytail like she did when she flew. He liked her in casual clothes. But then, Tris in uniform always turned him on, especially when she wore her pilot hat. Something about the way her hair popped out from under the hatband...

Danny had on his blue uniform pants and a golf shirt. A pilot sitting reserve was easy to spot. If his pants weren't obvious enough, his black lace-up shoes surely gave him away. Since he could be sent out on a trip any minute, he could only pack a few non-uniform items. No room for tennis shoes in his small overnight bag.

"You could always come back to the airlines. I'm livin' the dream." He thought this would make Tris smile, but she looked at him solemnly and swallowed.

"Seriously, Danny, I've thought about it. After almost eight months, I still have, what, only a hundred fifty hours of flight time in the Astral? 'Only experience leads to expertise,'" she said, mimicking

Bron's voice. Danny laughed, but the spot-on imitation made him uncomfortable. It was as if Bron sat right next to them.

"Well, what about this upcoming Europe trip? Won't that get you ready? What countries are you headed to?" Danny wanted to encourage Tris, keep her from waving the white flag. She'd quit her job at Clear Sky to become a captain. And if that's what she wanted, he wanted it for her.

"Geneva, Zurich, Berlin, Vienna, Luxembourg..." She recited the list of destinations she'd clearly memorized. "I haven't been to any of those places. Have you?" Danny shook his head. "But I'm just an observer-crewmember, so I'm told. That means lots of serving the passengers, no flying."

They sat quietly for a while in the cool afternoon sun, eating their donuts and sipping their coffee.

"You know, I was just awarded that job in the training department. The one..."

"Bron's old job?" She looked at what was left of her donut in the small white bag.

"Well, yeah...I mean, they held it open a long time. Out of respect."

"Yeah, they did. Or maybe they just couldn't find someone as good to replace him until you raised your hand!" She smiled up at him.

He couldn't hold back any longer. "Look, Tris. I don't even know why you and Bron broke up. One day you were together and then—" He stopped abruptly.

All of a sudden, despite their close proximity, Danny sensed that Tris was no longer there. She had a look—not blank, exactly, more like vacant. Gone.

"I knew we'd get back together. We weren't done." She wiped a coconut flake off of her lip and whispered, "We weren't done."

Danny's mobile phone rang. The caller ID said "Screw Desk,"

his code for crew scheduling. He was still on call and had to answer. If they assigned him a trip, he had two hours to get to the airport.

"Ok. Yeah. Three days? Ok. Ok," Danny said before hanging up. "Three days, five legs, including a DC overnight. Not a lot of flying, but the overnight in DC is decent."

"Have fun at *National*," Tris said, smiling at Danny. President Clinton had signed a law changing the name of the airport, but neither of them could bear to think of it by that other name. Politics was one of the many things they had in common.

They both loved the DC overnight at Clear Sky. The crew stayed in a block of hotels near the airport, just a short walk away from a small downtown area that had tons of restaurants.

"So we're heading back, right?" Tris stood up and gathered their trash.

"Yup," Danny replied. "I'm on, Flygirl!"

When they got to his car, Tris hugged him tightly. "I don't know what I'd do without you," she said.

Wrapping his arms around her in a friendly hug would be somehow dishonest. He wanted to hold her with his whole heart, to show his feelings instead of tamping them down. As he gave himself permission to embrace the woman he was in love with, he gently raised her chin until their eyes met.

"Tris, I want us to be together."

She froze. Her eyes were empty again, her face expressionless.

"No." Her voice sounded strangled, guttural as she pulled away.

"Please, Tris."

She bent over slightly and started to cry. He stood powerless, his arms now dangling at his side.

She mumbled something, but he couldn't make it out.

"What?"

Tris looked up at him, her eyes red. Her left hand was balled into a tight fist.

"I can't."

"Why?"

"Because..."

"*Why?*"

"Because I still love him."

Thirty

TRIS FORGED A path in her bedroom between each of her three alarm clocks to confirm they were set for 2:00 a.m. Show time was 4:30.

She needed rest but was too agitated to sleep. The Ball Buster launched the next day and everything seemed to have gone wrong in the week leading up to it.

Instead of calmly explaining to Danny how much she cared about him, how she valued him, she broke down and blurted out the truth. She'd hurt him.

A call to Danny's mobile phone later that night went straight to voicemail. Tris hoped he'd missed it because he was out with his crew at one of the cool restaurants in DC. But that was days ago, and he still hadn't called her back. Danny was so important to her; she couldn't lose him, too.

The very next day she flew with Deter. He was even more distant, more abrupt than usual. Tris assumed it was because his Gulfstream training had been delayed. She decided to treat it like any other trip.

After all, he was still supposed to train her. At one point, she asked him something about the Astral's hydraulic system, and he just detonated.

"Goddamn it, who gives a shit," he roared and walked away.

Deter's outbursts struck Tris the same way every time. Her arms tingled, her vision narrowed. Sometimes she forgot to breathe. Deter performed this particular rebuff right in front of Willett. They were both standing near the flight-planning computer and Willett passed behind her and whispered, "Let it go."

Tris stiffened in response to loud voices ever since she was a child, which made the effects of Deter's belligerence harder to hide. She grew up in a family where conversations were just a lot of noise, people obsessed with their own needs. She could never truly express herself because no one was listening. And if no one was actually listening, why bother to speak?

At almost thirty-five years old, she flinched at the sound of Deter's voice raised in conflict. Sometimes, its sheer volume transported her right back home, to when she was eight years old and no one had heard her say her stomach hurt over loud family "discussions." Or at twelve, when her mother was so busy arguing with her aunt about when to plant the tulip bulbs, her quiet pleas for help with her first Maxi pad were ignored.

But, she wasn't a child any longer; she was responsible for people's lives. Out of necessity, her silent tolerance was evaporating.

Later on during the trip, Tris flew an approach into Detroit and she asked for flaps. Deter refused to lower them.

"Too soon," he growled.

Unless it was a matter of life or death, the flying pilot configured the airplane as they saw fit. She took a deep breath and made sure the aircraft was under control.

"Flaps twenty-five. *Now*," she commanded. Following an exaggerated sigh, Deter lowered them.

If Deter had pulled that crap on another pilot—*any* other pilot—Tris was sure he'd have been spoken to, even at Tetrix. After that trip, once she was sure Deter had gone home, she went to Ann-Marie to vent her frustration.

Ann-Marie saw what went on behind the scenes at Tetrix from her unobtrusive perch at the front desk. She'd been around even longer than Zorn. She took every call that came into the department, opened each interoffice envelope, even those marked "Confidential." Tris had come to trust her.

"Deter being a dick?" Ann-Marie asked matter-of-factly when Tris had finished, as if she were observing the weather.

Tris didn't hesitate. "Oh yeah. Why, is he like that to you?"

"No way." Ann-Marie laughed. "I do the *schedule.*"

"Right. I think I have to say something to Zorn. Or Willett."

"Don't do it," Ann-Marie shook her head and crossed her arms in front of her in an "X," the same signal a ramper would use to stop an airplane in its tracks.

Tris hadn't detected this sense of urgency from Ann-Marie before.

"They don't like him either, but, in a way, they kind of *worship* him. I mean, his military service, and all those carrier landings…" Ann-Marie let her voice trail off. She didn't need to continue for Tris to get the point. She'd heard this before.

"Seriously? So, he gets away with how he treats people because of that? I thought the navy fighter pilots were supposed to be jerks. This guy, what, flew supplies or something?"

Ann-Marie nodded solemnly. "Just hang in there," she said. "You'll be going to school, and hopefully he'll move on to the Gulfstream soon." But both women knew that was unlikely.

"So this really is the way it works. Sit down and shut up?"

Ann-Marie put her finger to her lips and then motioned to Tris to follow her into the mechanics' smoking room.

"Tris, look, the way everyone is here, basically…you want to stay out of Zorn's way. Seriously." She hesitated for a moment. "Zorn and Willett will never do anything about Deter. If you were ever going to dump on Deter, it would have to be something big enough that they couldn't ignore it."

"Like?"

"I have no idea. I can't imagine anything worse than what he's already done!" They both laughed. Ann-Marie's advice was based on good information. Unless Deter's behavior escalated, Tris would stay quiet.

And now, on her last night at home before the Ball Buster, Tris checked again to make sure her passport was in her bag. Finally, she grabbed a book. At 9:30 p.m., after reading the same three pages in Toni Morrison's *Paradise* for the umpteenth time, she turned off the light and closed her eyes.

But she couldn't sleep. Danny, Deter, Ann-Marie—their words played in a continuous loop in her mind.

Thirty-One

*"**THAT'S THE THING** about being a pilot," Bron said as he slid his uniform pants over slim hips. "You gotta have a plan, a goal. Something to work for. How can you call it a career if you don't upgrade to captain?"*

It was a cool, bright April morning and they had spent the past two days lying in bed together talking, eating pizza, and making love. Bron had to go back to work. He had a four-day trip.

Bron had just been awarded Exeter as a crew base, and was about to leave regular line flying for a job in the Clear Sky training department. Now that Bron would be based in Exeter full-time, they wouldn't be scheduled to fly together as crew anymore.

They had discussed whether he'd find a place or move in with her. Bron wanted them to live together, but Tris wasn't sure she was ready. So they did what pilots always do—they put it in the "for later" compartment.

"Right," she said after thinking for a bit. "But what about people who just think flying is fun? What if they don't want the responsibility of command?"

Tris woke up with Bron's alarm at 5 a.m. and saw no point trying to go back to sleep. Might as well just make coffee and hang out before he left. She was on her last day off before she had to head back to the crash pad, to her Arkansas crew base. She didn't have enough seniority yet to hold the Exeter base. Soon.

Bron slid his starched white shirt over his broad chest and back, which looked out of place atop his long, spindly legs. Now in full uniform with four captain's stripes on his shoulders, he sat down on the bed and put his arms around her. "If they don't want command, then they're not professional pilots," he said and hugged her. "We'll pick this up when I get back. See you soon, baby. I love you."

Her body began to respond and she countered it by turning around to face Bron. "Fly safe, young'un." Bron laughed. He wasn't that much younger than Tris, but she still teased him about it. She kissed him, and he was gone.

⊶⬥⊷

"I love you," echoed inside her car as Tris sat with her foot on the brake. His voice, its scratchy, sexy tone, right there in the car. A freight train inched by in the pouring rain. Traffic was stopped.

Tris hadn't told anyone, not even Danny, that she still heard Bron's voice. Random words, now and then, things he'd said before. A real-time replay, but his *voice*, the sound of it was present, audible, and unmistakable. She hugged herself against her memory.

The Tetrix parking lot was pitch black when Tris pulled in at 4:20 a.m. Lights were on in the pilot area, and she could see Ross and Deter through the glass. She dragged her two black roller bags through executive parking, using the shortcut all the pilots took when Zorn and Willett weren't around.

By the time she entered the hangar, the two men stood in front

155

of the airplane, drinking coffee. Tris waved at them as she tried to roll both bags to the Astral's baggage door at the same time. Grasping one bag with each hand, the larger one kept tipping over, and she had to pull it along as it scraped against the concrete floor. Neither man moved to help her. In a way, she appreciated that. Generally, common courtesy would rule, but given the lack of professional duties she had on this trip, she was pleased to be treated like one of the guys.

Ross called out to her.

"Just a minute," she answered above the sound of a 737 taxiing by the hangar.

He leaned casually against the nose of the Astral.

"Ready for your first big international trip?"

"Oh yeah. I just wish I had more to do."

"Nah. You don't." Ross grimaced. "Seriously. I'm not looking forward to this trip. The last time it went out, the crew had maintenance trouble in just about every city. So, when we decided to take a third crewmember, Deter begged Zorn to let us take a mechanic." He checked himself immediately. "Oh. Sorry."

So Tris wasn't just an extra body, she was someone they were carrying instead of the mechanic they really needed.

"No, no problem. I get it. I never thought about that. I'm happy to be along. I'll make myself useful." She almost offered to step aside and let a mechanic go, but there was no way any of them could get packed in time.

"We were looking at the overnights. There's one long one in Vienna toward the end of the trip. We know it well." Ross dialed up his heartthrob smile. "Vienna's really fun. There's a neat bar near the airport. Live music. That is, if you'd be up for it."

"Sounds like a plan," she replied and turned the conversation back around to the work at hand. "Anything I can do to help?"

"Sure! Why don't you go put coffee and ice on the airplane?

And check on the catering. It's scheduled to arrive at five fifteen. Keep a lookout for it, ok?" Ross turned to walk back to the pilot area.

"Hey, you pre-flight yet?" Tris called to Ross's back.

"Deter's going to," he said without even turning around. She'd hoped she could do it but didn't want to ask Deter; she couldn't risk setting him off before the trip even got off the ground.

As Tris filled the ice bucket, she heard the loud bang of the hangar door locks release, followed by the unmistakable screech of cables and pulleys. The eighty-foot wide door rose slowly, noisily, and settled in its metal tracks high above the concrete floor. Tris hefted the bucket into the cabin, and listened to the sound of fuel trucks pumping, tugs pulling aircraft, and the usual cacophony of takeoffs and landings.

Once inside the Astral, Tris inhaled its signature smell, a combination of leather cleaner, metal, and dust. The navigation system clicked as it spooled up, all part of the low-level hum of the Astral rising early along with its crew.

Ross would fly the first leg. Tris recognized his headset on the left seat. She smiled at the sight of the custom-fitted earpiece attached to a microphone. Most pilots wore traditional headsets, with two ear covers, but rumor had it that Ross didn't want to mess his thick, wavy hair. The small leather bag he used to carry it, embossed with the initials LRR in gold, lay on the left seat.

Tris finished her duties early. It gave her some time before the maintenance crew pushed the Astral out of the hangar to treat herself to a few minutes alone on the ramp. Just to watch the show.

Airplanes executed precise turns and revolutions, taxiing in step with the choreography designed by ground control. Aviation equivalents of stop and yield signs kept them from harm as they traversed the blue, yellow, and white pathways on taxiways and runways. Other airplanes rose in rhythm to the takeoff commands of the tower controllers.

Tris closed her eyes to identify the manufacturer of aircraft engines from the sound they made on takeoff. She inhaled deeply. She counted off the seconds in her head until she heard the gear come up once airborne, felt the split-second timing of planned positioning. The canon of aircraft movement at the airport; the only true ballet.

"No. We can't," Deter said.

"Why not? Who cares? We'll be right there."

"But Zorn didn't approve it. I'm telling ya, man, don't do it."

"He'll never know if we don't tell him," Ross said, exasperated.

That was all Tris heard through the door to the pilot area. Deter and Ross both looked at her like she was the last person they expected to see when she walked in. Deter threw his hands up, shook his head, and walked away.

Ross turned to Tris. "I was pleading your case for some legs in Europe. I'm sorry."

"What case? What?"

"I thought we should give you a chance to fly a couple of legs." He took a breath and looked away for a second. "It would give you the experience and us a break, which we're gonna need at some point." He shuffled a massive stack of paper that was probably trip information. "But that's not what Zorn approved," he continued, lips pursed in distaste. "If I let you fly and Zorn found out, it's my ass, since I'm PIC on the trip. Well, both our asses, we're both captains. We can't do it."

"No, I get it," she said to Ross, moving quickly from excitement to disappointment. "No problem."

Tris finished her indoor chores and walked outside for a few more precious moments alone on the ramp. The sun rose to her right. It lit up piles of slush pushed to the edges of the taxiway by airplane tires. Some sparkled from the previous night's new snow, others were crusty with dirt-covered frost. Tris opened her overcoat. She already felt the heat.

Thirty-Two

"YEAH, WE JUST got here from Zurich," Ross told Devon over the speaker on the hotel room phone. "I wanted to try and reach you guys, talk to James, just check in."

He moved around the bed, pulling what he'd need for the short overnight out of his suitcase. They were in Berlin for the night, off to Vienna in the morning. Luckily the crew had a long layover there before heading to Luxembourg and then back across the Atlantic.

"Hey, Dev? Can you hear me?" Ross thought he might have gotten disconnected. Devon hadn't said anything. For the last two days, he'd called their home line and her mobile phone, but hadn't reached her. He'd left at least three messages on their home machine. Finally, he caught her.

"No, still here," she said, although she sounded very far away. Well, Exeter *was* far away.

"So," Devon continued, "that girl, that Tris, she's on the trip with you all?"

"Yeah, she's an observer. I told you that before I left. Dev, I don't make the schedule. You know that." He heard his wife take a deep, dramatic breath.

"You brought her home with you. You were alone with her *in our house.*"

"Dev, I had too much to drink at O'Slattery's. She *drove* me home. She didn't *come home* with me. You should be glad she did that!"

"I just..." She paused, then got a head of steam. "Look, Larry. The last couple of years have not been great for us. It's not just that girl, it's so many things. Your drinking. It's getting out of control and—"

He raked his fingers through his hair. "Hang on a minute. Just you wait now. I don't drink liquor at home anymore. And that's because of *you,* Dev. You asked me to stop and I did. I just have a couple of beers at home. You know that." Ross heard the panic in his own voice. *Calm down.*

"You still get drunk at home. It upsets James," she said quietly.

"How would you know?" Ross responded a bit too loudly.

"Well, he has asked me a few times why Daddy walks funny or laughs when nobody says anything."

Those words practically stopped his heart. His *son* noticed this? Or was she just positioning? If so, she had a position of strength. She had James.

"Ok, Dev. I'm so sorry. I am really sorry. I'll stop. I promise."

"Well, I hope so. I really hope you do. And, until you do, James, Buddy, and I will be at my parents'. We got to the ranch yesterday."

His legs buckled and he landed on the edge of his hotel bed. The room began to spin and his stomach lurched in revolt. And he hadn't even had a drink yet.

It took several seconds before he could speak.

"You left the house? You're not home? What...? When...?" He stammered.

Devon held her silence and drew in a long deep breath. "We

started driving the day you left on your trip." Her voice first sounded shaky and uncertain but quickly hardened. "We're just taking a break. Let's talk more when you get back home, ok?"

Ross thought he might be sick, that he might actually vomit. Buddy, too? She took the dog? He lowered his head between his knees and managed to say, "May I speak to my son, please?"

"Not today. When you get home, ok?"

His face flushed. He should demand that she put James on, order her to do it. But they weren't in the Astral; she didn't have to comply.

"Ok, Dev," he said.

He pressed the speaker button on the phone to disconnect his wife.

Thirty-Three

A SMALL, NONDESCRIPT entrance door on a dingy street near the airport in Vienna opened to a large room with tables, an L-shaped bar, and a wide dance floor. They'd just arrived from Berlin. The leg was uneventful, another routine trip from one airport to another.

Tris finally understood why the Tetrix pilots called this trip the "Ball Buster." She was exhausted from the long days, short nights, and lack of downtime. She just wanted to go to the hotel and relax.

But Deter and Ross couldn't wait to get to this place. It sure didn't look like much. There was a coat check area where they could park their luggage. Predictably, Ross and Deter walked straight inside to grab a table, leaving Tris to collect the claim checks.

As she shoved the stubs in the back pocket of her jeans, she fingered the familiar form of her spare house key. She must have forgotten to put it back in the kitchen drawer after grabbing it to run down to the laundry room in her building. Tris dreamed of twisting it in the lock of her front door and walking inside her home.

At the table, Deter motioned to a waiter.

"*Ein beir, bitte.*" Deter spoke halting German. Tris shook her head. Every pilot knew the word for "beer" in multiple languages.

The waiter nodded toward Tris and Ross. "*Zwei mass, bitte,*" Deter added. The waiter walked off and soon returned with three one-liter glasses of beer. The overnight had officially begun.

"I'm starving," Deter said. "You ordering lunch?" He asked Ross.

"Oh yeah. Tris?"

"Definitely." They stumbled through mispronounced menu choices.

"A toast," Deter announced. "To getting home," he said as their glasses clinked.

Ross was at the bar when lunch was served. While Tris and Deter ate, Ross drank. He'd grab a shot of tequila from the bar, do it halfway back to the table, then turn around and get another one. Each time, Ross positioned himself next to a different woman.

Tris found herself alone at the table with Deter, grasping for conversation.

"This happen a lot?"

Deter thought for a minute before speaking.

"You know, for most of the guys, a week away from home is a nice break." He sipped a cup of coffee. "Not sure what's going on in his world right now."

Ross weaved back and forth on his feet, trying to stroke the hair of an older woman who twisted away, and pushed her outstretched arm against his shoulder as she repeated, "Nein. Nein."

"Let's go get him," Deter said, as he rose from their table to guide Ross away.

Tris settled in her hotel room just before midnight. They had an evening departure to Luxembourg the next day, so she wasn't in a rush to get to sleep. Deter practically had to carry Ross to his room, he was so drunk. The night at O'Slattery's wasn't a one-off.

She cycled through all available TV channels, but only CNN broadcast in English. Tired of the news, she pulled out *Comanche Moon,* the prequel to *Lonesome Dove.*

Tris wedged herself deep into an overstuffed divan in her otherwise austere room. A thick, soft comforter covered the bed that she'd settle into soon enough.

Then she heard a knock on her door. Turndown service? Had the "*Bitte Nicht Stören*" sign fallen off the door handle? Tris had already stripped off her work clothes, slipped into the big cozy T-shirt she liked to sleep in and thrown on a pair of soft white tube socks. Two suitcases and she'd forgotten to pack slippers.

"Hey, Tris. Open up." She could hear Ross fumble with the doorknob.

"Larry. What's wrong?" She said from inside the room, the door still closed and locked.

"Can I come in?"

"Uh, why?"

"Really. It's important. I have something important to tell you."

"Is there something wrong?" she asked again. "Something with the Astral? The passengers?"

"Me! I need to tell you something."

Good grief. "Hang on a second." He replied with a grunt. She threw her jeans back on. There wasn't time for her bra, so she'd just cross her arms over her chest. He knocked again. *How is he still awake after all that drinking? Why hasn't he passed out?*

Tris flipped the safety bar off and opened the door. The smell of him knocked her back. Alcohol, cigarettes and urine. A dark stain spread on the front of his pants.

"So, how's it going?" he asked casually. He wore his uniform jacket over jeans and a sweater. He grasped at the doorjamb to stay upright and seemed even drunker than when Deter steered him to his room. *Must have hit the minibar.*

"Going good. Getting ready for bed."

"Oh yeah?" He leered at her breasts. She involuntarily took a step back.

"Yup. Off to bed. See you for breakfast in the morning?" This would be her only try at diplomacy. She hoped it would work.

It didn't. "Yeah, yeah, bed. Bed now. Lemme in."

"No, Larry. No. No. Your room is two floors down. Remember?"

He shouted. "I have something to tell you. It's really important!" Tris heard a couple of doors open elsewhere on the floor.

"Look. Have a good night. See you tomorrow." She stepped back further and pushed the door closed.

Ross grabbed the doorknob and leaned his full weight forward. "Let me use the key." He grabbed her around the waist and poked at the knob with his room key.

Tris put both hands on his chest and shoved him hard. He stumbled backward and caught himself against the door to the room across the hall.

"Larry, this is *my* room. Your room is two floors down? Do you know how to get back to your room?"

"I am here! I live here! Come on, Tris. You know you want it." He made a loose fist and moved his wrist quickly up and down, in a gesture that could not be mistaken for anything other than what it was.

"You need to get out of here, Larry." She heard more doors open on the floor. If she didn't call security, someone else would.

He stared at his room key and muttered what sounded like, "That's the way it's gonna be, ok." As he took a step in the direction of the elevator, he tripped over his own feet and almost fell. He literally hung on to a wall sconce in the hallway.

She couldn't handle this alone. "Wait. I'll bring you a chair. You can sit while I call the concierge."

Tris made sure Ross held on to a doorjamb as she ran inside her room to grab the straight back chair at the desk. She dragged it outside and put it against the wall, adjacent to a room service tray with a half-eaten hamburger and French fries on it.

"Sit here. I'll be right back." Tris hoped no one would come through the hallway until Ross was gone. She quickly called the concierge and returned to Ross.

Ross slumped in the chair, nodding off. Then, all of a sudden, he reached over and grabbed her thigh. She slapped his arm, but he held on tighter. Tris wrenched away and moved a safe distance from him.

She was more disgusted than afraid.

"What are you doing? What is so important that it couldn't wait for tomorrow?"

He mumbled something completely indecipherable. Maybe "buddy" or "my buddy."

Finally, the elevator door opened and a man in a uniform wearing a nametag appeared.

This discreet gentleman obviously had some experience with this type of situation and looked apologetically at Tris as he helped Ross up. "Sir. *Guten tag.* Let me escort you to your room, yes?"

Ross didn't say another word. "Good night," she called, as the concierge propelled him toward the elevator.

Thirty-Four

TRIS OPENED HER eyes to streaming sun the next day. She was safe in the soft folds of her hotel bed. The thermostat kept her room a cool 70 degrees, and she curled the covers beneath her chin and wondered if last night's episode had been a dream. Tris lay on her left side for a few seconds, then flipped over to her right. Surely she imagined it.

When she propped herself up in bed, she looked under the covers at the very real black and blue mark blooming on her thigh.

It made no sense. Sober, Ross always behaved like a professional. Outside the cockpit, he'd be friendly, joking around. He did nothing overtly suggestive. Last night he said he had important information, something she needed to know. Was it all bullshit? A ruse just to get into her pants?

And then logic set in. Ross was sloshed for sure, but lucid enough to figure out what room she was in, go to the elevator, push the right button, knock on the correct door, and proposition her. *Part of him knew exactly what he was doing.* That night at O'Slattery's— was he more conscious than she thought that night, too?

Her thoughts spun as she touched her thigh. A captain assaulted a crewmember on the road. No, no, she had to walk that thought back. Tris had to fly home with him. Luckily, he and Deter would be in the cockpit. She could hang in the back of the Astral with the passengers. She'd avoid the jump seat altogether.

She'd faded in and out all night, tempting sleep but never fully attracting it. Tris threw the covers off and walked to the window. Outside, the city's ornate rooftops looked thousands of years old. Paintings of old-world scenes in gilded frames were bolted to the walls of her room. Seen in the light of day, the high-backed chair Ross sat in resembled a small throne.

Everything about Vienna screamed history, and Tris wanted to scream right along with it. Instead, she paced. Bed to door to window and back again.

She looked at the antique style phone in her room, creamy ceramic complete with gold accents and a rotary dial. Tris had to talk to Danny. But it was 4:00 a.m. in Exeter, and he still hadn't returned any of her calls.

She'd just take it one step at a time. Breakfast, the flight to Luxembourg. One more night, two more days, three more legs, and she'd be home.

Tris found Deter sitting by himself in the hotel restaurant reading *The New York Times*. Although he faced the entrance, he didn't acknowledge Tris until she hovered right next to him.

"Good morning," she said brightly, sitting at his table. It was a strange day when being with Deter made her comfortable.

Deter peered over the newspaper. The scent of coffee and bacon surrounded them as silverware clinked against porcelain plates. *Should I tell him?*

"Hello, Tris," he said. "Sleep well?" Odd question coming from him. Why would he care how she *slept?* Or was she just being paranoid—after all, she'd heard a door open during Ross's hallway performance last night.

"Yeah, not bad. I'm over the hump," Tris said. Jet lag. "I'm officially on GMT." Deter smirked in response, although he never took his eyes from the paper.

"Bulls lost to the Pistons last night. Damn," he said.

Tris shared his love of sports. And they were both Bulls fans.

"Shouldn't matter. They're going all the way this year anyway," she replied and poured some coffee from a pot on the table.

Deter nodded in agreement and put the paper down.

"Have you heard from Ross?" she asked.

He didn't hesitate. "Nope. After I dropped my bags last night, I went back down to his room and put a chair in front of his door. That way, if he went out again, he'd have to move it." He took a sip of coffee. "When I checked this morning, I saw it had been moved. Can't imagine how that happened. Probably housekeeping." Deter folded his newspaper. "Or he went out again."

"He really loosened up last night, eh?"

"Yup," Deter said as he picked up the paper again.

"Anything else going on?" Tris still believed that Deter knew more than he said.

"Do you want to join me on a bus tour of downtown Vienna? Otherwise, we might as well be in Detroit." He repeated the joke Tris had made earlier in the trip and they both laughed.

"Uh, did you ask Ross to join you?" If he was going, she'd politely decline.

"Nah. Let him sleep it off."

"Right. Ok, I'm in."

"Meet me in the lobby at 11:00." And with that, Deter left Tris to finish her breakfast.

He never saw her bow her head and let out a long, slow breath.

Tris and Deter returned to the hotel mid-afternoon. He stopped at the desk to pick up some flight planning documents that were faxed to him.

They took the elevator together, casually reliving the last few hours. "That was actually a pretty good bus tour," Deter said.

Tris nodded. "Yeah, at least we saw the Vienna State Opera and St. Stephan's Cathedral. Too bad there was no time to stop and go inside."

Deter's minimal German helped them navigate the menu at the café they stopped at for lunch. Conversation between the two of them was forced and superficial. They talked about the weather and getting home. There was no mention of, or even allusion to, Ross.

Tris and Deter were on the same floor, his room further down the hall. They parted ways at her door and were back in the lobby two hours later, packed and in uniform. Ross was there when she arrived. His back was to her as he stuffed a piece of paper in his pocket.

She was torn. This was not the place or time to confront him. Which meant that Tris had to be cordial. To pretend.

"Hey, Larry. How's it going? You have a good day?"

He flinched when he heard her voice.

"Oh yeah. Watched TV in German!" He neither turned nor looked over as he spoke. Instead, he assumed his haughty pilot pose, chest out, eyes forward. Yet his voice was friendly.

"I hear you guys saw the town—or some of it." Ross nodded at Deter, who was still at the front desk.

"Yeah. It was a pretty good bus tour."

"Oh, I've seen it before. You know this ain't my first rodeo." Ross chuckled at his own joke. Tris rolled her eyes.

They packed themselves and their bags into the hotel van. On the way to the airport, Deter went over every detail of the day's leg with Tris and then passed her the weather package and flight plan documents. Ross read a magazine.

At the Executive Terminal, Tris rolled her bags toward the reception desk to ask about catering.

"Come on, Tris, follow me," Deter called from the exit to the ramp. Surprised, she caught up to him, and when she was astride, he said, "Your pre-flight. You're upfront for this leg."

Tris felt her chest constrict and her hands tingle. She actually dropped one of her roller bags, which met the ground with a loud clunk. She wasn't sure if it was nerves or excitement. Either way, once her initial reaction passed, she realized she hadn't reviewed any charts, wasn't sure of the flight plan, and was otherwise simply not ready.

"Thanks! I appreciate it." Did Zorn know? Had they cleared it with him? When? Maybe this was what Ross tried to tell her last night. Was "buddy" a reference to Zorn? Did he have a real reason to show up at her room?

She shook it off. There was simply no time to worry about it. *I'm First Officer on this leg, and I have work to do.*

Thirty-Five

TRIS STOOD ON the ramp in the brilliant Vienna sunshine. It was a crisp fifty-two degrees with light winds—a perfect day to get out of town. Each leg brought her one step closer to Exeter. To home.

Ross came outside during her pre-flight. He walked right past her with his suitcase; he didn't say a word to her.

Her focus on Ross turned from last night's behavior to today's crew change. "Hey, Larry. I didn't expect to be flying this leg. What's up?"

He responded as though he hadn't heard. "Ok, I'm heading back in to check on catering." As he walked away, Tris asked him if he'd ordered fuel. He nodded yes without missing a step. He hadn't looked her in the eye since the night before.

Powered by nervous energy, Tris finished the walk-around and climbed the Astral's airstairs two at a time. She found Deter and Ross sitting in the back of the aircraft. Ross bent over in his seat and spoke softly to Deter, who listened with his usual deadpan.

She thought she heard Ross say, "Don't call him."

"Ok, you can start it up anytime," she called to Deter from the front of the Astral. It was Deter's leg, so per procedure, he needed to start the APU so they'd have power on the ground.

"Get it started, Tris," Deter responded, and went back to his conversation with Ross.

"Sure. You want me to program the nav system?"

"No. I'll get that. You do everything else."

With the APU running, air poured through the environmental system. That and the whine of the engine made it too loud for Tris to tell if Ross and Deter were still talking. She felt the vibration of someone walking up the aisle and down the airstairs. Out the cockpit window, she saw the two men head back into the terminal.

The trip came together in routine fashion. The fuel truck finished pumping and pulled away from the wing. Ross loaded the ice and coffee and spread out the *USA Today* and the salmon-colored *Financial Times* on an empty seat.

Tris went to stand on the ramp for a few minutes and try to make sense of things. Jets pushed back from their gates, positioned to taxi. One-One was active, and Tris had a clear view of aircraft moving on and off that runway at regular intervals.

Once it got closer to the top of the hour, she'd get their clearance. Last reported winds were from the southeast at thirteen knots. All she had to do was look up into the clear blue sky to know they had good weather for departure.

Back in the cockpit, Tris found Deter programming the nav system. He'd placed the company flight manifest on the center console. For each previous leg, the manifest listed Ross as Captain and Deter as Co-Captain—an acknowledgment that while both held the same position in the Astral, Ross had more time in service at Tetrix. They split the flying evenly. After their names, she saw "Miles, Patricia F.—Crew Observer." Although these were only internal documents, Zorn was particular about paperwork.

She held up the manifest. "You want me to move Ross into the observer seat and me into the second-in-command spot for this leg?"

"What?" Deter didn't like being interrupted.

"Ann-Marie's probably at her desk. I can call home and have her change the paperwork."

"Change the paperwork? Why?"

"Why? You told me I'm sitting right seat on this leg. I figured Ross would be in the jump seat. Don't we need to amend the manifest for the crew change? Or at least tell someone back at Exeter?" She checked her watch. It was well into the business day back home.

"Don't do anything. I'll handle it."

"Hey, what's going on?" Her confusion turned into concern.

"*I'm* the pilot-in-command. I control the paperwork. You just keep up. Let's get to Luxembourg, ok?" Deter's patronizing comment scratched at her already stimulated nerves. Tris flexed her left hand to keep her nails from digging into her palm.

"Yes, master," she said, a bit louder than she intended. Deter pretended not to hear.

Within seconds, Deter had their flight plan up on the navigation screens on both sides of the cockpit and bounded out of his seat toward the terminal. He hadn't taken the manifest with him and hadn't penciled in any changes.

Tris hugged herself and rubbed her palms on her upper arms. Did anyone back home at Exeter know about the crew change? Did Deter decide to make her the co-pilot to Luxembourg? Or was that Ross's call? And why?

The Astral had a satellite phone. She could use it to call the office and talk to Zorn, or at least speak with Ann-Marie. In an environment that depended on crew coordination and communication to stay alive, Tris was alone, with a problem, and no one to talk to about it. Nothing about this situation felt right.

I'm calling. She walked to the SAT phone, which was embedded in the armrest next to one of the passenger seats. She picked it up and jiggled the hook to get a dial tone. Tris heard the hum, then depressed the hook and held it in. She had to organize her thoughts before she dialed.

She was co-pilot for this leg. They told her at the last minute and didn't say why. As drunk as Ross was last night, this trip departed at 7:00 p.m. Working backward, Ross would still have to be drinking at *11:00 this morning* to be outside the eight-hour bottle-to-throttle rule.

And at that moment, it finally made sense. Of course Ross wasn't concerned about the eight-hour rule. He satisfied that easily. But the rest of the regulation prohibited anyone with a blood alcohol level of .04 or higher from flying no matter when they took their last drink.

Ross was smashed last night. He's afraid he'll blow .04.

Tris looked at the receiver. Every nerve in her body fired, and she didn't know how to make them stop. She sat down, then stood back up, the phone still in her hand. If she told Zorn what she thought, this trip would be over. Deter would be furious, but that was the least of her concerns. And Ross. A drunk. A predator. "Erratic," Ann-Marie had called him.

Tris still didn't know exactly where she'd start when she released the hook and dialed. She'd punched in the numbers 0-1-1-1 when someone stepped on to the airplane. Ross stood at the galley carrying a number of plastic bags and a tray. The rest of the catering. Deter moved slowly behind him with the passengers in tow to give Ross a chance to get the food onboard.

Tris had to abandon her plan and reluctantly put the receiver down. Ross wasn't flying. If he had begged off for the reason she thought, they were legal to launch. She'd be fine. *They'd* be fine.

She went to help Ross with the food, and their eyes finally met. Her visceral reaction was to move back and shield her face. In response, Ross's eyes softened, and he slumped forward. He knew what he did.

He opened his mouth, about to speak what she hoped was an apology. "Here's the stuff," he said. "The food in these trays needs to be heated. Can you turn the galley ovens on?"

Technically, that was his job now that she was flying. She elected not to argue; she just did it. Even if she did push back, she had no support here, and she knew it.

But Tris had to try to get some answers one last time before the passengers boarded. "Hey, look, I'm happy to fly to Luxembourg. But did Deter change the paperwork?" That's when she realized she'd only thought about the Tetrix paperwork. That was an easy fix. But every time the Astral flew anywhere in the world, the crew had to file an instrument flight plan with the FAA. And it had to have the name and number of the pilot-in-command. It was the law.

Tris squared her shoulders and faced Ross. "Hey, are you still PIC on the flight plan?"

A look of panic crossed Ross's face, and then quickly vanished. Surely they'd taken his name off; in case something happened, authorities would call the captain. And today that wasn't Ross.

Ross ignored her, but she kept going. "Larry? Wait! Did you change it?" Ross continued walking to the back of the airplane.

Frustrated and angry, Tris turned so suddenly she knocked a bag of paper plates and plastic utensils on the floor. They scattered all over and blocked the narrow aisle in the cabin. She bent over to pick them up just as the passengers boarded. *Focus. Focus.*

The two executives nodded and squeezed around Tris, who, in a crouch, apologized while she cleaned up the mess. She grabbed the hot meals and popped them in the oven, then ripped the cellophane cover from a cheese tray big enough to feed a dozen people.

"Have a seat, gentlemen. We'll get going in a few minutes," Deter called back to the passengers and climbed into the left seat. "Get the clearance, Tris."

"Standby." Tris still hadn't sat down in the co-pilot's seat.

"C'mon, c'mon. Radios set?" Deter pushed.

"Hey, wait a second. I'm working as fast as I can." She clicked her seat belt and shoulder harness, quickly tuning in the departure frequencies.

"Work faster."

It was go time.

Thirty-Six

WITHIN MINUTES, THE Astral settled at cruise altitude en route to Luxembourg. With no one but ATC to speak with, Tris concentrated on her stunning view of the Swiss Alps. They looked so close, like she could touch the tips of their peaks.

Their flight plan took them over Nuremberg, south of the Czech Republic, and around Frankfurt into ELLX, the local airport in Luxembourg. The plane performed perfectly, and tension in the cockpit had dissipated. Tris leaned back, letting her shoulders drop for the first time in hours.

She loved the peace of a stable cockpit, where she could appreciate this view of Europe from her special perch at thirty-eight thousand feet. Tris and the Astral were part of this vista, the uneven terrain, whitecaps that hovered over wide-open valleys below. This was the real prize. It answered the question she asked herself more and more frequently about why she had chosen Tetrix.

Tris turned around to check on their three passengers. The executives were working. Ross laid asleep, his head thrown back, tie loose, the top button of his shirt open and his uniform jacket removed. His hands were folded neatly in his lap.

She checked the navigation program, which could correctly estimate within seconds where they were along the route. They had at least twenty minutes before they could begin a descent into Lux.

Deter hadn't said much since takeoff, mostly operational talk. She rotated in her seat to face him, but he kept his gaze straight ahead or on the instrument and radio panels. Tired of trying to edge her way into information, Tris flat out asked him what she wanted to know.

"So. Why isn't Ross flying this leg?"

It took a few seconds for Deter to acknowledge her. "He wasn't up to it. He wasn't feeling well. He called me right before you and I met for sight-seeing."

"Why didn't you tell me? We were together all afternoon." She could have had hours to prepare for the flight.

"I briefed you in the van and told you once we got to the airport. You had almost two hours to get ready. He took over your chores. What's the big deal?"

"Did Zorn ok this?" She thought she saw his jaw tense, just slightly. There was no way Deter could make a crew change without notifying Zorn first.

"I had a qualified co-pilot on the trip with me, and as pilot-in-command, I made the decision to have you fly the leg. And that's the end of it." With that short twist of words, she was dismissed. Her own anger rose, a vise that tightened in her throat to the beat of its own pulse.

"Astral November Nine Tango X-ray, Wien Center. Descend and maintain flight level Two-Four-Zero and report leaving Three-Eight-Zero." Tris glanced over as Deter nodded.

Tris could only do her job. She keyed the mike to answer ATC.

"Wein Center, November Nine Tango X-ray leaving Three-Eight-Zero for Two-Four-Zero."

"November Nine-Tango-X-ray, expect the Vetil Two Mike Arrival into Luxembourg."

"Roger, Nine Tango X-ray will expect the Vetil Two Mike."

Tris entered the details of the arrival into their navigation system. The straightforward procedure would put them on a long final approach for Runway Two-Four.

Tris studied the airport diagram and saw that it would be a short taxi to the executive ramp. They were slightly early, and the ground handlers confirmed that the limo was waiting with engines running. Soon they'd be at their hotel for the final overnight in Europe before the long flight back over the Atlantic. Tris could not stop thinking of home.

Just then, ATC cleared them down to nine thousand feet. Once they flew below ten thousand, conversation upfront was limited to items essential to flight. She wasn't done with Deter. But for now, it was a relief to focus on approach and landing.

At five miles out, Deter called, "Slats and flaps fifteen." The aircraft rumbled and slowed as the wing expanded. A minute later, they were cleared by ATC for a visual approach into Luxembourg and told to contact the tower. As the approach controller spoke, Deter asked for more flaps. Tris answered ATC and lowered the flaps simultaneously. A second later, she heard the expected increase in engine power. The aircraft's nose pitched up slightly. They were fifteen hundred feet above the ground. Tris checked on with tower.

"Welcome to Luxembourg, Astral November Nine Tango X-ray. Runway Two-Four, cleared to land, wind two-five-zero at six knots, right turn off." Tris acknowledged the landing clearance.

"Gear down, before landing checklist," Deter said.

Tris grasped the handle that lowered the Astral's landing gear. She kept her left index finger pointed at the three lights that would turn green when each of the plane's wheels were down and locked. After a few seconds, Tris saw the left main and nose gear lights illuminate, but the right gear light remained dark.

"I do not have three green. No three green," she said quickly. The aircraft was just six hundred feet above the ground.

"What the fuck?" Deter screamed but took no action as the Astral moved closer to the ground.

Deter hesitated so Tris made the call. "We don't have three green. Go around!"

"*Go around!*" Deter slammed full power on the aircraft. He swore under his breath as the airplane's nose hesitated, then pitched up.

Tris lifted the gear handle to stow the gear. Maybe raising it would shake something loose, and that third light would come on next time they tried to put the wheels down. But first, the Astral had to get away from other air traffic.

"Tower, Nine Tango X-ray, missed approach. We can't confirm that the landing gear is down and locked. We need a vector to an area where we can diagnose the problem." Deter nodded along with her demand.

"Roger, Nine Tango X-ray, fly heading two-four-zero, climb and maintain six thousand. Let us know what happens."

"What is wrong with the goddamn gear? Recycle it! Now!" Deter's words landed like blows, his anger unrestrained. Tris recovered quickly; she had to. And she couldn't punch back. The five souls aboard the Astral were in real danger. They weren't on the ground with options—they were in the air with none.

Tris lowered the gear again, as Deter commanded. Still only two green lights.

Someone traveled toward the cockpit. Ross stood behind them. He hadn't said a word.

"Larry, let the passengers know we had to go around. Up to you what explanation you want to give them." Tris gave the order.

"We'll keep recycling the gear and see if we get three green," Deter said, more composed. At least he'd lowered his voice. Tris took a deep breath and exhaled slowly.

The Astral flew in a holding pattern away from other airplanes, with the autopilot on. Now Tris could think. They survived a calamity close to the ground. With the immediate urgency over, the action in the cockpit slowed. It was something she'd learned at the commuter; the first thing you do in any emergency is take a breath.

Ross talked to the passengers. She couldn't hear everything he said but knew his velvety baritone would soothe them. The executives simply nodded and returned to what they were doing. Tris had to grin—Ross had a way with people. All things considered, Tris was glad Ross spoke to them.

In the captain's seat, Deter quietly reviewed the emergency checklists. As sweat stains spread under the arms of his uniform shirt, Tris smelled the strong scent of fear.

Her hands hovered over the yoke as the autopilot slowly rotated it to the left. The sound of the ambient air traveling over the aerodynamic arms of the Astral changed only slightly in the turn. But Tris could feel it: the initial, subtle resistance of the aircraft, disturbed from equilibrium when the right wing rose and then descended as the autopilot finished its leisurely turn.

When Tris flew as a passenger she would guess the configuration of the airplane solely by sound. A slight rumbling accompanied by barely discernable bumps—the slats poking out of the front of the wing. A bang, the aircraft slowing briefly, followed by twenty seconds of movement and a loud click—that was the gear. The run-up of engines, pitch of the nose, and feel of the wing expanding to slow the aircraft—final flaps down, aircraft with the nose up high, ready to touch down on the runway.

Inside, the airflow would increase with altitude and then decrease all the way to its final dump as the aircraft depressurized near the ground. She would sit in her aisle seat, close her eyes, and fly every airplane down the pipe by those sounds.

"Ok, Tris, gear down." Deter sounded like he was underwater. He addressed Tris by name, which he rarely did in the cockpit. A testament to the gravity of the situation and, she hoped, Deter recognizing the need for calm, concerted action by the flight crew.

Tris reached across her body toward the gear lever, a long switch with a round plastic handle that poked out of the middle of the instrument panel. She grasped and raised the lever to remove it from its safety lock. Tris glanced at the airspeed indicator to make sure they were still at a safe gear down speed. If they flew too fast, the gear could be ripped off the airplane as it lowered.

Tris slowly extended the handle to the full down position and waited. She heard the gear doors click open. The airplane buffeted slightly as the gear assemblies lowered. But how many?

She saw the first green light. The left was down and locked. Then came the second green. The nose wheel was in position.

There was no green light on the right main.

"I have two down and locked. What's next?"

"Aw goddamn it! Useless fucking *cunt.*"

The sheer force of Deter's roar threw Tris back in her seat and up against the right side window. The glass was freezing against her cheek. Her heartbeat raced as though she were running from a loaded gun, cornered with no means of escape.

As the slur reverberated in the cockpit, Tris forced herself back into the moment. Yes, he said it. Finally said it. She pressed her lips

together, her jaw tense and eyes narrow. She wanted to scream too—
at Deter to shut up. *Just shut up and fly the plane!* But she couldn't
get into it with Deter now. He'd lost his grip, with the plane in the
air and passengers in the back.

Long seconds passed before anyone spoke. "Come on! Keep
your voice down!" Ross finally said as he glanced back and forth at
the passengers. "Keep it together, man. I'm not upfront. I can't help
you here." Tris blanched at the implication. Even if there was some
practical benefit to Ross being in a pilot's seat—which there
wasn't—neither Deter nor Tris could get up now. It would further
alarm the passengers, who were sitting only ten feet away watching
the pilots' every move. And if what she suspected was true, if Ross
was legally drunk and sat in the cockpit, or took one single action as
a pilot, it could cost them all their careers.

"November Nine Tango X-ray, contact approach one-one-
eight-decimal-nine-zero. Are you declaring an emergency?"

Deter shook his head "no" so hard she could feel his seat wobble
in its tracks.

"Negative. We'll contact approach," she said.

"It's probably a light," Deter offered, as if the events of the last
few minutes never happened. Like the word, "cunt" wasn't still
bouncing back and forth off of all three of them. She shot a look at
Ross, who had nothing to add.

"I can do a quick light check. Make sure it's not a burned out
bulb." Tris pointed to the button she'd press to make all the indicator
lights on the panel come on. This way, if the right main gear light
stayed out, chances were it was just a burned out bulb and the gear
was actually extended.

"Good idea," Ross said. She saw Deter nod out of the corner of
her eye.

"Ok. But when I do, the red lights will go on, too. Some of them will flash. Larry, can you tell the folks in the back in case they notice it? They are probably already a little freaked out." She looked directly at Deter, her expression taut and purposeful. Tris welcomed the measured sound of her own voice.

"Good idea. Hang on a minute." Ross spoke briefly to the passengers. Seconds later, he stood behind the pilots. "Go ahead." He pointed to the test button. Tris pressed it. The green right main gear light came on. *Shit. It's working.* The problem wasn't a bulb.

Tris had another idea. "Right. Ok. Let's try putting them down again and ask tower for a flyby."

Deter jumped back in. "Yeah, we can," he said, "but let's say they see three gear down, even though we aren't getting three green lights. I'm concerned that the right main may be down, but not locked, or worse, crooked. The only way anyone can know for sure they are properly extended *and* locked down are three green lights. If the right main buckled on the runway, well, that could be catastrophic." Tris knew he was considering numerous scenarios, including the worst case—the gear collapsing, the right wing hitting the ground and bursting into flames.

"Think we have enough to make Paris?" Ross nodded toward the fuel gauges. Paris had an Astral repair station located on the field. If they had to make an emergency landing, that was the best place to do it. All three of them looked at the fuel remaining. Tris could almost hear the air being sucked out of the cockpit. They had enough gas to stay aloft another forty-five minutes, tops. No way they could make Paris.

"I wish," Deter said. "This is as good a place as any. The runway is long, and they have crash, fire, and rescue trucks." Deter tapped his fingers on the yoke, his posture stiff, muscles rigid as he looked from Tris to Ross and continued.

"Here's the plan," he said, resuming his role as pilot-in-command.

"Let's try to lower them again and do a flyby. If the tower doesn't see three down, we'll come back out here," Deter said, gesturing outside the cockpit windshield, "and consider our options." He looked past Tris to Ross. "I think landing with two down is better than gear up. You?"

"Yep," Ross and Tris answered at the same time.

"We can use engine thrust and the rudders to try and keep the right side of the aircraft from falling to the ground until the airspeed bleeds off enough to prevent a fire, even if the right side hits. Larry, make sure both passengers are sitting on the left side of the plane. We need as much ballast on that side as possible, and they stand the least chance of getting hurt on that side. They can get out quickly." He paused. "If the worst happens."

"Roger. I've got it."

"Ok. Gear down."

Tris reached over, released the handle lock, and pulled it down. And, again, only two green lights illuminated.

"Ok. Raise the goddamn gear." Deter erupted again. "And tell approach we need a flyby."

"Hey! Keep. Your. Voice. Down. The passengers already asked me if you were ok up here," Ross said sharply. Tris looked straight ahead. If Deter lost it again, if in *her* professional judgment he could no longer be trusted to safely control the aircraft or make decisions, she'd relieve him of his PIC duties and take control of the airplane. She'd have no choice.

A few beats passed. "If we have three down, we'll make the approach and pray the right main doesn't collapse. We'll prepare for a two-wheel landing." Deter's composure faded back in. "Ok. Bring the gear up again."

Tris's heart slammed against her chest as she raised the gear handle. *Maintain the majestic calm.* Despite Deter's cavern of disrespect, she was crew on this airplane. And it had to land soon.

"Luxembourg Approach, Nine Tango X-ray. We are not getting three green lights when we lower the gear. Requesting flyby to see if tower can confirm the gear is down. The light we're not getting is the right main, so requesting right traffic." This was what she trained for. Tris let *her* demeanor set the tone in the cockpit.

Deter nodded at her request for a right turn in front of the tower. It would give Luxembourg the best view of the right main gear.

"Roger, Nine Tango X-ray, understand. Fly heading zero-six-zero, vectors for flyby Luxembourg Tower. Contact tower now, one-one-eight-decimal-one-zero. Good luck!"

"Over to tower, thanks." Tris dialed in the new frequency. Before checking in, she asked Deter if he wanted Luxembourg to roll emergency vehicles, just as a precaution.

"Not yet," he replied. "We need to lower the gear one more time for the flyby. If the lights finally come on, no need. If they don't, which, well, we're all expecting, yes, roll the trucks."

Deter clicked off the autopilot and hand-flew the airplane. Tris checked on with the tower. Tower responded quickly. "Nine Tango X-ray, yes, we understand you need visual confirmation of the gear. Descend to pattern altitude and fly a close downwind. We'll let you know what we see."

"Roger, tower."

"Gear down," Deter called from what sounded like very far away. Once again, and for what she hoped was the final time, Tris pulled the lever and lowered the gear. As the handle clicked into position, Tris heard the familiar change in airflow as the gear assemblies dropped from their sheltered positions in the bottom of the fuselage. She felt the left main gear lock into place and then the nose. Tris had no tactile signal from the right main.

But then she saw the light.

R. D. KARDON

"Three green. I have three green," Tris announced breathlessly, almost beyond belief. "The gear is down and locked. I'll continue with the Before Landing checklist." Her voice was calm and strong.

Deter responded in the clipped tenor of command. "Ok. Let tower know. Tell them we'll need to swing around to a long downwind and can turn final in another mile."

"One hundred, fifty, twenty, ten," the Astral's synthesized voice droned, ticking off the airplane's distance from the ground on final approach. Emergency vehicles with their lights flashing were positioned along the edge of the runway. Deter flew the aircraft. Tris communicated with ATC. Ross briefed the passengers on emergency evacuation procedures if the Astral's gear collapsed.

Tris looked straight ahead during those final seconds of flight. Deter's shirt was soaked in sweat as he gently pulled the power levers to idle. The Astral rolled forward.

The gear held.

"Astral November Nine Tango X-ray, welcome to Luxembourg," tower chirped. "Contact ground control for taxi."

Thirty-Seven

THE CRASH TRUCKS sped away with their lights off, back to their garage. "Shutdown checklist," Deter called as he set the parking brake and moved the Astral's power levers to the shutoff position. The flight was over, but unfinished.

The passengers ran out of the plane as soon as they could without saying a word to any of the pilots. Deter followed them inside. They had an early departure the next day to Gander, Newfoundland, where they'd fuel up for the nonstop leg home.

Tris felt another set of footsteps walk quickly down the airstairs. Ross jogged into the terminal.

Relieved to finally be alone, the stress, the fear, the anger she'd sloughed off just to get down safely shrouded her. Tris closed her eyes as her shoulders slowly collapsed, her stoic façade with it. She realized her hands were shaking.

Cunt. More than just an insult, it sent the shameful message that a person's genetics, their physical characteristics were reason alone to despise them. That's what made it insidious, and why it hurt so badly.

"No. Oh no," were her only intelligible words. Her throat tightened, and every nerve ending tingled. She pulled her knees to her chest, hugged them, and bent her chin. Her right foot shoved the co-pilot seat as far back as it would go.

Curled up and crammed into a corner in the cockpit, her head pushed against the circuit breaker panel, its tiny plastic knobs pressed into her skull. She never felt as insignificant or alone.

Her instincts implored her to fight back at the highest possible decibel. *Take those feelings and shove them down. You're an expert at it.*

She'd done it with her family. She'd done it with Bron. And for the sake of her passengers, the safety of the flight, and her own life, she'd done it on the way to Luxembourg.

Tris forced her body harder into the metal, plastic and Plexiglas corner of her co-pilot seat. There, in that tiny space, the trauma, outrage, and sorrow she'd endured this last year twisted around her like a tornado's vortex. Her brain was thrown into overload.

Memory took over. She thought of a small picture of her and Bron standing next to their airplane on a Clear Sky trip in Roanoke, Virginia. Bron brandished his trademark toothy mug. She wasn't smiling.

He was the one who had wanted to take that picture. It was their last trip together as a crew, although neither knew it at the time. He'd called his buddy in crew scheduling and requested Tris as his first officer.

"Hey, the company loves it when we fly together. They save money on a hotel room." Bron liked that everyone at Clear Sky knew they were together. Tris would have preferred to keep the information close.

"Hey, can you get a shot of the two of us in front of the plane?" he'd asked the ramper. She remembered feeling impatient, like she'd had enough photography for one day. They'd already taken a bunch of pictures on the trip, but for some reason, this one was important to Bron. And Bron was important to her, so she stood next to him, with her arm barely draped around him. Why couldn't she just let go and enjoy him? There was doubt behind every moment, each experience cloaked in it.

No, it wasn't the best picture of the two of them, with her standing stoically next to the man she loved, but it ended up being the last. Barely a month later, she answered the phone in the middle of the night to learn that Bron's twisted body had been pulled from his car by the Jaws of Life.

Her heartbeat thrummed, just like it had during their Luxembourg leg. Tris stared at the empty captain's seat beside her and mouthed something, but made no sound. She was sure, in time, she could make the right noise pass her lips, put together the letters and make a word, then a sentence. Then a prayer. A prayer for Bron. But mostly for herself.

Yet she didn't have time. There was no time. Weary from the fight, she had to face the rest of the crew.

Thirty-Eight

ROSS RAN UP the steps of the Astral. Tris unfolded her body and wiped her face with a catering napkin. The last hour's events replayed in her head. Irregular procedures, especially if the crash trucks rolled, always led to questions. As crew, she'd be interviewed. And possibly urine tested. Maybe that's what Deter and Ross were doing inside. If so, she'd be next.

Without saying a word, Ross walked from seat to seat, filling a trash bin.

Finally, he spoke to her. "Did you have fun up there?"

Had he lost his mind? Tris responded to what she hoped was sarcasm. "*Fun?* Are you kidding? I wish it had been you, man. Why didn't *you* fly this leg?"

He hesitated. "It all worked out. You guys did a good job."

She flashed a hard, unforgiving look as she unloaded on him. "*It all worked out?* That's it? Deter nearly lost it up there. You saw it! And he finally said what he's been thinking since the day I started here."

193

Ross stood there, his head hanging woefully. Something was happening, *had* happened to him, she was now sure of it.

His posture stooped, arms sagging at his sides, Ross stepped toward Tris. She involuntarily backed away.

"What did you want to tell me last night?" She softened her voice to invite his confidence yet kept a safe distance between them. But Ross simply shook his head and turned away.

"You came to my room late at night and now you're not going to tell me why?" She pushed harder.

Ross stopped but did not turn around. "My wife left me. Ok? She took our son. She even took the dog."

That's what he wanted to tell her? Why her?

Tris's mouth had dropped open. "When?"

"Toward the end of the trip. She's making all kinds of crazy threats. Like she says she's never coming back. I'll never see my boy." His voice began to break.

"I'm so sorry." She tried to make eye contact.

Ross avoided her gaze. "We've been having trouble at home for a while. Then that night you drove me home, well, she heard about it. Someone told her I brought a woman home." His voice hardened.

"You were drunk! I drove you home. She should be glad I did."

"Look, it's not just that. She has a lot of complaints about me." He faced Tris, his nostrils flared with rage. A bolt of fear forced her to step further back.

Tris bit her lip and looked down at the scuffed men's lace-ups she wore with her uniform.

"Your family. It's awful. Still..." There was no right way to finish that sentence. They shared the hopelessness of a loss they each thought they caused. But she didn't owe him any apology.

Ross grabbed some magazines and jammed them into seat pouches.

"The plane's going into the hangar overnight. There's a mechanic coming to safety-check the gear for tomorrow."

Just then a young ramper stuck his head in and spoke to them in French-accented English.

"Larry Ross, if you please, come inside. Call for you. Inside. Please." Then the ramper ran off to marshal a jet that was just pulling in.

Tris stood in stunned silence, caught in a complex mesh of anger, sadness and fear as Ross shoved a trash bag into her hand and hurried toward the terminal.

Thirty-Nine

EXHAUSTED AND LONG past angry, Tris wanted to get away from Ross and Deter, from the airport, from all of it. At the hotel, in the peace of her room, she could sort it out—unless she got another visit.

Neither man thought to take their overnight bags off the plane. Tris either had to lug all of their bags inside by herself or wait for them to do it. She was in no mood to wait.

It took Tris three trips to drag all the crew bags inside, including her own. Once she finished, she went to the ladies' room. *Almost done*, she thought, more a rallying cry than acknowledgment. She took her time at the sink, wet a paper towel, and held it to her cheeks and neck. A small comfort, but so welcome.

Once outside the restroom, Tris noticed a large conference room on her right. Inside, Deter, Ross, and two men sat in business suits wearing airport security badges.

She caught Ross's eye from outside and mouthed, "Should I come in?" He shook his head. This distracted Deter, who said something to

Ross and then said "no" so loud Tris could hear him through the glass.

"Hi. I'm with the Astral. What's going on?" she asked the woman behind the reception desk, motioning toward the conference room.

"The, uh, fireman, trucks," she said, struggling to speak English with a heavy French accent. "They come, so the managers, they wish to speak to the PIC."

"The PIC?" But it made perfect sense. Airport authority in the U.S. would want to interview the crew if they had to roll crash, fire, and rescue trucks. Luxembourg would naturally have the same procedure. But why was Ross in there?

What was going on in that conference room between Deter and Ross and the local airport authority? *Ross didn't bring the airplane down. Why is he in there instead of me?*

He never changed the flight plan! He's still listed as PIC. Was he urine-tested? Did he pass?

Her anxiety increased as Tris was once again excluded from crew communication.

"Also, there is a message. From the phone, yes?"

The woman handed Tris a pink slip of paper. "N9TX" was written on the "to" line, and the number that followed was Zorn's. Tris looked into the conference room again where Deter, Ross, and the two men remained heavily involved in conversation. *To hell with both of them.* She'd call Zorn herself.

She asked where she could make a call using her international calling card. The Tetrix PIC was issued a portable SAT phone capable of making overseas calls. Tris wished she had it on her.

Instead, she sat in a public phone cubicle, pulled out her card, and punched in the endless codes. She struggled to make sure her fingers, still surprisingly unsteady, didn't press the wrong buttons. She couldn't calm herself. Tris still wasn't sure what Zorn already knew or what she'd tell him.

A few seconds later she heard Zorn's voice. "Ed? Larry? What's going on?" His caller ID must have shown an international exchange.

"Hi, Brian. It's Tris. I saw your message and wanted to get back to you. Ed and Larry are in some type of meeting with the airport authority."

"What? What are they doing?" Was it possible no one had told him anything?

"I'm sorry. I'm not sure whether you knew." Zorn breathed into the phone like an animal ready to charge. She thought he might be craving information, so she kept talking. "We recycled the gear numerous times, and we kept the passengers advised."

After a few more sentences, Zorn cut her off again. "I need to speak with Larry Ross. *Only* Ross. As soon as possible." He sounded as angry as she'd ever heard him. Zorn hung up without saying anything more, including good-bye.

Ross? Why Ross? He wasn't even flying.

She loitered outside the conference room and waited, anxiously shifting her weight from side to side. She had to get to the hotel, had to figure things out. She couldn't get her bearings with these people around her.

Tris handled the gear emergency consistent with her training and knew she had done well. But everything surrounding it—Deter, Ross—there was no checklist she could consult for erratic crew behavior. They were late; she was tired, hungry, still stressed from the mechanical, furious at Deter for today's attack—and at Ross for the one last night.

"Remember, Tris, it's up to *you*," Bron had said, more lecture than instruction. "If the PIC does not respond appropriately to a situation, when they're not thinking straight, *you* take control. It's your airplane." They were reviewing a training scenario where the PIC becomes incapacitated, and the first officer assumes command. Tris realized she'd just experienced it in real life.

Just then, the conference room doors opened. One of the local officials told Deter in a heavy German accent that he would "call this man Brian Zorn." All four men shook hands.

The officials left the building, and Deter and Ross shuffled back into the conference room. Tris strode in behind them. That vise in her throat tightened, the one she had become so used to; the one that kept her from forming the words she wanted to speak.

"What do you *need*?" Deter yelled. He stared at her as if amazed she hadn't crumbled in response. Her eyes narrowed and shoulders squared as she matched his gaze.

In the dark, without any advantage or support, Tris played the one and only card she had.

"I talked to Zorn."

Ross and Deter froze. A second later Ross moaned. His renowned countenance fell away and he practically shouted, "What did you tell him?" Then he writhed in his seat. "Oh my god, oh my god," he bleated.

Tell him? "There was a message at the desk for a crewmember to call him, so I did."

"You should have let us handle it," Deter said.

"Why? I'm a crewmember. A *crewmember*. Not a *cunt*."

Deter's face twisted into a horror mask. He rose halfway out of his chair, and stopped.

"Crewmember? Not since we shut down, you're not," he seethed.

As Deter fired back, Tris heard brakes screech outside on the ramp and what sounded like claps of thunder. She jumped back, but it was just a tug hauling an aircraft out of the hangar. Her exasperation, Ross's panic, and Deter's anger fell in torrents, the three of them striking each other with words that sliced like machetes. Tris used all of her remaining will to stay composed.

"Zorn wants you to call him." Tris tossed the words at Ross, along with the crumpled phone message. "Provided you're sober enough to dial."

Ross audibly slumped in his chair. His uniform jacket scratched against the cheap upholstery. "Oh my god, oh my god," he mumbled, his eyes closed, while his right hand ran from the top of his head, through his hair, to the collar of his uniform shirt over and over again. "Jesus, I can't tell him. He can't find out."

"I'll call him if you want," Deter said quietly.

Ross's eyes stayed closed. "Nope. I'll...think of something."

"What are you going to tell him?"

"I don't know yet."

Tris evenly suggested a plan. "Ok, let's hash this out. Let's go over what happened, so when we talk to Zorn, we'll be consistent. So, first thing, did you guys do a whiz quiz? Do I need to do one?"

"No. No, no. No one's peeing in a cup. I've got this!" Ross yelled so loud Tris saw two people stop walking outside the room and look in at them. She and Deter glanced at each other, his anger replaced by a look of concern mixed with fear.

"All right, just calm down. *Calm down.* We'll figure it out." Deter tried to soothe Ross.

"Figure *what* out? What exactly did we screw up?" Tris was even deeper in the dark than when this day started.

But the two men just got up and walked past her toward where Tris left their bags.

"Get us a ride to the hotel, will you?" Deter practically threw the words at Tris.

The crew was crossing the Atlantic the next day.

PART III:
ALBEMARLE
and
VAUGHN
April 1998

Forty

TRIS SAT OUTSIDE on the patio with a cup of coffee after a sleepless night. The Astral had landed back in Exeter yesterday, but her body hadn't adjusted to Central time yet. She paced, tried to read, watched TV. Finally, she gave up and just stared at the digital clock for the rest of the night and watched the minutes click by.

Tetrix had a thirty-six-hour blackout period for pilots who just returned from international trips. It was a window during which they couldn't be scheduled to fly or even be contacted. Tris thought if she kept looking at the clock, those hours would pass more slowly. And she'd have more time to think, to make sense of what had happened.

The crew made it back to Exeter without further incident. After Luxembourg, Ross sat upfront, and Tris returned to serving the passengers. The tension between Tris, Deter, and Ross ended any levity or camaraderie. At one point, Tris sat in the jump seat folding a navigation map, as she'd done hundreds of times before.

"What's that goddamn rustling?" Deter snapped.

Ross raised his hand and mouthed "shhh" to steady him. Tris

wanted to tell him where he could stick his "rustling" but kept her mouth shut and eyes fixed on the navigation clock that ticked down the flight time remaining until they landed in Exeter.

During the long trip across the Atlantic, Deter and Ross spoke to the passengers, a bit to each other, and little to Tris. Anything they needed to ask or say to her was communicated with a grunt or a hand signal. And nobody—*nobody*—mentioned Luxembourg.

Tris called Danny as soon as she got home, hoping he'd answer his phone. Luckily, she caught him on an overnight in Sioux Falls. There was nothing to do there, and Danny sat in his hotel room with his new notebook computer; he'd just discovered aviation message boards.

At first, he said he was too busy to talk.

"Please Danny," she begged.

"Ok, but I only have a few minutes."

He rushed her off the phone, but not before he agreed to come by her place after his trip concluded this morning.

She watched Danny approach and went to greet him. "Hey," he said and walked by her into the living room without even a friendly hug. She read the hurt on his face.

Tris plopped down into the new leather recliner she'd treated herself to after a couple of months on a corporate pilot salary. Instead of sitting on the couch near her, Danny chose one of the old club chairs Tris had bought second-hand.

Tris described what happened in Vienna—and after. But he barely commented; mostly, he just sipped the cup of coffee he'd brought with him. Just an odd "hmmm" or "really?" punctuated her story.

Tris bent and straightened her legs as she talked. She couldn't get comfortable in the slick new chair. At some point, Tris knew she would have to address what had happened between her and Danny before she left on the Ball Buster. But first, she just needed his help.

"I don't think he went out again. But I don't know. Maybe the minibar? All I know is he should have been coming down from the drinking he did at the pub by the time he came to my door." She looked over to see if Danny had anything to add.

He pursed his lips and shook his head before he spoke. "Doesn't really matter. He knocked on your door, obviously wanted to come in. Are you sure you didn't invite him in?"

"No. Of course not." No matter how many times she replayed that night's events, she could not begin to fathom how drunken crewmembers making late-night visits to her hotel room had become part of her world.

"So, the night before the whole gear incident, a crewmember shows up at your hotel room door, obviously drunk. This doesn't seem random. Did you get any sense from Ross what he wanted?" Danny leaned forward in his chair.

"No." Another partial truth. He told her, just not that night. She absent-mindedly touched her thigh. She'd keep that part of the story to herself.

They were both quiet for a minute. Danny looked lost in thought. Tris had to tell him the rest.

"Danny, uh, there's more. I have to tell you about Deter."

"What, he make a pass at you, too?" Danny said and rolled his eyes.

His sarcasm stung. Tris forced a quick, insincere laugh and looked down. She rubbed at a coffee stain on her sweatpants.

"Look, it was crazy up there when we couldn't get three green. I get that. I must have raised and lowered the gear a dozen times. Once, when I put them down and the one light didn't come on, Deter really... Well, he lost it."

"Yeah?" Danny was used to her stories about Deter losing his cool. "He said something worse than all the stuff he's said before? Hard to believe."

She spoke softly. "He yelled the c-word."

Danny looked at her as though he didn't understand.

"Look, he called me a 'useless cunt.' Well, he just yelled the words," she quickly added, "I don't know if he was referring to me or what. I don't think so—"

"He *said* that? To *you*? Wow. I mean, we swear upfront all the time, you know that. But the c-word? What did you do? What did you say?"

"Me? Nothing. We had two in back. Ross was dealing with them and with *himself*, and we couldn't get the gear down. And I swear, Danny, I can't say for certain he called me and not the plane...that word. We couldn't get the gear down, and he started to unravel. But I gotta say, it stopped me cold."

She let a few more seconds pass. "It was like I was the only one up there keeping it together." She choked on the last few words.

"I have to do something. I have to tell someone. But who?"

"Tell?" Danny vehemently shook his head no. "Don't tell anyone!"

This caught her short. Keep this a *secret?* No way. "Danny, what are you saying? I can't let this go. This is a new level of disrespect. You know that! And in the cockpit during an emergency? That's when he's supposed to be at his most professional. And he lost it. Why not tell Willett? Isn't that what *you'd do?*"

Danny sighed. "Probably. But this is tricky under the best of circumstances. Even in a situation like this, when just saying that word makes someone guilty, politics still plays a role. You're not one of the guys, Tris. They'll protect their own."

"But Zorn and Willett. They'll find out, I'm sure. Ross heard him. The passengers, I'm sure they heard him too!" She pressed Danny for another answer. Didn't she have a *duty* to report this?

"Tris, this type of thing will come right back on you if you talk to someone. This isn't the airlines, where we have Pro Stans." Danny referred to Clear Sky's internal affairs group. "Deter deserves to get in trouble. And he would be in trouble— for a little while. Maybe get his wrist slapped, maybe more. But this could blow up your career!"

"*Me*? How does this come back on *me*?" Tris rose and started to pace. One captain grabs her, the other calls her a cunt. And *her* career was in jeopardy?

But she knew. Of course she knew.

"If you complain, then you've played 'the woman card.' That type of story, that you tried to get some kind of advantage, or get someone in trouble, would spread like fire. Soon, it won't be 'well he showed up at my room drunk and horny.' It'll be 'she came on to *me*.' And Deter? He'll come up with something you did wrong, or should have done. And it will follow you everywhere you go. Any interviewer who knows a guy who knows someone at Tetrix, gets their buddies to make a phone call. That's how it works."

They were quiet for a long time. The thought of leaving Deter and Ross unscathed burned like acid. Her own self-respect was at stake. How could she let them get away with it? It was flat-out wrong.

Danny waved his hand. "Forget them, Tris. Get your type rating and move on. It's your ticket out."

A dog howled outside her patio door. She nodded slowly to Danny. He was right. She could tell nothing but the absolute truth, and still, the whispers, the comments, the wariness would follow her forever. Deter and Ross would get 'spoken to,' and go on with their lives. And she'd be destroyed. No one would trust her again.

Training was so close. She'd get the type rating. Get qualified to be a captain, and then move up or get out.

As if he read her mind, Danny asked, "When do you go to school for your type?"

"I leave a week from Sunday."

"When's your ride with the FAA?"

"My type ride is May third," she answered immediately. This was the date she'd been focused on since she received her training schedule.

"Any chance they would cancel it on you?"

"Why?"

Danny sighed. "Tris, have you been listening? You've gotta get that type before those guys turn on *you!*"

"Maybe they could, I guess, but Ann-Marie told me they've already paid the training center. They'd lose the money if they canceled."

"Who is riding with you? Someone at the facility?"

She huffed. "Ross. Can you believe it?"

"*Ross*? You know, that's actually good. You've got some dirt on him, something you could use if you needed it."

Tris swallowed hard.

"Look," Danny said, "I'm not saying you should actually do it, but you know *why* he pulled himself off of that leg, don't you." It was more a statement than a question.

"Probably his BAC. He probably figured he'd be above the minimum." And then she remembered that moment in the conference room in Lux. Ross freaked out about talking to Zorn.

"It's not that he didn't fly or that he was drunk or his blood alcohol level. Well, it is, but it's more than that. He's afraid of *Zorn finding out he didn't fly*! But why? Who cares?" Again, the behavior of the pilots at Tetrix flummoxed her.

Danny nodded. "Who knows. These guys are just different, no figuring them out. But Ross isn't going to mess with you. And he also heard the, uh, comment Deter made. He's probably glad that it happened. He wants the spotlight anywhere but on him."

Danny's voice suddenly became more purposeful. "You got two

choices, Tris. You can tell the chief pilot, or the boss, the whole deal—the c-word, Ross coming to your room, you flying the leg. But if you do, there will be consequences. For Deter and Ross for sure. But for you, too."

He spoke as he would as PIC. "Get the type. Just get the type. Hold out a few more weeks, until you pass your training. Once you have the type rating, it's yours. They can't take it away."

So much to consider. All Tris wanted to do was sleep.

Danny walked over and sat on the edge of her chair. He leaned in and put his arm around her, and drew her close to him. But her body felt like a puzzle piece being forced into a place it didn't fit. She moved outside the reach of his arms.

"What's wrong, Flygirl?"

She shook her head. As much as she needed his support, she could not give him what he wanted right now. Why couldn't he understand that? Did she have to hurt him again?

"Danny, I don't think I can stand their crap another day."

He rose to his full captain stance and threw his shoulders back. "Oh yes, you can. This sucks. But it's what happens, you know, when there are no rules. You gotta get that type. What would all this crap be worth if you didn't?"

Get through training. Pass her check ride.

"But what if I can't? You know..." What if she froze up, couldn't handle the V1 cut, failed *again?* It would be humiliating, especially in front of Ross. She was so tired, tired of fighting, tired of taking blows.

"You mean the check ride. What if it were...like at Clear Sky."

She nodded. "They won't give me a second chance. If I don't pass, they'll fire me." And then she thought of an even worse possibility. "Or I'll be stuck there. A co-pilot forever."

"Just guard your six, keep your head down. You can do it. You *have* to do it."

It was too much.

She changed the subject. "I'm starving. I'll call for a pizza. Would you mind picking it up?"

"Sure. Mario's?"

"Yup. Extra cheese half pepperoni. As usual." She smiled. Danny grabbed his keys and left.

Tris moved over to her comfortable old couch. She reached for the blue Trimline phone she'd had since her fourteenth birthday. Last June, almost a year ago, she picked up the receiver and heard Danny crying on the other end. He struggled to find the words to tell her.

"Just let me read what the policeman wrote down, ok," he'd said. It was 3:06 a.m., and she was confused. What was Danny even talking about?

Between sobs, she heard his voice. "The decedent's car was headed east on Albemarle. After impact from the defendant's car it came to rest in the strip mall on the northeast corner of Albemarle and Vaughn." Tris knew the location. It was the way to Bron's crash pad.

"What's this about, Danny?" She asked, still half-asleep.

He sounded like he was hyperventilating for several seconds before he could continue. "It was Bron's car, Tris. Bron's car was hit. He was on his way to the pad. And he died."

Tris touched the phone's cord and ran her finger along the knotted curls in the plastic. How many times had Bron straightened it out? He'd sit on the couch, exactly where she sat now, and patiently twist it this way and that. It was always tangled again the next day.

Forty-One

ROSS'S FINGERS PLAYED a virtual drum solo on the steering wheel of the Cutlass. When it started to vibrate, he stopped.

He reached the turn to the hangar and pulled over. He had forty minutes until he had to show for the trip. Plenty of time for a cigarette.

Ross slid a Marlboro Light out of the pack he'd bought a couple of days ago. Devon wasn't home so he could smoke if he wanted to.

He'd stayed in last night because of today's trip with Zorn. They were overnight to Los Angeles and back tomorrow. His first trip since the clusterfuck in Luxembourg.

When he walked in the door after the Ball Buster, he almost thought he was in the wrong house. He kept expecting to hear the *tick-tick-tick* of Buddy's paws on the tile floor. He still couldn't believe she'd taken the dog.

Devon had waited until he was deep into the Europe trip to announce she'd left him. Sly of her. He wondered how long she'd been planning it. The timing was perfect. He was on the backside of the trip when it made no sense for him to come straight home, to try and talk her out of it.

She and James were on their way to her daddy's ranch while he was thousands of miles from home trying to reach her. Just when he was about to ring a neighbor to make sure his family was still alive, she'd answered her phone.

Those fucking Europe trips. They dragged him away from everything familiar, shook him up, and put the lives of strangers in his hands while his life—his real life—fell apart.

Ross's cigarette burned down, a line of ash teetering off of the filter. He stubbed it out in the ashtray and slid another out of the pack. He placed it between his lips and sucked in as he pushed the car's cigarette lighter against the open end.

When Devon had first dropped her bomb, he'd panicked and wanted to get to Montana. If he called Zorn, explained the situation, said Tris could finish the trip, he'd have to explain why. The questions, the rumors, the gossip that would create. And for what? To fly a thousand miles away from home in the opposite direction from where he was to argue with Devon from a shorter distance? With her father close by? *No way.*

Ross had another fifteen minutes to get to the hangar. He took a long pull on his cigarette to steady himself. His phone rang last night right on the tick of thirty-six hours. Zorn had called Ross himself to tell him about today's trip and asked him to be early so that they could talk about Luxembourg.

Luxembourg. He tried to fill in the missing pieces. He'd made a great landing in Vienna the day before. He remembered that. But everything that happened later was fuzzy. The next morning, after several cups of coffee, he vaguely recalled a bar. Maybe two bars? There were women, lots of smoke, and polka music.

Like every pilot, he knew the "bottle to throttle" rules and wasn't going to try and massage them just to fly to Luxembourg. He'd have passed the eight-hour rule, no problem. But there was that damn .04 BAC regulation. If his blood alcohol was above .04 and they got randomly tested, or—God forbid—something happened, an accident, or incident that *required* the crew to be tested, he'd be toast.

Ross tried to be responsible. When he called Deter to explain why he didn't think he should fly, Deter understood. Say what you wanted about him, and Ross had said plenty over the years, but when Deter learned about Devon, all he wanted to do was help. As much as Ross and everyone else joked about Deter and his military countenance behind his back, Deter had commanded men on active duty. Surely he could manage this problem.

Deter suggested they put Tris in the right seat on the Luxembourg leg. Why not? She was qualified, and she was there. They talked about the paperwork. The company manifest was no problem. Nobody really looked at those after a trip, Deter had reasoned.

But the flight plan had to name the pilot-in-command. If he couldn't fly the leg, Ross couldn't be PIC on the flight plan, which had already been filed. They'd have to change it.

"I'll change it at the airport," Ross had told Deter. "I'll put your name on it."

"Yeah, what's the worst that can happen? And if Zorn ever finds out, just say you were sick. Guys do it all the time," Deter said matter-of-factly.

"Right. Ok. I'll take care of it," Ross had promised. He figured he'd have plenty of time to make the change. Zorn would never notice the switch.

But he forgot, and then the passengers had shown up early. The crew had to rush and get the flight off the ground. It wouldn't have mattered, as long as nothing went wrong. Nothing ever went wrong. Right up until the moment it did.

Deter almost came out of his socks when the authorities showed up at the terminal in Luxembourg asking for "PIC Lawrence Ross." The men were from the local airport authority. Speaking with the PIC was standard procedure when emergency vehicles were deployed.

Turned out the Luxembourg officials simply called the PIC contact number they found on the flight plan. Ross had used the office number back at Exeter, which he had been doing for years whenever he flew Tetrix planes. And, predictably, Ann-Marie took the call and forwarded it to Zorn. From there, the situation took on a life of its own.

Ross realized that even if he'd amended the flight plan, he'd still have to explain to Zorn why he didn't fly. He could say he was upset about Devon, but he knew Zorn wouldn't buy it. They complained about their wives to each other all the time and could still fly.

All the times they'd gone out on the road, so many nights they stumbled back to their rooms. But Ross was always ready to go when the bell rang. Until Luxembourg. He'd convinced himself that if Zorn found out, he'd be considered a liability. It would just take an anonymous tip to the FAA for them to check Ross's driving record. His career would be over.

But he could spin this with Zorn. He hadn't realized it before, but Deter provided the perfect cover. Hell, it didn't even matter who flew the leg. Deter's fuck-up was way worse than his.

Which left him here, pounding the steering wheel with his right hand, throwing the remains of cigarette number three out the window with his left. He started the car and headed toward the hangar. By the time he made his way into the parking lot, he had his Tetrix mask firmly in place. Eyes blank, reactions stunted.

He had to keep his job. No way Devon would come back if he didn't. Fueled by nicotine-induced courage and some volatile information, Ross was ready.

Forty-Two

THE SECOND ROSS opened the door to the pilot area, there Zorn stood with a stack of papers in hand. Zorn had probably monitored his track from the parking lot. Christ, those window walls turned the lot into a fishbowl.

"Hey man," Ross offered in his typical, easygoing manner. It was a performance that had never been so important to maintain.

Zorn didn't buy it. "Shit man. And I mean *shit*. You're swimming in it."

Ross lowered his gaze and navigated to his cubicle. Slowly, he put his briefcase down. He pretended to notice two messages on his desk, scrawled in Ann-Marie's handwriting on the time-honored pink form. Ross knew this ploy—it was Zorn's way of teasing out anything Ross might feel responsible for, making him play defense. But Ross was running his own game. First, he needed to find out what Zorn already knew.

"Is that so? Can we possibly talk about this somewhere private?"

Zorn looked like a police detective about to interrogate a

suspect. "Let's go into the smoking lounge. I don't want people to see me talking to you in my office or the conference room. Best to keep it quiet. For now." Ross chuckled involuntarily, immediately wishing he hadn't. Zorn shot him a hard look.

Ross grabbed some coffee and a pack of Famous Amos cookies before walking to the cigarette-infused conference room. He turned on the lights and inhaled the remnants of a recent smoke. How Ross wished he had one now; he had to focus. He knew how quickly Zorn could turn on him. *Just ask RJ.* The poor guy was still having trouble finding a job.

Seconds later, the door cracked open, and Zorn entered carrying the stack of papers he'd had in his hand when Ross first saw him. He clutched a pad under his arm and a pen in his mouth. His left hand held a Diet Coke and a bag of M&M's.

"Hey, ok, let's get going," Zorn said as he put down his load on the small, oval table. His gut spilled over the top of his belt when he sat.

"Larry, what the fuck happened? You were flying pilot from Vienna to Luxembourg, right?"

"No, that was Deter's leg." So far so good.

Ross leaned back in his chair and looked into the distance behind Zorn at the bare wall painted in commercial off-white. He could see scuff marks by the plastic trim which met the brown Berber carpet, probably made by the cleaning crew smacking into it with their vacuum.

"Well, you guys had a gear problem. You were flying around out there for quite a while. And then, what, you declared an emergency?" Zorn looked down at a sheet of shiny thermal fax paper.

"It was an emergency. We couldn't get the gear down."

"Well, you rolled the trucks, so the airport authority had to investigate. I guess they pulled the flight plan and called the PIC's

218

number." He thumbed through his stack of papers and pulled out another document. He nodded. "Yours, since they asked for you when Ann-Marie answered. And it was the first I'd heard of any problems." He looked up at Ross. "Why was that? You had a SAT phone on the plane. And you could have had the handler send a message."

This was going way better than Ross imagined. Zorn's ego was bruised. He didn't like being the last to know. If all Zorn was going to do was chastise him about failing to give him a head's up, Ross had already won.

"There was a lot happening during that leg. We had no time to call." Ross sounded like he was the aggrieved party. "I mean, really, what would *you* have done?"

Zorn rustled the documents in front of him with his brows creased and chin lowered. He was just yanking Ross's chain to remind him that *he'd* have handled the whole thing differently, that if it were *him*, the gear lights would have come on the first time. It was crap, but that was Zorn.

"Our money man was one of your passengers," Zorn said as if Ross didn't already know. "I mean, Emerson's the CEO, but your passenger Robert Christianson's even more important to us. He's Willett's direct boss." Zorn glared at Ross. "And Willett's mine."

"And?" Ross wondered where this was going.

"Well, Willett called me and said that Christianson wants a meeting with him as soon as possible. He didn't want to wait but Willett's out of town for a few days. What's he gonna say?"

"Look, everything happened just the way I told you when I called you from Lux," Ross said, elated Zorn wasn't angry at him. "And the way Deter told you," he said deliberately.

"I haven't talked to him. He's on vacation for a few days. Started during the blackout."

"Well, then I'm not sure what else I can tell you, man."

"Yeah, I hear you. I get it. Look, next time something like that happens, you've gotta call me. I sure as shit didn't love getting a call from the Luxembourg airport officials, for chrissakes." He smiled warmly at Ross for the first time since the conversation started. "I'm glad you were there. No one I'd want more to be up there. Except for me, of course." Both pilots laughed.

Ross forced himself to breathe normally, in and out, in and out. That was the only way to control his emotions. Because out there, somewhere, was the record of a flight plan with his name on it, when there was a very good reason why there shouldn't be.

Ross thought they were done and moved to get up and prepare for the Gulfstream trip.

"So, how did it go with the girl while all this was happening? What was she doing?" Zorn shifted the thrust of the conversation as he reclined in his chair and took a long drink from the red and white can.

"Not sure what you mean."

"Well, could she handle it? How did she do in a stressful situation? You know, things being what they are, tight financially and all, at some point, if I have to make some hard decisions..." Right. The budget. It was always the budget. "And we're just about to send her to training. We paid full boat for her course on the Astral."

Ross thought about what would make sense to say next. "She was fine. It was her first trip to Europe. She did everything she was supposed to do." He could have gone on to say that she handled the gear thing just fine, but that would invite more discussion.

"And Deter? The girl and Deter? How'd that go over ten days in Europe? You come to her rescue?" Zorn smiled lasciviously.

Zorn was trying to goad him. But instead, he provided an opening for Ross to shine the spotlight on someone else. He didn't owe Deter anything, not really.

"You know how Deter can be. He let some pretty salty language fly during the whole gear thing. It was tense, as you can imagine."

"Oh yeah?" Zorn laughed. "No kidding? What did he say this time?"

Ross paused to create the impression that he was thinking about his response. But he'd hoped all along the conversation would take this turn.

"He called her a cunt." An involuntary wave of guilt swept over Ross as the words came out of his mouth. *Well, if I don't say it, she probably will.* And just like that, Zorn focused his full attention on Deter and away from Ross. *Deter can handle it.*

"Holy crap. Oh, *goddamn him.* Well, what did she do?"

Ross bent forward in his chair, then pushed himself back and crossed his legs. "Well, you know, we were dealing with the emergency..." His voice stepped carefully around the truth.

Zorn made a note and started to rise from his chair. "Anything else I should know?" Zorn asked before standing up. "Are you sure she didn't yell back at him? What *did* she do?"

Ross had to get out of this. "She did her job, man, all right? Her job," he said and walked out of the room. Zorn was busy making notes and didn't look up.

Ross walked directly to the men's room, locked the door behind him, and leaned face-first against the cold, tile wall. How easy it was to manipulate people. Zorn, Deter, Tris, everyone. How easy it was to put Deter under the hot lights.

He wanted to rinse the shame off of his face but couldn't look at himself in the mirror.

Forty-Three

ZORN PARKED HIS BMW next to Willett's Mercedes in the private garage. Willett always arrived early when he called a meeting, when he thought he had control of a situation. Zorn figured that Willett would bombard him the moment he walked in.

Sure enough, Willett loitered by Zorn's office door. His posture was stiff and exaggerated his brows cinched close together, his eyes like slashes. This attempt to look serious didn't jibe with his short, round body. Zorn stifled a grin.

"Meet me in the smoking lounge in ten." He flung the words at Zorn and walked away.

Willett clearly had a bug up his ass. Zorn grabbed a Diet Coke from the fridge and headed toward the stock room. He lingered by the small packages of M&M's and engaged in his usual internal struggle. To eat or not to eat the M&M's? *Crap, I'm putting way too much energy into this decision.*

He grabbed a couple of packages. Soon, he settled into his favorite chair in the tiny room. He reclined and pressed the bottom of his foot against the edge of the table. Willett was already there, with a stack of papers and his laptop in front of him.

"Smells like someone was just in here." Willett sniffed the scent of cigarettes and squeezed his eyes closed while his nostrils flared. He shook his head.

"Brian, I...uh, well, I just got off the phone with Robert Christianson," Willett said.

"Right, yes, the budget," Zorn interrupted him and motioned with his hand trying to move the conversation along.

"Yes, the budget. But something else. About Luxembourg. We might have a problem."

Zorn straightened in his seat, put both feet on the floor. "Yes? What about it?" Willett had his attention, although he was sure he knew what was coming.

"Robert, who sat directly behind the cockpit on the flight, heard quite a bit. He mentioned something that went on between Patricia and Ed during the leg. Do you know anything about it?"

Yep. Deter. "Well, I know they were under stress. Who wouldn't be?" He elegantly skirted the question. Zorn wanted to be smart here, make the best political play. He'd let Willett go through the motions and think he could best Zorn by dropping a bomb. But once again, Zorn's sources would prove superior; his buddy Ross gave him the heads up.

Willett searched through his pile of papers, found the one he wanted, and reviewed it. Then he held it up as if he were going to read it to Zorn.

"Robert complimented Patricia on her handling of the crisis." He paused. "And he wondered why Deter was yelling at her." Willett checked his notes closely, squinting like he couldn't read his own writing. "Apparently, he yelled something, uh, completely inappropriate. Robert swears he heard Deter call Patricia a 'cunt,' believe it or not. Robert almost couldn't say the word. I had to drag it out of him. Then Ross yelled at Deter." He looked over his notes again. "They don't know what Patricia did." He placed the piece of paper on the table and locked eyes with Zorn.

"Of course they couldn't see Patricia since she was in the right seat."

Zorn had so much experience keeping his expression unreadable, he couldn't look surprised if he wanted to. But this was unexpected. Where was Ross?

"That's bad," he said, nodding at Willett. "That's really bad." Willett got him after all! Tris was flying? How did Ross leave out that salient detail? And why?

"Did you know about this?"

"No, of course not." Zorn lied. Well, only half a lie. He knew about Deter. But he had no idea that Tris was in the right seat.

Ross. Zorn needed a few minutes alone with Ross. But he had to finish with Willett first. One fire at a time.

"I haven't heard a word about it from Tris," Zorn said. "I'm talking to her this afternoon when she gets back, but, seriously, if that happened, don't you think she'd have said something right away?"

Willett looked perplexed. "Well, maybe. I don't know. I've never had to deal with anything like this before. We've never had a girl here before."

Willett said nothing, but gave him a look Zorn read as, "And whose idea was that?"

Zorn was on the verge of something unfamiliar, that rare chance for Willett to one-up him. He continued slowly. "Well, at the very least, Deter's gotta do a pass through charm school." Their slang for Tetrix diversity training. "I'll tell him about it. I'm meeting with him today, as you know."

"And what was she doing in the right seat? Weren't Ross and

Deter supposed to do the flying? She was an observer, right?" Willett kept pushing.

Zorn needed to think of something. He had to get Willett to hone in on the Deter thing. That was the true management nightmare.

Willett graciously obliged. "So, how was it working out with them? Deter and the girl? Surely you kept up with that, as chief pilot."

Zorn ignored Willett's dig. He leaned over the conference table, his arms crossed. "I thought it was going ok. Ross said Deter was hard on her, but not unfair. And we both know Deter didn't want her. But even he's said she really works hard. I had no idea it might be this bad."

"Now that we know, what are we going to do about it? What if she's afraid to tell us? I had to call HR, alert them. They said if she's intimidated by Deter now, afraid to tell us, that creates a whole new set of problems. Already we have a red flag on sexual harassment." And then a thought energized Willett and his words rushed out. "What if she's just lying in the weeds, talking to a lawyer before she says anything to us?"

That was possible, sure. Zorn had to admit to himself that he never saw this coming. She was quiet around him, but he figured she was just doing her job and trying to work her way up the chain like he'd expect her to. Now, Zorn wished he'd paid more attention to her.

He relied on Ross to keep him informed. Ross liked her. But that could be about something other than her piloting skills.

Willett looked at his notes again. "Well, Robert was pretty clear about what he heard." He sat upright in his best bird colonel pose. "What the hell is going on with your crews?"

Willett intended to toss this steaming turd into his lap because he didn't have either the guile or nerve to resolve this situation. But Zorn already had the seed of an idea.

"So, what do *you* think?" Zorn wisely asked his boss before disclosing his own plan.

"Truthfully, I think one of them has to go. If Deter said, uh, cunt, well, it probably has to be him." Willett licked his lips as if he'd just tasted something bitter.

Zorn agreed but could tell by the look on Willett's face that he didn't want to fire Deter. And neither did Zorn. But maybe they didn't have to.

"So, if we can only keep one, it should be a captain, right?"

"Ideally," Willett said, not catching on.

"But she's *not* a captain. Well, of course, we could consider her for upgrade." He paused for effect. "*If* she passes her training."

A knowing look finally settled on Willett's face. Zorn had to admit, from time to time, Willett showed flashes of actual comprehension.

Willett exhaled slowly. "Ok. You're in charge of training. Let's see how it goes and then make the call. Unless she approaches us first, but I don't see her doing that. Starting a sexual harassment scandal right before she goes to training? She's a smart girl. No way she does that. If she passes, she may come back and demand to be a captain. And, you know, hold that whole Deter thing over our head."

"I've heard that some women have done that. Forced a company to move them up before they were ready. Certainly, we wouldn't want to do *that*." Zorn wasn't concerned. He was way ahead of Willett, and already had his next move planned.

"Yeah, I say let's see how training goes. The decision may be made for us. I'll make sure to set her up for her ride with, what's his name? That guy in Dallas who is always trying to take us out for drinks?"

"Jensen," Willett offered. "Jim Jensen. He's, uh, *approachable*." Willett wrinkled his nose and looked away. "And he won't rock the boat." Willett paused. "Stinkin' business, eh?"

Zorn wasn't exactly sure what part Willett referred to. Far from foul, it seemed like the perfect solution. If it worked, it would avoid problems now, and in the future.

"Yep," he said to placate Willett. But it was utter brilliance.

Both men went about their mornings without further discussion. Zorn grabbed another bag of M&M's. For energy, he told himself as he crunched the small, round candies. Deter was next on his schedule. He'd better not bitch about charm school, especially after what Zorn was planning to save his ass.

And when the Astral landed, he'd talk to Tris. He was curious about what she'd say. Not about Deter so much, but about flying the Luxembourg leg.

He also needed to talk to the person who made the decision to let her fly. Zorn added a conversation with Ross to his mental itinerary. Oh, they would talk all right.

But not yet.

Forty-Four

THE MINUTE HER blackout period ended, Ann-Marie called
Tris to give her a trip. She could have waited since the flight didn't
leave for a few more days. But she wanted the scoop on the Ball
Buster. Everyone in the office was whispering about it.

"What the heck happened on the way to Luxembourg?
Nobody's saying anything, but there's a ton of whispering going on
and I can make out the word 'Luxembourg.'" This time Ann-Marie
needed information from Tris. They had returned from Europe too
late for anyone besides maintenance to meet the Astral, and the
blackout prevented anyone at Tetrix from talking to the crew.

"Well, you probably know about the gear emergency. It was
pretty tense in the cockpit while that was going on. And I'm not sure
how much of the story Zorn knows. Do you have any idea?"

"Nope. But there was a call between Willett and one of your
passengers. They probably talked about it. Did anyone get hurt?"

"No, not at all, thank goodness. I know they were freaked out.
But Deter and Ross and I were all working the gear issue. So I can't

say for sure." Not clear who knew what, Tris hesitated as her brain spun various information scenarios. She was unsure of her footing, and even though she trusted Ann-Marie, she needed to form her own plan of action before confiding in her. "We'll find out soon I guess."

"Yeah. So, sorry about this trip. Hate to send you out again right before your training. Deter's on vacation, and Basson is going out with Zorn on the Gulfstream the next day. So you'll be with Ross."

"Ok. Got it."

"One more thing," Ann-Marie hesitated. "Zorn told me that he's gonna want to talk to you when your trip gets back. About Lux. So be ready for that."

"Ok. I will be."

Questions clicked around her like the tongues of snakes. Once they were aloft, she'd get some answers from Ross.

Ross stood at the bottom of the Astral's airstairs talking to the mechanics when Tris walked into the hangar. He had on his leather bomber jacket, the one all the Tetrix pilots had. His name was embossed in gold on a patch over his heart, mimicking the ones that military pilots wore. Tris thought they were pretentious. But she was an outsider in so many other ways, no sense making it worse by refusing to buy a jacket. She passed on getting a name patch, and left it at Tetrix where it hung over her desk chair.

Ross cleared his throat. "Ok, Tris, we're ready for pre-flight." He spoke quickly and then dashed off to handle his PIC duties. The few times their eyes met before flight, he'd look down and pretend to study a flight plan, or walk away from her mumbling about something he had to do.

The flight came together in routine fashion. With the Astral level at thirty-seven-thousand feet, and a solid hour to go until they had to descend, Tris glanced in the back to make sure their passengers were settled. Ross sat quietly in the captain's seat.

"Astral Nine Tango X-ray, Center," ATC's call broke the silence.

"Astral Nine TX go," Tris responded.

"Astral Nine Tango X-ray, light to moderate turbulence reported, all altitudes, for the next ten minutes." Tris looked over at Ross, who shook his head. They'd stay where they were instead of climbing or descending in search of smooth air. "Thanks, Center, Astral Nine TX, we'll stay at Three-Seven-Zero."

"Roger, Nine TX."

Tris watched Ross burrow his left hand through his dark brown hair. It started at the crown and worked its way to the collar of his shirt, back and forth, over and over. The last time she saw him do that was in the conference room in Luxembourg. He coupled the movement with a melodic sound she vaguely recognized. Ross was humming.

He seemed haggard and frail like he was being crushed under the weight of his life. His shoulders, which appeared broad in his best, most confident moments, looked bony and close together. As she watched him rhythmically stroke his hair and hum along with the motion, she felt a flash of sadness for his family predicament, which quickly faded into wariness.

Ross turned to her and smiled broadly—but it wasn't his real smile, the grin that belonged in a toothpaste commercial. It was that cheek-stretching, plastic one he used for the passengers.

He glanced back toward the passengers who were both still seated. She could barely hear Ross's voice over the buzz of the instruments.

"Tris, I talked to Zorn. About Europe." His eyes were steady and fixed.

Ross continued in the same calm, professional voice he'd use to tick off the details of a takeoff briefing in the most dangerous imaginable weather.

"Well, Tris, you know, you did a really good job up there. It was rough, I know it." He shot her a knowing glance, but it didn't reveal where his conversation headed.

"So, the airport guys wanted to talk to the PIC about it after the flight. You know, the *PIC*," he said.

"Yeah. Well, Deter was there, right?" Tris flipped her left shoulder up in a questioning shrug.

The airplane suddenly twisted ten degrees to the left. Ross instinctively moved his hands toward the yoke but stopped short of grabbing it. They watched the autopilot bring the Astral back to level flight. Ross inhaled deeply.

"Tris, they wanted to talk to *the pilot-in-command*." His left hand once again began smoothing his hair. "They wanted to talk to *me*."

Tris could hear the whoosh of the environmental system in the cabin. Just inches away, right outside the window, came the sound of sub-sonic flight: the constant complaint of air being disturbed at over four hundred miles an hour by this seventy-five-thousand-pound fiberglass bird. She thought she heard one of their passengers turn the page of a newspaper.

"You guys changed the name of the PIC on the flight plan before we took off, right?" But she knew the answer as soon as she asked the question, knew it that day. After the gear deal, she'd just forgotten about it.

They looked at each other like strangers, each taking their measure. Ross cocked his head to the side and leaned forward just short of the yoke. He grabbed his water bottle, took a drink, and twisted his plastic smile back on along with the bottle cap.

The plane hit a series of bumps. Tris could see the culprit—the pulsing red center of a thunderstorm crept into view on the outer edge of her radar screen.

"Well, uh...you know, the passengers arrived early..." Ross continued after a long pause. "But, you see..." He shot a quick glance behind him to make sure the passengers weren't listening. One executive read, the other was asleep—as if they would have the faintest idea what the two pilots were talking about.

"Look, this isn't a big deal, Tris. Nothing happened. There was no accident. There's no formal investigation by Luxembourg or U.S. authorities. Or so Zorn says. He called them, you know." He rolled his eyes as he spoke about Zorn, the man who called Ross his best friend. "Well, it's really about Deter. He was pretty agitated during the whole thing." Ross lifted his water bottle to his mouth and finished drinking just seconds before the plane hit a pocket of turbulence that would have sent water dripping into his lap. Always the lucky one.

The rough air passed and the plane settled back at altitude. "Well, you know, he said some stuff...in the cockpit." He looked at Tris, eyebrows raised.

She barely knew the guy sitting next to her, the man she'd once thought of as a friend. Who she helped at O'Slattery's that night. The man she turned away in Vienna before his behavior had worse consequences than just a bruise.

This stilted conversation was excruciating, so she tried to move it along.

"Yeah, I know. The 'cunt' remark. Did you tell Zorn about that?" *And did you tell him what you did?* The Luxembourg situation had so many moving parts, all tenuously lumped together. Like the story each crewmember told was part of a stack of lemons arranged in a grocery store display— prod one and they'd all tumble to the ground.

232

"Well, you know, not too cool of him. You were doing the best you could under the circumstances."

Tris couldn't believe his arrogance. She was about to ask him what he would have done differently when the Astral hit a huge air pocket, bounced up three hundred feet, and dropped back down. Both pilots instinctively moved their hands to guard the yoke and power levers. But Tris could only shadow Ross; he was the pilot-in-command.

Their sleeping passenger was knocked awake. "We're ok, just some turbulence," Ross called to the executives and then picked up the conversation right where he left off. "So, with the airport guys asking questions, the passengers bitching, and Deter, you know, losing it a little, Zorn and me, well, we never got around to talking about who was actually, you know, up there." He paused. "Instead of me, that is. But we did talk about Deter. You need to tell Zorn and Willett about it. Deter shouldn't get away with...well, what he said."

He spoke as if the facts supported no other conclusion.

"That's what you want me to do, is it? Tell Zorn all about Deter. Does he know who flew the leg?"

Ross recoiled as though he'd been struck. "Hell, who cares? There was no magic to what was happening upfront. The gear light finally came on. Not like it was a flight maneuver that required an *experienced* crewmember." He nodded toward the gear indicators, all extinguished now that the gear was up and locked.

Tris swallowed hard and looked away, as if searching for some stunning retort in the vast expanse of the sky just outside the cockpit window.

"You didn't do anything wrong, of course," he said again. "But the real story was Deter. You know, him losing it like that. That's the real story," he repeated, his head nodding with conviction.

Tris closed her eyes. All the compliments and encouragement

Ross had given her since she joined Tetrix eight months ago. The tips, the shortcuts, the support, the real training as opposed to Deter's "aw, hell, just watch me" approach. She was just starting to fit in at Tetrix, and it was primary due to Ross. He was popular, a leader. He always treated her with respect in the hangar, in front of the other guys—in public.

Tris realized now that she was just another co-worker, someone Ross could easily dismiss with an eye roll.

She wondered if he'd gone out drinking last night.

"What do you want from me?" Tris remembered the plan she and Danny agreed on. Low profile. Get the type.

"Right. Ok. So, you're gonna talk to Zorn?"

"Yep. Today. As soon as we get back."

"Look, I'm not asking you to lie. I'm not. But I talked to him a couple of days ago. He never asked who was upfront on the way to Lux. And it doesn't matter. I can't tell you what to do. But I'd really appreciate it if he could go on thinking that. You know..."

"Have you talked to Deter? He knows you weren't up there. What's he going to tell Zorn?" She raised her hands slightly and let them fall hard back into her lap. No way Deter would lie for him. Of course, who could predict what these guys would do.

"Deter's on vacation. By the time he gets back, he'll have to deal with his own issues. I mean, he's the one who *really* fucked up."

"Ok, I've had enough of this crap. *Why* weren't you upfront on that leg?" She deserved to hear him say it. It was time for the truth even if it was just between them. But Ross's face remained blank.

"Tris, look. I'm really sorry about coming to your door that night. I was out of it. I shouldn't have done...what I did. I apologize."

"Well, ok. Thanks. *But why* was I in the right seat? Why?" Tris pulled against her shoulder harness for emphasis. She could unclick it. She would be free. But there was nowhere to go.

Ross put his fingers to his lips to quiet her. Obviously, he didn't want the passengers to hear. She shook her head.

"We wanted to give you a leg!" he said brightly, his synthetic smile firmly in place. She couldn't believe how brazen he was, floating such patent bullshit. Tris finally recognized the fake grin for exactly what it was: the look of a good old boy covering his ass.

"Who cares whether you were up there or not? And, seriously, pilots call in sick all the time. Luckily, you had another pilot there to take the leg. So what? Why lie?" Tris tried to reason.

"No, no, no, I'm not asking you to *lie*. I mean, I don't think he's gonna ask you about who did or said what with the gear thing, you know. I don't think he's gonna ask who was where. I think he wants to hear about *Deter*," Ross continued as the aircraft bumped along. The turbulence was continuous now as the big red ball on the radar screen grew bigger, moved closer.

The voices of every flight instructor, every airline trainer, and every single captain she flew with at the commuter, including Bron, ran in a continuous loop in her head. *'It's what's right, not who's right.' 'Take responsibility. If you fuck up, fess up.' 'Tell the truth about what happened, or next time someone dies.'* Trite, but remarkably powerful, conversational shortcuts that rang all too true.

Tris caught a glimpse of Ross, his eyes cast down. For a split second, she felt his defeat. Just as quickly, his façade had returned. And her emotions hardened.

While she tried to figure out the best way to tell him to go to hell, he continued casually.

"And, you know, I'm really looking forward to flying right seat for your type rating. If I'm in trouble, Zorn could pull me from the schedule. Hell, Zorn could decide to fly it himself!" He put his hand on his lips, as if ashamed of them for what he just implied. Then he smiled and winked. "Or he can send you with Deter."

The hours she'd spent in the right seat of the Astral, listening to Deter, Ross, even Basson bloviate about what it took to be pilot-in-command. The knowledge, the judgment, and skill to fly maneuvers to the tightest possible tolerances. The ability to make decisions, stay calm during calamity. And the one thing they left out: a little deception.

Tris glanced at the ominous red ball on her radar display. A storm was surely coming.

Forty-Five

THE SECOND TRIS entered the pilot area, Deter flashed her a look that would have instantly turned a river to ice. This latest version of his withering, reproving gaze startled her with its sheer force. She thought she'd memorized every expression he had—impatience, frustration, anger, arrogance. But this was pure hate.

He sat in his cubicle with his coat on. She and Ross had just flown in on the Astral, and he wouldn't be flying the Gulfstream. He must have been called in, probably about Luxembourg. She knew he hated coming in on non-flying days. Yet, the level of his anger spoke to something much more than that.

"Hey, Ed, what's up? What brings you in today? Aren't you supposed to be on vacation?"

A vein throbbed in his neck. "Patricia."

Huh? Since when? She waited for more. Nothing came.

Then Ross breezed in, carrying a can of Mountain Dew and a bag of pretzels.

"Hey, Larry. How are ya, buddy?" Deter smiled at him.

"Good." Ross looked around to make sure no one else was around. "Meeting go ok?"

Deter gave Tris another hard look. This had to be about Luxembourg.

"Ok, considering I had to cut my vacation short for it. I'm gonna try and salvage the rest of this day. I'm outta here. Talk to you soon," Deter said and clapped Ross on the shoulder on his way out. "Thanks, man. Good to see you."

"You too," Ross said gaily to Deter's back, simultaneously rolling his eyes in Tris's direction. Ross was playing both sides, and she despised him for it.

Zorn walked in and stood by the flight-planning computer. "Hello, Tris. Excited about training?"

"Yeah, I am. It will be nice to get the type. I've been working hard."

"I know. I know. Everyone's had nice things to say." He glanced quickly at Ross. "Just remember, Tris, the type rating is a license to learn." Then he added, "Let's talk when you get a minute. I'll be here." He walked away without waiting for a response.

Tris couldn't put it off any longer—Zorn wanted to question her about Luxembourg.

"I've gotta head outside and finish up," Ross said, sprinting back into the hangar.

Tris thought she understood loyalty. When she was a child, loyalty was as simple as not telling on someone. As she got older, it became more complex, about taking sides, being in someone's camp, their clique.

Over the last few years, Tris had learned about loyalty from studying, teaching, and flying with imperfect people. Aviation taught her that you have to trust the guy—male or female—sitting next to you not to file away every mistake you made or exasperated thought you expressed to use against you later. If they did, you couldn't work with them. In the cockpit of an airplane, distrust killed people. It was that simple.

Such were her thoughts as she sat in the small, smoky conference room listening to Zorn wax on about his version of loyalty.

"We need to avoid, uh, drama here, Tris. You know, everyone needs to support the professional way we do things here at Tetrix." His words had no relation to the way things were. They sounded like undecipherable taxi instructions from a deranged ground controller.

Bron used to say that when things went bad, like an accident or aircraft damage, the first thing to do was duck, so people pointing fingers at each other didn't poke you in the eye. Tris agreed, adding that people pointed fingers at everyone but themselves.

Early on, role models like Diana, Bron and Danny helped Tris to develop her sense of responsibility as an aviator. She'd always taken whatever part of the blame she was responsible for if something went wrong. Ever since she was a child, Tris was the first to say, "I'm sorry." It cut off arguments. People liked to think they'd won—and she'd let them.

"Remember, Flygirl," Bron would say when Tris over-apologized, "*you* didn't sink the Titanic!"

But it was Zorn who spoke now, not Bron.

"You know, Tris, your primary duty is to the company. The company that brought you here, took you out of the cockpit of a turboprop, and put you in an *Astral.*" He might as well have said, "space shuttle" the way the word "Astral" glided out of his mouth on magic breath.

Clearly, he'd found out about Deter. But how? The passengers? Ross? Had to be Ross. Ross was in deep on this one. And that would explain why Deter had ignored her earlier. He probably figured she'd ratted him out. Ross continued to disappoint. She was equal parts pissed off and melancholy.

Not particularly bright in the best of circumstances, Zorn was out of his element trying to talk his way around the issue. His allusions to Deter's outburst were about as subtle as a bird blasting into the windshield on takeoff.

"Well, we understand that it was very, uh, tense in the cockpit. Was it?"

"Oh yeah. Very. We couldn't get the gear down."

"And, you know, Tris, in the heat of the moment, sometimes people say things they wouldn't otherwise."

"Right. Of course."

It was the community she'd been fighting to be a part of that worried her. Ross might be trying to set Deter up. Deter obviously thought she'd complained. Now Zorn treated her like she was a landmine he had to tiptoe around.

Deter was an asshole. She could barely tolerate being with him before Luxembourg, and he was completely unapproachable earlier today. But he came to work and did his job. He expected that she would do hers. Once she had that type, the second the ink dried on her Temporary Airman Certificate, her training was officially over. Deter would be just another line captain to her. Until then, though, she had a choice to make.

Danny was right. If she brought up Deter's explosion, it would never be told the way it really happened. As pilot after pilot gossiped, facts would get muddled, part myth, part mystery. All of a sudden, the story would be that *she'd* attacked *him* in the cockpit during an engine fire, or started crying because he asked her to lower the gear. No. That kind of talk would color any job interview she ever had, be the subject of hushed conversations when she walked into crew rooms. And if she tried to explain, it would be just as Danny had said.

She played the woman card.

As much as she'd love to stick it to Deter, she couldn't do it, not like this. The very idea was dirty, unseemly. Tris wondered when Zorn would shine a light in her face to get her to break down, but this wasn't an episode of *Perry Mason*.

Then again, maybe Zorn wasn't as stupid as she thought. Unable to dazzle her into throwing Deter off a cliff with his interrogation techniques, Zorn moved on to something he could win.

"Tris, who was in the right seat on the leg to Luxembourg?"

Zorn had her attention. He must already know.

She thought about Ross, whom she once believed respected her. But she was just a potential conquest to him. A target.

And then she remembered another conversation with Zorn, months ago at her interview. When she had the chance to come clean about her training problems at Clear Sky—and didn't.

Loyalty, yes. But first and foremost, self-respect. And that meant the truth.

"I was."

Zorn leaned in, his eyes narrow. "Without my permission?"

This information had consequences for people. Possibly even for her. Definitely Ross. She simply nodded.

Zorn was building momentum. "Did you ask if I gave permission for you to fly? I'm the one who assigns crew." He visibly attempted to puff his chest out beyond his belly, but only strained the buttons on his shirt.

Tris was fueled by the kind of confidence that only comes from the unembellished truth.

"I didn't even know I was flying until we got to the airport that day. Deter told me when we arrived at the terminal. There was just no time to question the *PIC's* decision to put me in the seat."

She hit Zorn squarely in *his* moral code. Nothing was more important to him than the final authority of the pilot-in-command.

Tris heard the faint sounds of movement in the hallway, probably Ross loitering outside the room. He would want to know what she'd said to Zorn. She hoped he was gone by the time Zorn finished up with her. She and Ross couldn't speak freely around Zorn anyway.

Ross was scheduled to sit in the right seat for her check ride. Whatever the consequences to Ross or Deter from that crazy leg to Luxembourg, she hoped they'd be over and done by then. Nothing could change the past, although that was precisely what Tris wished for every single day.

Suddenly, Zorn flashed a chilling smile, gathered his papers and headed toward the door.

"Thanks, Tris. Good luck in training."

PART IV:
WHAT'S RIGHT
April 1998

Forty-Six

"I DON'T UNDERSTAND, Dev. How can we work this out if you aren't *here*?" They'd been on the phone for ten minutes, but it seemed like forever. Ross forced himself to hold his temper, keep his frustration in check.

"Aw, Larry, really? Don't you get it? It isn't about *me*..." That's how she got him, every time.

"Cut the crap, Devon. James is fine. Well, he *was*. He keeps asking me when I'm coming out to join you guys on *vacation*. Yeah, vacation, while school's in session. I'm sure he knows what's going on."

"All I've told him is that we're spending some time on the ranch."

"Yeah, I'll bet your dad is filling in the blanks for him!" After all these years, Devon's father still didn't think Ross was good enough for her.

It gnawed at Ross, how things had turned for him and Devon. He had to remember to remove that happy-go-lucky family picture from his desk at work. They'd taken it on the beach in Maui, their first Hawaiian vacation with James. It was, what, five years ago? They'd been so in sync then.

The photo used to cheer him, motivate him through the difficult trips, the days he had to spend on the road with nothing but dead time in front of him. Now it just mocked him. The happy family in that photo was long gone.

"Can I please speak to my son?"

She didn't answer, but he heard her call to James in the background.

"Dad?" James asked. He sounded taller. How much had he grown since the last time they were together?

"Hey, pal. What have you been up to?"

"I've been horseback riding every day, Dad. I rode Jet and a new horse that Granddad bought named Bruno. When are you coming?"

"Soon, son." He walked over to the fridge and pulled out a beer. Ross hesitated, but only briefly before tossing his head back and letting the amber nectar trickle down his throat. "But you and Mom may be heading back this way soon."

"Do we have to drive? Buddy threw up in the car, and it still smells." James whined like he did when he was small. It sounded like nails scratching a blackboard and usually made Ross cringe. Today it made Ross miss him more.

"Well, we'll see. I think so. When you get back here, how 'bout you help me shampoo the rug and the upholstery? Sound like fun?"

"Ugh. No way, Dad. Hey, I think Granddad is heading out to the stables. See ya, Dad," he said. "Have fun," Ross heard Devon say before a door slammed shut in the background.

He knew he was defeated. Devon simply held the winning hand.

"What do you need me to do to come home?" He practically whispered, afraid that if he spoke any louder, he'd start to cry.

He looked around his house while he waited to hear her demands. Beer bottles spilled out of the garbage can. Paper plates lay stacked next to greasy pizza boxes, beside a mountain of dirty plastic utensils usually used for cookouts or emergencies. He would call a cleaning service. It would take Devon at least a week to drive home. Plenty of time to get the place clean.

"Larry, no drinking. Nothing. No beer. Nothing."

Yep, there it is. Well, the last time she had said he needed to go to AA. At least she realized that wasn't going to happen. She was so dramatic about the beers. All the other guys he flew with were lucky; their wives let them relax in their own homes.

Yet he knew he had no choice. "Ok Dev. You win. Consider it done."

"You say that all the time, Larry. How do I know you mean it this time?"

Man, she just won't quit. "Because I'm telling you. Anything else?"

"And no more flying with that girl." Her tone had shifted from whiny to demanding.

"You mean Tris Miles? Christ, Devon, you know I can't promise that." He thought she'd dropped that after he explained, again and again, that there was nothing going on between them.

"Why don't you just tell Brian you want to be on the Gulfstream all the time?"

"Are you kidding? I can't tell him *that*. The Gulfstream is his baby. He runs the schedule like..." He wanted to say, "like you run me," but luckily stopped himself. Instead, he said, "Like it's his own private kingdom. You know that, Devon. I tell you that all the time. And so does his wife when the two of you get together for your little bitch sessions." *Whoa, buckaroo. Hold up there.*

He walked to the fridge and grabbed another beer. Ross wisely bought MGD in bottles with a twist off cap. If Devon heard him popping the top off of a can right now, even if it were just Mountain Dew, her next call would be to a lawyer.

"Dev, how 'bout we just wait and see if I get on the schedule with her. If I do, well, I can just say something to Brian. Or call in sick."

"How's that going to work long-term?"

The long-distance minutes ticked by. Ross could almost hear his phone bill going up. "Let me figure it out, Dev. Can you guys be home next week?" Luckily, she'd still be gone when he headed to Dallas in three days. He was scheduled to support Tris's check ride. He'd prefer not to go, but it was his job.

It was quiet on the other end of the line. "Let me see. I'll call you tomorrow," she said finally. He definitely had to schedule the cleaning service; the place smelled awful.

"Ok, baby. Talk to you tomorrow. Tell James I love him."

"Bye, Larry."

He had to get his son back, and if that meant giving in to Devon's demands, even temporarily, so be it. Once they were home, he could come up with a better plan. For now, he just promised Devon whatever she wanted. To get James home.

With the details of his surrender hammered out, he prepared to head to O'Slattery's. 10:00 p.m.—the polished wood bar, brass chair rail, and comfortable stools beckoned. He loved those barstools. They had backs, so he could recline and even slump down a bit. There wasn't a single chair at home that felt so inviting.

Ross was already negotiating around Devon's demands in his head. In the short-term, maybe he could ask to just be on the Gulfstream, or do his Astral time with Basson and Deter. Flying with Deter always put him in a bad mood, but it would only be temporary. After a while, Devon would forget about Tris.

And maybe Zorn would make Tris a captain after all. Ross

would try and persuade him when she passed her check ride. He was Zorn's favorite. Maybe he could trade on that goodwill.

With a new captain on the Astral, he wouldn't be needed to fly it as much. Things could go back to normal. He and Zorn, Gulfstream trips by day, the bars of the road by night.

Forty-Seven

ROSS PACKED FOR Dallas a day early. His suitcase was in its usual spot on the bed, open and ready to receive his offering of underwear, socks, khakis, and T-shirts. Training was business casual, so no uniform was required.

He loved his own training sequences. Four nights away from home, no passengers. After two type ratings and recurrent training twice a year on two airplanes, he could run through the simulator profiles half asleep. And sometimes he did.

It was the quietly held opinion of his fellow pilots that Ross was the one they wanted upfront during the challenging landings on short runways or in bad weather. The guys at Tetrix—everyone but Zorn, of course—considered him the premier pilot in the department. That was important to him, especially now, with his family gone. His professional reputation was all he had.

His front doorbell rang, and he jerked his head back. He wobbled and swayed until he could grasp the back of a chair with both hands. The wall clock in the kitchen read 6:30 p.m. For a second he thought it might be Devon. But no, she was still on the road—and had a key!

Wait a minute. He needed to bring his uniform tomorrow after all. He'd told her he was flying the Gulfstream. He'd better have it on when he got home from Tris's check ride in case Devon and James were already here.

Ross planned to head over to a new local bar about a mile away and see what they had on cable. Maybe he could catch a baseball game, drink a beer, eat some chicken wings, and top it off with some tequila for dessert. He wanted to enjoy what was left of his bachelor-hood while he could still drink as much as he wanted, whenever he wanted.

Distracted by his reverie, Ross forgot about the front door. The doorbell rang again. He scowled and peeked out the stained glass sidelight. Zorn stood on the porch, facing the street. *What the hell?*

The door swung open. "Brian?"

"Yeah. Can I come in a minute?" Zorn breezed in past him.

Zorn wore jeans, so Ross figured he had just stopped by for a beer. Zorn walked directly to the refrigerator and pulled out a Miller Lite. He twisted off the bottle cap and took a long pull.

Ross glanced around the kitchen and saw a quick image of his home as a bachelor pad: friends coming and going, drinking what they wanted without fear of reprimand, kicking back. James outside in the backyard, playing with his friends.

But since this was his family home, the home he built and shared with Devon, James, and the dog, he needed to claim his space. "Brian, hey, so, good to see you. You just stoppin' by for one? I wasn't expecting company, you know..." *Did the piles of trash in the room just grow?*

Zorn's eyes were wide, whites gleaming. His expression put Ross on edge. Ross's hand unconsciously pushed strands of dark hair away from his face. When did that habit start? Devon always pointed it out, as it frequently began mid-argument. He commanded his hand back to his side, but it wouldn't stop. Ross was never quite able to reconcile his ability to make an airplane do whatever he wanted with his utter powerlessness over himself.

Zorn stood at the kitchen sink and quietly drank his beer. Finally, he was ready to talk about why he'd shown up, unannounced, at Ross's home, on a random weeknight.

"So," he began.

"Why don't you sit down?" Ross pointed to an empty space on the couch next to a pile of old newspapers. "You want another beer?"

Zorn glanced over to the fridge for a second and then turned back. "No thanks. And I'd rather stand."

When Zorn acted like this, Ross knew something bad was coming. Before he even heard the charge, Ross started to defend himself. "Brian, I—"

"Who was upfront from Vienna to Luxembourg on the Europe trip? And, please, tell me the truth."

So, it wasn't over after all. Ross bee-lined to the couch and started stacking the newspapers that covered its cushions.

"Hey, sit down man. Relax. Let's kick back and have some beers."

Zorn didn't move.

"You know, I was just thinking how convenient it would be to keep our garbage cans in the back alley, you know, have trash picked up back there. I hate draggin' those things out to the curb every week. Makes sense doesn't it?"

Zorn wasn't smiling. "Who. Flew. The. Leg? Not who was on the paperwork—we know that was you. Who flew it?"

"Brian, I.... Really, just listen..."

"Man, I'm not playin'. Did you fly the fucking leg or not?" Zorn stepped heavily back and forth in the kitchen, all the while shaking his head.

"No. I didn't. I was in the back. I dealt with the passengers, and it was a good thing, because..." He paused, now resigned.

"How did you find out?"

"How did *I* find out? From Willett. You know how *he* found out? His boss. One of *your* passengers!"

Zorn's face was red and his lips pulled back into a snarl. Ross had never seen him this hot.

"No. No. This is not how it goes. This is not how we do it. What the hell, man, why the fuck weren't you upfront? That's your goddamn job. And I've gotta find out from *Willett*? Why didn't you just tell me?"

So Tris didn't tell him. *What a good girl. She'd probably let me have a beer after work sometimes.*

"I was sick. I didn't feel well, so I took myself off the leg. That's what we're supposed to do, isn't it?" All he had was this shot from a now-empty barrel at an opponent he could not hit.

"Sick? Yeah? Sick from what?"

"Well, you know, we were overnight in Vienna. You know that place?" He smiled broadly at Zorn. "And I just got the news from Devon the day before. Things got out of hand, Brian. You know."

Zorn shook his head. Ross thought he might be softening, coming over to his side.

"You're in trouble, Larry. I didn't see it before. But I get it now." Zorn was lost in thought for a second and then recovered. "This. The DUIs. At least the ones I know about."

"They're the only two, man, I swear," Ross said as he bent over and rested his right hand on a countertop for support. This was the conversation Ross dreaded. He had moved into the kitchen, closer to Zorn in an effort to try and explain. To bring back his best friend. Where was that guy?

"I know. I should have told you about Lux. But I was afraid you'd...reach the wrong conclusion. I can always go. You know I'm always ready to fly. It was a one-off. It will never happen again."

Zorn stood there and sipped his beer, so Ross kept talking.

"I'm so sorry. But what I told you about what Deter said was true. It was really stressful up there. Did she tell you about it? Oh god. Does Willett know?" Ross was desperately trying to throw the spotlight on Deter. It had worked before.

"He sure does. At least I knew about Deter before Willett told me. We're sending him to 'charm school.' And he might lose his bonus this year. But both you guys are on my shit list."

"What about Tris? What did she say?"

Zorn smiled. "Nothing. She said nothing. She didn't accuse him of anything. At least not yet. That's what I want to talk to you about."

"Look, man, even if you were there—"

"Oh, fuck it, if I were there, we wouldn't even be talking about this right now."

"What's going to happen to me?" It was all Ross could think of to say.

"I don't know yet. But one thing's for sure. You're off the schedule for a while. Until we get some things worked out."

Ross brightened. "So, I don't have to fly with her? At the sim?" he asked hopefully.

"Oh, you're going to be her sim partner. And, under the circumstances, I think you can help me and yourself out."

"How? She doesn't need my help. She'll zoom through it. She's a good stick. After all that pissing and moaning by Deter, turns out she *can* fly. And she has great judgment. Man, you should have seen her upfront during the gear emergency..." He kept talking, assuming Zorn would be excited about his prize hire passing the check ride at last. But he soon realized Zorn wasn't listening.

It took Zorn only a few minutes to brief Ross on what he had in mind, what he'd sold to Willett, how Ross could support the plan. And if Ross came on board, all would be forgiven. He'd offered Ross a way out.

"Right. I get it," he told Zorn. They said good-bye, and Ross watched Zorn walk over to his car like what they'd discussed, the revolting pact they just formed, meant nothing at all to him. Ross bent over, a little queasy. *She'll recover. She has no one depending on her, no reason she couldn't work somewhere else. Eventually.*

Ross let the front door click behind him and looked over at the clock. 7:42 p.m. He threw on his tennis shoes and grabbed his keys. Ross had a lot of things to think about. The central, most important goal was to get things back to normal at home, do whatever it took to make that happen. And Zorn just gave him a way to solve the problem of flying with Tris. If he could give Devon that, she might lighten up on her other demands.

When Ross left his house for the bar, he was on a mission. He'd have to draw on all of his experience, his judgment, and know-how to execute Zorn's plan.

All he needed was another beer.

Forty-Eight

"BRIAN, LEMME GET this straight..." Jim Jensen coughed into the phone. A chain smoker, Jensen could barely make it through a two-hour simulator session before heading outside for a cigarette. "Are you asking me to...just what are you asking me?"

"Jim, I'm just saying, you know, she's gotta really *earn* it. No mistakes. She's gotta nail everything, no exceptions. Hold her to the same high standard you'd hold me." Zorn was a twenty-year captain.

He hoped that Jensen knew what he wanted. Maybe it wouldn't be close. She'd learned the Astral 'by the book,' but could she really fly it to the standards of a pilot-in-command? Zorn thought about some bonehead moves Tetrix pilots made in the simulator from time to time, and Jensen always passed them—because that's what Zorn usually wanted him to do.

Jensen was one of those guys Zorn knew he'd never become—a former chief pilot, laid off when his CEO instituted cost-cutting measures. Cost-cutting always equaled unemployment for corporate pilots.

Luckily, Jensen made a soft landing with his instructing gig. He was in his mid-sixties when he lost his flight department to a NetJets contract, and too old to get hired by the airlines. Federal law required airline pilots to retire at age sixty.

Now, Jensen was well connected at the FAA, always good for job security in aviation. After a few years teaching in the simulator, he became certified as an in-house check airman, qualified to give check rides and issue type ratings. He was an old-timer—a member of the club—and Tetrix was a huge client of the flight training company. Jensen only got paid if he had a crew to train or a check ride to do. If Tetrix requested Jensen as an instructor or a check airman, that put money in his pocket. If Jensen hopped on board with the plan, Zorn would make him the designated instructor for Tetrix.

"Well, ok, Brian. I know Tetrix is a really important customer here, you know. But what you're asking…"

Zorn hoped that Jensen's defenses would fade in the wake of the money he'd make on Tetrix crews. All of the Tetrix pilots were trained on the Astral, and they each came through recurrent training twice a year. That amounted to serious income for Jensen.

"We'd really appreciate the help, Jim. We'll make sure the head of the center, whoever it ends up being, knows that we do." Zorn referred to the fact that the training facility was about to hire Jensen's new boss.

"Tetrix has very high standards, as you know," Zorn repeated. "I just want to make sure everyone is treated *equally*."

It was quiet on the other end of the phone for a few seconds. Zorn wondered if he'd heard. But then he responded. "Oh, I hear you loud and clear, man. Whatever you need, we want to give it to you," Jensen finally said.

Good. Zorn was pleased, and ultimately a bit surprised, how easily Jensen came on board. But then again, he had promised to make a substantial deposit in the Jensen family bank. Everyone had their price.

"Hey, when are you coming down here for Astral recurrent? Might as well get that on the books. I see the other guys on the schedule, but not you." Jensen harped on setting up Zorn's recurrent training for a few minutes. This guy wanted to be sure he'd be appropriately compensated for his help.

"Yeah, I've been spending more of my time on the Gulfstream these days. When I get to fly at all..." Zorn looked over at the scale model of a Gulfstream on his desk. "I've got a number of responsibilities as chief pilot that keep me out of the cockpit."

"Oh yeah, I know that. Ok, Brian, I've got you covered. Now, get yourself on the schedule, and we'll have a cold one when you come down here."

"You bet. Thanks, Jim."

It was a strange day. He remembered a few years ago when he begged Jensen to make sure one of his pilots—Willett—*passed* his check ride. Today was the first time Zorn had asked a check airman to do what he could to make sure it went the other way.

If Tris failed her check ride, they'd have a bulletproof excuse to fire her, save the department from any potential lawsuit, and return the group to the status quo he'd sent ripples through when he hired her. It could have been different, might have worked out. If only Deter had kept his big mouth shut. Idiot.

One way or another, he'd keep them all together, safe from attack. Willett would owe him big time.

Forty-Nine

TRIS SAT IN the left seat of the Astral. They were on their way to Binghamton. She looked over and smiled at Willett, who sat as co-pilot in the right seat. The sky was clear, visibility unlimited. She could hear the passengers laughing in their leather recliners. All they had to do was drop the executives and head back to Exeter. Short day, easy trip.

She turned the Astral parallel to the runway. "Slats and flaps 15," she commanded. Willett just sat there and smiled. She asked again. He folded his arms across his chest. Binghamton Tower was calling them, asking them to slow down and follow a Falcon 50 ahead of them. Willett didn't answer; he just kept grinning and staring at Tris.

"Dave, I need slats and flaps fifteen right now. *And you need to answer ATC," she said again. "Do I have to do everything myself?"*

He responded by taking a sip out of a bottle of water. His gaze never left Tris. She reached over, quickly lowered the slats, and keyed the mike and responded to ATC.

"Binghamton Tower, Astral Nine TX, request immediate landing clearance. We are declaring an emergency—we have an incapacitated

pilot upfront." More laughter from the passengers. As she'd been trained, she yelled back for someone to come up and help her.

Ross's voice called out, "Oh, we're not worried. We know you've got it!"

Tris opened her eyes, expecting to see the center console of the Astral and Willett sitting next to her with an otherworldly grin on his face. But she was in bed, alone, in a hotel room in Dallas. It was 5:30 a.m.

Today was the day. Her training complete, Tris would fly for the right to be a captain on the Astral and fulfill her unspoken promise. To Bron. To herself. Despite constant distractions, Tris stayed focused on her end goal.

She knew if a corporate pilot busted a type ride in the jet she'd been flying for eight months, her career would be over. And she'd have failed Bron again.

Anxiety built in her chest and throat. Tris welcomed the game-day stress. She'd done the work and today she'd get the payoff.

Her ride was scheduled at 10:00 a.m., exactly when she wanted it. Get in there, get it done. Her examiner, Jim Jensen, was supposedly a "good guy," according to her instructors. No-nonsense, by the book, so she'd heard from some of the other pilots she ran into at the training center. They'd begin with an oral exam. Tris wasn't con-cerned about the oral. She knew the Astral's systems and structure as though she'd fastened every rivet, hung every valve herself.

She climbed out of bed and stretched. It was still dark outside as fading stars began giving way to the sun. She tossed a single-serve packet of grounds into the in-room coffee machine. Impatient, she paced as she waited for it to stop dripping so she could pour the coffee into one of the complimentary Styrofoam cups. Experience had taught her that hotel room coffee smelled better than it would taste. Still, she loved this particular perk.

When her room phone rang, she thought it was housekeeping. Training hours were odd, and they were always wondering when she'd be out of her room.

"Hello?"

"Tris?" It wasn't housekeeping. They always called her Miss Miles. "Tris, Brian Zorn here. Got a minute?" *A good luck call?*

She realized she hadn't answered right away and forced out a tentative "Sure."

"Tris, some news. Not sure if you've heard." Zorn always gave an initial nod to the rumor mill. "Tris, Larry Ross was in a car accident a couple nights ago. He isn't in town to fly your check ride with you."

"Oh my god, what happened? Is he ok? Where is he?"

"Not sure of the details yet. He's at St. Luke's. Tris, it was really bad." Zorn sounded uncharacteristically upset. Tris didn't think anything could get to him, but this did. "He had surgery last night and he's still unconscious." Zorn stopped abruptly. Tris thought he might say more but didn't.

"Surgery? What kind? Oh my god, was anyone else hurt?" She immediately assumed he was driving drunk. And this time, she couldn't stop him. His personal life was collapsing, and somehow this accident was the last domino.

Zorn sighed. "He hit another car. It had a woman and her two children in it." He stopped, and she heard him swallow hard. "They all died. The three of them. They're dead. Larry's the only one who lived, as far as we know."

She had no idea how much time had passed when she felt her left palm begin to throb. This time, her nails were dug in so far she'd drawn blood.

Tris released her grip, shook out her hand, and forced herself to focus on the check ride.

"I mean, I know this is a totally unexpected situation, and, god, poor Larry... " And there was more hesitation on the other end of the line. "And, so, what about the ride?" The words left a gritty aftertaste in her mouth.

"Look, Tris, we know this isn't ideal with everything that's going on. We don't want to lose the schedule." Pause. "We sent Deter. He's on his way now. I talked to Jim Jensen, and he pushed your ride to 2 p.m. Deter'll meet you there."

Tris shivered. She'd prepared for every possible contingency in the simulator but never imagined flying this ride with anyone other than Ross. Certainly not with Deter.

"Brian, look, well, the last time I saw him, Deter that is, it...he and I haven't talked much since Europe. You know..."

"I know. I know. I'm sorry, Tris. We could try and put it off if you want. Not sure when we'd complete it though. Maybe you could go next year if the money's in the budget. We don't want to force you, or make you *uncomfortable*."

Bullshit. "Have you spoken to Deter about this?"

"I have. Look, he knows how to support a check ride. He did it for years in the military. And he flew support for Dave Willett's ride in the Astral," Zorn said, even though Tris knew Willett had failed the first time. "But I'll handle it however you want. Will you agree to ride with Deter? Take a second and think about it."

Tris assessed the odds. The Astral required two pilots upfront for a reason. She needed someone to be the kind of co-pilot she had always been for the captains she flew with, someone who could anticipate, have their hand already touching a switch before she asked for it. To prompt her when it got busy, cue her for what came next. Would Deter be that person?

Still, it was her check ride, not Deter's. Only she could pass it.

If she didn't go today, she wouldn't get another chance.

Maybe this flying thing wouldn't work out after all. She and Bron always joked that they could become florists if career options seemed bleak. Gallows humor. She grimaced at the receiver before she spoke.

"Ok. Let's do it."

Fifty

TRIS SLEEPWALKED THROUGH her daily routine after the call with Zorn. She showered, dressed, loaded up her flight bag. Tris could barely lift it since it was stuffed with so many manuals. Outside she walked through a steady drizzle to her rental car, but didn't even notice until she had to turn on the windshield wipers.

Tris flew the required maneuvers again in her head as she drove her white Grand Am through the streets of Dallas to the training facility. She issued imaginary commands that were followed by Deter's clipped, one-word responses uttered as he nimbly did what she directed. She was so engrossed in her mental preparation, she almost drove past the simulator building's tiny industrial parking lot.

Today, she would finally prove to Deter she wasn't just some ponytailed, big-breasted accessory in the cockpit. His distrust of female pilots plunged deep, and the whole brouhaha over Luxembourg made things worse.

She still had no idea how they'd found out about his remark. That one comment, one word, uttered during unimaginable stress.

She still wasn't sure if he directed it at her. Yet, if Deter couldn't keep his head in an emergency, that in itself was serious.

But that *word*. Horrifying in a vacuum, but, given the circumstances, even worse. Tris was his co-pilot, an *asset*. Yet she'd been obliterated right where she sat.

Deter lashed out that day in the way bullies do. He attacked someone he saw as weak and could crush. As she moved closer to a critical moment in her career, for the first time Tris wondered whether Deter's comment was even directed at her, or just the explosive product of an extraordinary situation and an angry man.

There was no time to figure it out. "Keep your eyes on the prize," Danny told her last night. She was relieved when he called to wish her good luck. "Just ignore distractions, get the type." As though the whole rutted landscape of her experience at Tetrix could even out with that one accomplishment.

For so long, Tris believed that making captain would somehow even the count, be the huge success that would zero out her mistakes: her Clear Sky training, her relationship with Bron. At least she'd have something to show for the parade of horribles she'd been subject to.

But it could change nothing, replace no one.

Tris walked through the training center's sliding glass doors with her two heavy bags of books balanced on her shoulders. The first thing she heard was Deter's voice. He stood at the reception desk with a cup of coffee, chatting up the woman behind the counter.

Deter saw Tris and looked away. No greeting, no wish of luck. As she approached him, he finally turned to her. "Ready?" he asked.

"Yes," she responded. "Do you know what briefing room we're in?"

"Two."

"Ok. I'll head over there."

"Ok. I'm right behind you," Deter said. There was no support required during the oral exam, where Tris would be judged based on her knowledge of the Astral. Tris couldn't figure out why Deter would want to sit in, but she didn't care. She knew the Astral cold.

"Ok, I've gotta go listen to this oral. Have a good one, Gina," Deter said to the receptionist before leaving with Tris. "I didn't expect to be anywhere near here today. I have a seven thirty flight out, so I'll say goodbye to you now. You'll probably be gone when I get out of the box."

The box—pilot-speak for the simulator. And it actually *was* a big, white box. It sat high above the ground on long, silver cylinders. When powered up, hydraulic lift provided tactile sensations of flight. Or something close to them.

Tris and Bron coined it "the stimulator." Much harder to fly than the airplane itself, Bron always said that it "just sucked the will to live right out of you."

Tris, Deter and Jensen sat crammed in a windowless briefing room. Outside, the simulator rocked in time to flight maneuvers.

Jensen fired questions at her. Deter said nothing as she dashed off thorough, correct answers to each one. She was pleased to show the depth of her understanding of aircraft systems, procedures, and operations. Deter never acknowledged it, but it meant something to her.

She and Deter were on a short break before the sim ride began. She pressed him for any information about Ross.

"Do you know how it happened?" She asked, but had her own suspicions. Deter's eyes met hers and he nodded slightly, knowingly. They both thought Ross had been drinking.

"Not really. Just what I saw on the news." Deter shook his head.

"His car looked pretty banged up."

"Is he going to..."

"Make it?"

Tris nodded.

"No idea. It was a bad accident, three people dead and all. And he's in the hospital unconscious. Poor bastard," Deter said as he walked to the men's bathroom.

Ross killed people. Could she have prevented it? Maybe if she had told Deter about O'Slattery's. If she'd told someone, anyone at Tetrix that he came to her room in Vienna, how drunk he was.

Tris looked down at the crisscrossed metal panel she stood on, through to the concrete floor twenty feet below. Ross lost his family. Now, this. Why, then, was she so conflicted, at once feeling partially responsible, yet angry at his drunken stupidity.

No. It was not her fault.

She did not cause those three deaths. Only the one.

Fifty-One

TRIS STOOD ON the catwalk a few yards from the simulator entrance. There was a chain in front of the metal door, the red "In Use" light illuminated on the square, white structure. She needed to wait a few minutes longer until the previous crew finished up. The box's hydraulic legs slid feverishly up and down. *Someone was working hard in there.*

She thought she was alone until she heard Deter and the man she thought was Jensen talking farther down the hallway. She heard laughter and someone—Deter, she thought—say loudly, "No kidding. You know him?" Aviation was a small community; with all the years Deter had come here for training, of course they'd know each other and have friends in common. Tris grudgingly accepted that she'd be sharing the 'stimulator' with a couple of country cousins for the next two hours.

Finally, the simulator door popped open. The exiting crew joked and slapped each other on the back. *Two passes.* With barely a nod between them, Deter and Jensen headed inside, and she followed.

When the two pilots strapped into their seats, Jensen set the sim's computer to Exeter and Kennedy airports for Tris's ride. She was familiar with both of them, though she preferred Kennedy with its long runways. Long runways, high altitudes, and extra fuel—a pilot's best friends.

Jensen started out the ride with basic maneuvers and non-emergency situations that Tris had to assess and resolve. Deter was a competent first officer who responded in rhythm with her commands. She made flight decisions quickly and correctly.

One by one, Tris completed the required maneuvers. She knew she flew the box within required tolerances. She kept looking over at Deter, hoping today of all days he'd show some signs of support. A smile and nod. A "looks good" now and then during a particularly tense maneuver. He'd occasionally jot something down on a small notepad.

The simulator creaked and bounced as Tris landed it for the third time. Jensen changed the visual setting to the departure end of the runway. He made sure Tris and Deter completed the after landing checklists and gave them a new takeoff clearance as they configured the Astral for the next takeoff.

Tris ticked off the list of required maneuvers quickly in her head to figure out what was left. Wind shear demonstration, visual approach and landing, and the V1 cut. Wind shear and the visual always came last. The V1 cut was coming up next—and she'd only get one chance.

Tris took a deep breath and looked over at Deter. He sat Zen-like as Jensen entered data into his control panel behind the simulated cockpit and out of sight of both pilots. Deter probably knew the check ride protocol as well as Jensen. But he didn't know Tris's training history.

Both engines would operate normally on the takeoff roll, then right as Deter called "V1, Rotate," she'd hear the sound of an engine spooling down, feel the airplane yaw left or right. If she aborted the takeoff after V1, they would crash. If she took off but didn't keep the aircraft climbing straight ahead, they would crash.

Jensen set the sim to Exeter. They'd depart on Runway Two-Four Right. Good. She'd make a right turn and climb to four thousand feet. *Just do it—block everything else out. It's show time.*

"Astral Nine Tango X-ray," Jensen said, using their aircraft's tail number to make the ride more realistic. "Runway Two-Four Right, cleared for takeoff."

Tris pushed the power levers forward. "Power set," Deter said. "Eighty knots."

She glanced at her airspeed indicator. "Cross-check." The simulated sound of the wind tripping by outside and the bumpy feel of the runway below them were the only tactile sensations.

"V1. Rotate."

As the left engine failed right at V1, Tris jammed the right rudder pedal to the floor and banked the wings. She lifted the heavy nose into the air, to get it away from the ground. *Maintain course, maintain airspeed, and, for God's sake, climb.*

"Left engine failure," she called.

"Positive rate." Deter confirmed they were rising.

"Gear up." Then, at four hundred feet, "Flaps up, stand by for engine failure memory items."

At that precise moment, Jensen-as-tower instructed, "Nine Tango X-ray contact departure one-one-eight-decimal-five, climb and maintain four thousand." Tris kept the aircraft under control and continued to climb. Deter said nothing.

"Tell ATC we've had an engine failure and ask for vectors back to the ILS Two-Four Right approach."

Deter did as he was told. "Departure, Astral Nine TX climbing to four thousand. We've had an engine failure, requesting vectors back to the ILS Two-Four Right at Exeter."

"Roger, Astral Nine Tango X-ray. Are you declaring an emergency at this time?"

"Yes. Have them roll the trucks," Tris ordered.

"Roger." Deter keyed the mike. "Departure Nine TX, we're declaring an emergency."

"Astral Nine Tango X-ray, understand. Do you want emergency vehicles standing by?"

"Affirmative."

So far, so good. No altitude, airspeed, or heading busts. They made it up to four thousand and Tris had the aircraft stable. She kept her right hand on the one good power lever, and opened and closed her left hand to make sure she didn't get the death grip on the yoke. Her palm was clammy and her fingers cramped.

"Is the emergency checklist complete?"

"It is," Deter replied.

"Thanks. Ok, descent and approach checklists, please." Tris began to configure the aircraft for the approach. Sure enough, the check airman vectored them back to Exeter before Deter finished the checklists—a standard training ploy meant to distract her from flying the airplane. In the real world, Exeter would have sent every other arriving aircraft into a hold to give priority to the crippled Astral. She'd need to get it on the ground quickly and safely.

Just then her scan moved over to the altimeter. The needle dipped beyond a hundred feet low. Shit. Why didn't Deter alert her? She glanced over at him while gently lifting the yoke to reverse the trend. Out of the corner of her eye, she saw a slight grin on Deter's face. He jotted down a quick note on his pad. *Oh shit. Did he notice? Did the examiner?*

"Astral Nine Tango X-ray, are you ready for the approach? Turn to the heading of Two-Six-Zero to intercept the final approach course." Jensen delivered the approach clearance.

Again Deter looked over at Tris, who nodded, confirming the instructions.

"Ed, are we ready for the approach?"

"Yes," he said, but then corrected himself. "Oh, wait, no. Let me finish the checklist," he said and started reading it aloud. He was almost done as the needles that would guide them to the ground vibrated, then came alive and slowly swept across the navigation screen. Tris turned on course.

"Approach checklist complete," Deter finally called, "pending your briefing that is."

They already had the first degrees of flaps extended. The airplane was in a stable descent, airspeed was constant. Everything looked good. The hard part was almost over, and she nailed it.

Tris quickly briefed the approach. The most critical decision was what they would do if they had to go around. Guaranteed that they were both thinking of Luxembourg. The memory caused a rush of nerves, but Tris shook them off.

The closer they were to the runway, the more sensitive their navigation system became. The slightest movement could cause their guidance to disappear, and then she'd have to put full thrust on her one overworked engine. *No, stay on course.*

"Small corrections," Bron said. "It wasn't your fault."

Just then, Deter made the first altitude call. "Five hundred feet."

"That checks," Tris responded. She scanned the instruments in double time to fly within the tight parameters required for a type rating. If Tetrix wasn't going to let her act as PIC, so be it. But it wasn't going to be because she couldn't do the job.

Airspeed held steady. Descent rate was six hundred feet per minute, exactly what she wanted. Tris was right on course, in the center of the chute. She included a quick outside look in her scan, hoping to see the approach lights. The simulator was set so that she wouldn't see them until she was two hundred off the ground, but she wouldn't always be flying a simulator.

"One hundred," Deter said.

"Nothing in sight," Tris whispered. It wasn't a standard call.

"Fifty feet to minimums." Tris was stable, and so was the airplane.

"Minimums," Deter practically shouted. There were the runway lights!

"Landing," Tris declared.

"*Wind shear! Wind shear!*" The airplane's synthesized voice screamed.

"Full power," Tris commanded as she increased to max thrust on the only reliable engine. *No configuration change, pitch up, ride it away from the ground.*

"We're losing altitude," Deter said urgently.

"I see that. Confirm full power."

"We have it."

"Can't change configuration," Tris said as she struggled to keep the nose up. Her voice filled with urgency as if willing the airplane to climb.

"Too much drag. We're sinking."

Tris fought to keep the wings level against the banging force of the simulated wind shear. And then, just as quickly as the simulation began, she heard the sound of a crash. The screen ahead was black. All the red warning lights on the panel flashed.

The examiner sighed heavily behind her. She crashed the sim. She was done. *This is how it ends.*

But Deter was pissed. "Jim, I need a minute, if you don't mind," he growled as Tris stared at the dark screen.

"Ed, you know I can't interrupt a ride."

"I *said* I need a minute." Red-faced, Deter turned all the way around in his seat. He stared Jenson down until the check airman flinched.

"Ok, we'll take five," Jensen said and reset the simulator. He and Deter flew out the door.

Tris sat dumbfounded in the left seat, surrounded by blinking lights.

Fifty-Two

"WHAT THE FUCK was that?" Deter said to Jensen as they stood side by side at the urinals.

"What do you mean? It was a wind shear demo."

"Uh-uh. That didn't look like a wind shear demo to me, Jim. It looked like the Delta 191 microburst scenario. Nobody ever recovers from that. Did you even train that with her?" Deter extended his chest, eyes intent on his target.

He was sure of what did and didn't belong on a check ride. And the Delta 191 microburst simulation did not. That deadly crash scenario was only taught as a cautionary tale. Jensen took a minute to finish his maneuver. He shook, zipped up, and walked over to the sink.

When Jensen didn't respond, Deter continued. "And no way that belongs on a check ride. What are you doing, Jim?"

Jensen looked straight at him. "Christ, Ed, you know what I'm doing."

"I don't. That pilot is flying the hell out of the simulator. Did

277

you make a mistake? Did you program the wrong demo?" Deter stood up close to Jensen at the sink. He stared Jensen down, trying to get him to admit what he'd done.

"Jim, did you do that *on purpose*? Why?" Deter had a striking moment of clarity—and a moment of surprising kinship with Tris. Both pilots were completely in the dark.

Seconds passed as the two men considered each other's mettle. Finally, Jensen stepped away from Deter and raised his arms.

"Ed, did you talk to Zorn before you came out here?"

"Briefly. Why?"

"Well, I thought he'd let you know," Jensen said, tentatively.

"Know what?"

Jensen washed his hands. He pulled several paper towels from the dispenser and dried one finger at a time.

"When did *you* speak to Zorn, Jim?"

Jensen patted his breast pocket. A pack of Marlboro Reds peeked out from the top, along with a book of matches. Jensen began to pull the pack out, but his fingers were trembling.

"Well, Zorn asked me to make sure this, uh, pilot, could really fly. That she was, you know, *worthy* of a type rating. Really earned it, you know?"

Deter had no idea what Jensen was getting at. Only that it smelled bad. It wasn't right, and he wouldn't have it.

"Jim, she didn't make one single mistake. And I'm wondering now, when I review the Practical Test Standards for the Astral check ride, the requirements published by the FAA—people that *you answer to*—if I'll find that they endorse giving a *microburst on final on a single-engine approach.*" He stared unblinkingly at Jensen.

"I don't know what you're doing, Jim, but we both know that's not in the rules."

Jensen's fingers fiddled with the Marlboros. Deter walked up to him and stood just inches away, shoulders square, neck muscles pulsing.

"Look, Jim," Deter said, his voice stilted as he slowly enunciated each word. "I'm sure you just made a mistake. Maybe pressed the wrong button? Yeah, let's say that's what happened." His eyes narrowed. "Let's go back into the sim, reset, and let her finish the approach." He paused, never taking his eyes off of Jensen. "Make sense?"

Even though Jensen probably outweighed Deter by thirty pounds, there was no doubt that Deter could take him hand to hand. Jensen looked down at his feet. No help there. Finally, he took the paper towel he'd been massaging in one hand and the cigarette he'd fondled in the other and tossed them both in the trash.

"Sure. Let's finish up. After you," he said and pointed to the door.

Fifty-Three

I CRASHED THE sim. I crashed the sim. I crashed the sim.

She'd flown that demo a dozen times. But they trained the maneuver on takeoff, with the gear and flaps already up, on two engines. Well, she had to be ready for anything—turns out she wasn't. *I just busted my ride. This is how it ends.*

She'd been so worried about the V1 cut. Tris laughed out loud. *Nailed it.* But the wind shear demo, she'd flown it to perfection every time during simulator training until the only day that really mattered.

Thankfully, Jensen had turned off the simulated sounds of the crash before he and Deter left the box. She was grateful not to hear the recorded loop of crash truck sirens and the crackle of burning fuel. Tris realized she couldn't feel her fingertips and she'd been holding her breath. She exhaled, then started gulping air.

Tris felt the heavy push of tears behind her eyes and pressed them back with her balled fists. Everything she'd worked for these past four years gone in just seconds. She unhooked her belt and tried to slide out of the seat. *What now? What now for me?*

Does it really even matter?

She pivoted to other endings, final moments, last words. That final night in her apartment. They argued. Well, *disagreed*. Bron didn't argue. He had a perpetually sunny disposition. She'd asked him once why he was always so happy. "Born this way," he'd shrugged. *Born this way.*

He wanted to move in. Not get married, not right away, but live together. He was ready.

She loved Bron with her whole heart but simply could not fathom he felt the same way, so she deflected her feelings and his. Tris had learned her childhood lessons well.

"But aren't things great the way they are? I'm very happy."

"Yeah, of course. But I just got the training department job here in Exeter. It makes sense right? I mean, we're together every night anyway."

She'd dreaded that day, which she always knew would come. He'd want more, and she wouldn't be sure she had it to give. Her feelings for him were so strong they coursed through her like white water. But she couldn't process them, couldn't control them. That flash of fear she'd get when he unexpectedly said he loved her. The same terror when she wanted him to say it, but he didn't. The daunting part of love.

She didn't understand what was inside her, so she shut it down. Right then, at that moment, all she had to do was let him in.

"I can't," she whispered.

"Can we talk about it tomorrow?"

"Well, yeah. But aren't you going to stay tonight?"

He grinned and put his hand on her shoulder, the touch that immediately relaxed her. "Not tonight. I'll head to the crash pad. We'll talk tomorrow, ok?"

They stood at the door of her apartment and held each other for a long time.

Bron's last words to her that night were, "I love you."

Hers were, "I know." And then he was gone.

Tris looked around and realized she was still in the captain's seat. She tried again to get up, but the sound of footsteps on the metal catwalk outside the box stopped her. She didn't want to run into anyone she knew, other trainees, or instructors. How could she face them?

Jensen and Deter walked back in like nothing had happened. Deter sat down in the right seat and fastened his belt and shoulder harness. Jensen took his seat at the control panel and pushed some buttons. She tried to get a sense from Deter what was going on but couldn't get his attention.

"Ma'am," Jensen said. "Let me set you up on final again. Just fly it down to the runway and land, ok?"

Tris turned toward Deter, who looked at her out of the corner of his eye. She mouthed, "What's going on?" He ignored her, jotted something on his notepad, and picked up the checklist.

"Sure, I can do that," Tris replied, still confused. She flew the approach again, single-engine, and put it down smoothly, right on the centerline.

"Astral Nine Tango X-ray, you have your engine back. Taxi back for takeoff," Jensen-as-ATC commanded.

Deter read the checklist. "Time for a two-engine takeoff and visual approach to landing," Jensen said. She had no idea why he made her fly the final required maneuvers. But the longer she was in the sim, the more time would pass before her failure was official.

Fifty-Four

ZORN HUNG UP the phone and took a deep breath. He'd heard Devon's words but didn't quite understand them. If he could only discuss it with Ross over a beer at O'Slattery's. But that wasn't possible. Ross was dead.

Just yesterday at the hospital, the doctors said Ross should regain consciousness and might not even have brain damage. Something to hope for.

Zorn touched the wing of one of the airplane models on his desk. Devon said Ross had a seizure overnight, leaving him brain-dead. Ross's parents were there, and the three of them had agreed to pull the plug.

She was crying so hard on the phone Zorn didn't press for details. He assured her that the folks at Tetrix would do whatever they could to help, and asked her to let him know the arrangements. The department would be out at the funeral "in force," he said. Devon quieted long enough to respond that they were free to mourn however they wished, but Ross's body was going home to Indiana.

Zorn needed to inform Willett, although he had no idea what he'd say. His mind was blank. The lights were off in Willett's office. He wasn't flying; the Gulfstream and the Astral were in the hangar, and he didn't hear the sounds of the flight planning computer spitting out printer paper or the laughter of crews. None of the typical pre-trip noise.

Then Zorn remembered there was a budget meeting downtown that day and Willett always went straight home after those. He lifted the receiver and pressed the number "3" on his speed dial: DW/Home.

"Brian?" Willett was surprised to hear from him.

He could tell that Willet didn't know yet. Zorn wasn't sure if that made it better or worse.

"Dave, we just got some bad news." He could barely spit it out. "Larry's gone."

"Gone? Gone where? Isn't he still in the hospital?"

Zorn felt like a character in a bad B-level movie. "Gone, Dave. Devon just called me."

"Devon?" Willett sounded confused. "So what's going on?"

"Larry died. Of his injuries from the accident. He's gone."

"That's...I don't know, Brian. Wasn't the accident just two days ago? He had surgery, right? *You just saw him*. You said he was improving. What happened?"

Zorn fell silent.

"Ok, Brian. Ok. I don't know what to say."

"Who does?"

"Ok. Well, I'll let the rest of the crews know. Unless you want to..."

"I'll call the center in Dallas. Can you call Basson? Thanks, David. This is...just...so...bad."

Zorn hung up. He covered his face with his hands and rubbed his forehead as he considered the devastating consequences of the accident. Even if Ross had survived, his life, as he knew it, was over. This would have been his third drunk driving conviction. This time, Ross's blood alcohol was .19.

According to the police report, Ross sped through a stop sign going sixty-five miles per hour on a residential street. He'd be convicted of voluntary manslaughter for the deaths of the three people in the other car, and he'd likely go to prison. There'd be no way to keep the information from the FAA. He'd never touch the controls of an airplane again.

Zorn wiped his face with the back of his hand and sniffed. His grief turned to anger as he thought about the cavalier way Ross had treated the privilege of being a pilot. His eyes caught a glimpse of the "World's Greatest Pilot" clock his son had given him. No way he'd toss his career away the way Ross did.

This would never happen to me. He got what was coming to him.

Fifty-Five

TRIS TAXIED THE simulator to a stop, and she and Deter ran the shutdown checklist. Deter had done his job. He'd been a good co-pilot. That was something at least. Tris was proud of her crew, and that helped her to stand tall, ready to accept the judgment that was coming.

As soon as the door to the sim opened, the receptionist Deter had been so friendly with earlier waited for them. She shifted from foot to foot with a piece of paper in her hand. As soon as he was clear of the simulator, she pulled Jensen aside and handed him a pink message slip.

Tris looked down. The color of the message slip was the same as the FAA check ride 'pink slip,' the one they gave to trainees who failed their check rides. She should know.

Tris headed to the ladies' room, Deter ostensibly to the men's, and both planned to meet up with Jensen in the briefing room. But the examiner cut them off before they had a chance to walk far.

"I've got an urgent message for both of you to call Zorn at

home," he said, waving the piece of paper at them. "Do you need the number?"

Tris and Deter looked at each other blankly. Deter breezed by Jensen and headed directly to the pay phone, whipping his calling card out along the way. Tris took the pink message and followed behind, figuring she'd have to wait until Deter was finished. She couldn't hear Deter's end of the conversation, which was short. He cast his eyes toward the ground as he turned toward her.

"Larry's dead. He died early this morning before we went into the sim." For the first time since she'd known him, Deter looked bereft. Tears pooled in his eyes. He kept them open and stood as though he'd frozen in place.

"Call Brian if you want, but that's what he's going to tell you." He turned away slowly, and Tris heard him mutter, "What a fucking waste."

Tris was paralyzed, watching Deter move forward, shifting his weight from side to side. As he walked, Deter's rubber-soled shoes twisted on the tile floor, the unique sound of his gait so familiar to her now. It struck her that the sound of every person's walk was different, unique. Such an odd thought, right then.

After a few steps, Deter stopped and turned back to face her. Tears spilled, but his eyes were never clearer, bluer, or more resolute than they were in that moment.

"For what it's worth, you flew a great ride."

Dizzy, Tris braced herself against the wall for support. She was back on the corner of Albemarle and Vaughn. If only she'd said yes. If only he'd stayed over. If only...then he'd never have been on that corner, at that moment. Ross, Bron, the circumstances of their deaths were jumbled in her mind. No, she shook her head vigorously. She wasn't responsible for Ross. It was Bron that she killed.

Her legs slowly collapsed under her as she slid down against the cold, metal wall. Crumpled on the catwalk, sobbing, the only other sound she heard was the simulator sliding up and down on cylindrical hydraulic legs, the staccato breath of a body removed from life support.

PART V:
RED OVER WHITE
September 1998

Fifty-Six

TRIS SIGHED AND turned off the ignition. She looked around the Tetrix parking lot and took a minute to consider the piece of real estate, what she always thought of as the transition area between real life and Tetrix life.

Deter's white Jeep was parked just a couple of spots away. She wouldn't see Zorn's car, but if he wasn't there, he'd be in soon. He had a trip on the Gulfstream in a couple of hours.

Deter sounded surprised when he heard Tris's voice on the other end of his home phone yesterday, and even more so when she asked him to come in early for his trip today so they could talk. Tris and Deter hadn't seen much of each other since Dallas. On their way to DFW for their flight back to Exeter, she had asked him what he and Jensen talked about after she crashed the sim. He looked away, shook his head, and grumbled something about old men and loss of bladder control.

It had been over four months since Tris got her type. At first, she still hoped to upgrade but felt it unseemly to ask. Ross's death cast a pall over everything in the flight department. It was impossible to pass his cube, now empty, without remembering.

Tris flew as co-pilot on Astral trips after training, mostly with Basson, once with Zorn. She planned to wait a respectable amount of time before she pushed to be captain. Now it wasn't even up for discussion.

Just two weeks after Ross died, Zorn and Willett announced that Dicky Lord would be joining the company. They sent him to Dallas right away to qualify as pilot-in-command on the Astral since they were short a captain on that airplane. Tris continued to fly as co-pilot over and over on Astral trips after training, including a couple of times with Dicky.

Tris wasn't considered for the open captain slot. That's when she realized that if she didn't leave voluntarily, she'd be stuck in the right seat forever.

Deter sat at his desk when Tris walked into the pilot area. There was no one else around. He got up when he saw her and motioned in the direction of the smoking lounge. Tris nodded and pointed to the coffee maker. She'd grab a cup and meet him in there, where she'd begin the first of three important conversations she would have today.

"First I wanted to thank you," Tris said when they finally settled around the table.

Deter had been looking at his hands, folded neatly in his lap, but raised his head at those words, his eyes wide. It was not what he expected her to say.

"That day, during the type ride. After the sim crashed. What happened between you and Jensen? Will you please tell me?"

"No."

"Why not?"

"You don't need to know."

"Whatever you talked about, I can't shake the feeling that you saved the ride. Did you?"

Deter's expression never changed, though she noticed a slight quiver in his Adam's apple. That was his only tell. He bent his head in the slight nod that pilots use to acknowledge their respect for other pilots.

"You earned it."

She returned the acknowledgment and took a deep breath. "But now it's time for me to tell you what flying with you was like for me this last year." She looked into his now translucent blue eyes, waiting for him to yell or storm out of the room.

"Go ahead, Tris. I'm listening." Deter settled back in his chair, and crossed his legs, his fingers laced together around his neck.

They spoke for another half hour. They both learned from separate sources that Ross first told Zorn about Deter's comment. And then, of course, the passengers who overheard it told Willett, and the situation took on a life of its own.

"I regret that comment," Deter said. "I shouldn't have said it. I lost my composure under stress. But you held up perfectly, professional to the last. You did a great job that day." Tris stifled her surprise at the compliment and again nodded her head toward Deter.

Deter kept his job at Tetrix on the Astral. Ann-Marie told Tris that he wouldn't see the inside of the Gulfstream for a long time, if ever. In addition to a swing through charm school, she confidentially shared with Tris that Tetrix had put him on 'super secret' probation. Tris figured the 'super secret' part was that they weren't supposed to talk about it, but everyone seemed to know.

In the end, Deter accepted responsibility for what happened on the Luxembourg leg. He stood tall in a way Ross never could.

After Ross's death, Deter and Tris were questioned again about that flight. They explained separately and consistently that Ross begged them to say he flew the leg. Ross told Deter he was afraid his blood alcohol level was over the legal limit. There was no way to test it, so they decided to put Tris in the right seat simply out of an abundance of caution. And now no one would ever know the truth about Ross, where he'd been, what he'd done the night before, and whether he could have flown that leg.

Tris never told anyone at Tetrix that Ross came to her room in Vienna, not even Ann-Marie. There was nothing to gain, no greater purpose to accomplish, by sharing that story.

Tris and Deter made their peace. Despite Deter's constant mistreatment, well, Tris wouldn't hold it against him. Deter was there when she needed him.

"Thanks, Ed." Tris extended her hand to him. "Now, I need to speak to Zorn," she said, mostly to herself, as they shook.

No one in the Tetrix flight department knew she would hand in her letter of resignation that morning. In fact, when she walked into Zorn's office, he shuffled papers around on his desk and said he had "just a few minutes" to speak to her. She simply placed it on his desk and waited.

Zorn tilted his head back and arched his brows after he read the two-line note. "Really? Do you have a better offer? More money?" He always said he couldn't understand why anyone would ever leave his department.

"No, no other offer."

"So you're leaving flying?" Zorn looked incredulous.

"I have no immediate professional plans."

Zorn thanked her, wished her luck, and told her he'd make sure she didn't fly but stayed on the payroll for the next two weeks. She could return her keys and clear out her desk that day if she wanted. So she did, taking her time before she headed out to have the third and most important conversation of the day.

Her last official day at Tetrix was 369 days after her first.

Fifty-Seven

TRIS LEFT THE Tetrix hangar for the last time and headed south for the two-hour drive to the cemetery. Located close to the edge of the state, it sat in a commercial zone next to a tiny airport called Orchard Field—the perfect place to put a cemetery. None of the residents would call the airport authority with noise complaints.

Each time she stopped at a light, she reached into her purse and fingered her new pilot certificate. She'd received it in the mail a few weeks earlier. It had the designation for the Astral, AsL1000, listed after the words, "Type Ratings." She'd done it, and she needed to tell him.

Tris parked in the familiar lot and left her bomber jacket in the car. It was unseasonably cool for September—around fifty degrees, but the jacket would be too warm. She checked the front of her blouse for gaps and ran her hands down her thighs to smooth her slacks.

She walked inside the small-shingled welcome building she

knew so well, with a sign that read "Maps & Directions" and then "Restrooms" underneath. Inside, an older couple perused reproduced maps of the grounds alongside a stack of brochures touting local attractions. Tris spotted the familiar ad for skydiving lessons.

The first few times she came here, that ad had seemed so misplaced. After a few visits spent in the welcome shack, she realized that people probably came from out of town to visit relatives and friends buried here, maybe they'd want to do something besides mourn while they were in town.

Tris didn't know exactly how many times she'd made this trek, but she'd yet to see his grave. She also couldn't bring herself to attend his funeral or the company-sponsored memorial service. She thought everyone would expect her to say something, have the right words. She couldn't face his family, his friends. What could she possibly tell them?

Tris exhaled in frustration. She hadn't had the right words in any situation for a long, long time. And she simply could not be with him again until she did. Until today.

The plot was a short walk from the parking lot. The sky shone an outrageous clear blue, an almost arrogant tint, as if daring any other color to interfere.

His grave sat in an open area near a large oak. In the spring and summer, it would be shaded. She knew he'd like that.

She wiped her hands against her slacks. Tris wanted nothing between her and the stone as she traced the engraving of his full name with her fingers.

BRON GREGORY MICHAELS

She used both of her hands. Right hand first, one letter at a time. Then left. And when she was done, she said his name out loud.

"Bron Gregory Michaels. Hi, baby." She choked out the last two words. He was really, really gone.

Below his name, the headstone read *Beloved Son and Brother*. Beloved.

He was beloved. She should have told Bron that her life was better simply because he lived. That when he walked into a room, everyone else disappeared. But those feelings sucked her down and swallowed her whole. They were so big, she couldn't control them, so she packed them away.

They'd take a break and get back together, she'd reasoned, after he left her apartment that last time. It was as though she'd tossed him out, but like a cat you'd fully expect to be back in the morning, she never thought it would be forever. On his way to the crash pad, by the Chinese greasy spoon on the corner of Albemarle and Vaughn, Bron was hit and killed by a drunk driver.

It was her fault, she was sure of it. So how could she face him? How could she get him to understand, *no, no, it wasn't that she didn't love him*? She just didn't know how.

But Bron would have never blamed her. He was simply too good a man.

"Coincidence, Flygirl," he'd say. "Just a really, really bad one."

Tris lugged her guilt around like a bag of stones she couldn't put down. It got heavier and heavier, harder to carry. She could have cast that burden aside in favor of Bron's memory, his lightness, the love he had given her while he was alive. Instead, she simply worked harder. Jurgis Rudkus indeed.

Tris finally accepted what she'd lost, what *was* lost, what left the world when Bron had died. She could not stop hearing the words Bron would use to soothe nervous airline passengers. "Hey. Don't worry. The most dangerous part of this flight was your drive to the airport!"

Tris had failed Bron that night; that's why she *had* to make captain, to show him that she'd heard him, understood him, at least about flying. Then she would be ok—or so she thought.

And there, as she faced his grave, it finally made sense. The answer wasn't a particular airplane, type-rating, or rank. It was love.

Bron wouldn't have cared if she had failed her training at Tetrix or if she'd given up flying altogether. Because he loved her.

Nothing could make up for the pain she caused by holding back her love for Bron. Tris had run from her feelings, a marathon paced to her beating heart. The race never slowed, never stopped, and she never gained any ground. She was exhausted from the sheer effort of restraint.

Finally, Tris could let go. The search for the right words was over. Today, she had every verb, noun, vowel, and consonant she needed.

Tris sat cross-legged at the base of the headstone, facing it at an angle. It still looked brand new. She loved the purples and blues of the granite, the sun reflecting off of it in several spots, shooting out prisms of color. Half of her body sat directly over where his casket was buried. Tris touched her heart with her left hand and the word "Beloved" with her right. Her voice had to be certain and strong.

As she opened her mouth to speak, Tris first swallowed back the tears. And then she realized there was no need. She cried openly as she began her final conversation of the day, the one she'd waited fifteen months to have.

"I love you. I wish I'd said yes."

Well into the afternoon, Tris sat over the grave, telling Bron all the things he needed to hear.

The things she had never, ever said.

December 15, 1998

IT WAS ONE of those hot and humid days in Miami, where it was sticky even in winter.

Today Tris would fly to Atlanta and then work her way back across the country with her student, an Exeter gastroenterologist. She enjoyed these long training trips, and her student was fun to fly with.

Before the Doc left for his meeting, they did a brief ground lesson on visual landing aids. She took out pictures of the red and white lights set on the side of the runway that told pilots if they were too high, too low, or right on course. Every student remembered the sing-songy memory device.

> *White over white, you're high as a kite.*
> *Red over red, you're dead.*
> *Red over white, you're all right.*

You're all right.

Tris loved the Doc's plane, a straight tail Beech Bonanza. The Doc enjoyed having a plane but didn't fly much. At least he was smart enough to know he shouldn't do a cross-country trip without an instructor sitting next to him. The Bonanza, with its turbocharged engine and retractable gear, was way too much airplane for him to fly alone safely by himself.

When she first resigned from Tetrix, she had marked her distance from the job by hours. A hundred and two hours since Tetrix. A hundred and thirty-two. After the first week, by days. Forty-six days since she worked there. Then fifty-six. Now it was almost three months. She counted as though that alone would widen the gap, make moments pass faster.

Tris kept in touch with Ann-Marie, who had secretly been in her corner during the whole Deter-Ross-Luxembourg disaster. Over a drink at O'Slattery's one night, Ann-Marie told Tris that when she quit, Willett took the heat for making a bad hire. After all, Tris left after just a year with the company, and just months after all that money spent to get her a type rating wasted. Zorn skated away from all responsibility, naturally.

Each time Tris visited O'Slattery's, she thought about Ross. Since his death, Ross had taken on saint status in the department, even though he killed three people. Ann-Marie shook her head as she told Tris that salient fact never made it into the "remember when" stories the guys told about Ross. Tris wondered how Deter felt about that, but it wouldn't matter. Deter would be a good soldier. That's what and who he was, loyal to the mission, to the core. And someone who would always protect what was his, even if it was only his honor.

She and Danny were back on speaking terms, but it would be a while before their friendship fully recovered. He told her about a girl he was dating, said it was getting serious. She was truly happy for him.

Now that she was instructing again, some of the other résumés she'd sent out the world over the years started to generate some interest. Danny offered to put in a good word if she wanted to return to Clear Sky. She wasn't interested in going back there. She filled out an application at another commuter airline, one that paid better than Clear Sky. They asked her to call for an interview date, but she hadn't done it yet.

The most amusing call she got came from the chief pilot of another large company in Exeter with three Astrals in its fleet.

"I heard about you," he said. She clenched a bit at first and realized he must have gotten positive information or he wouldn't be calling. Turns out Jim Jensen was a buddy of his. Jensen was always spying for good talent, he said.

According to Jensen, Tris "did an amazing job in the simulator under difficult circumstances." Tris still didn't know what had gone on between Deter and Jensen, but if Jensen was impressed, she'd take it. She found it amusing that Jensen was lying in the weeds, looking to help his buddy do some pilot poaching.

"Someday on the road, you'll have to tell me all about it," he continued as if inviting Tris into her own conspiracy. She listened politely as the chief pilot tried to entice her to interview for a job at his company. "And we don't only go to Europe, like Tetrix, you know," he said brightly. It was true. The company had manufacturing facilities in Asia and South America. She would love to travel to those regions. She still might someday. But not in their airplanes.

Tris listened politely as he bulled on. "We're trying to integrate our department, Patricia. We've never had a woman—a qualified woman—and it's time."

Maybe, but I'm not that girl.

"Thanks so much. I'm in a good situation right now. Let's stay in touch." As soon as she said it, she realized she truly believed it. When she had first instructed, it was simply a way to build flight time, a means to an end. Tris had seen what the 'end' looked like up close and she liked this better.

"Need fuel?" one of the rampers asked, startling her from behind.

"We do. But I want to wait until my student gets back from his meeting. I want him to decide how much we need and do the order."

"Got it. Just let us know. Will you need anything else? Ice? Coffee?"

Cleary the ramper wasn't sure what airplane she was on. The flight school she worked for required instructors to wear uniform shirts with bars, so she could have been crewing one of the many corporate jets on the ramp instead of her student's single-engine Bonanza.

She was happy at the flight school, glad to be back in a job where she made a positive difference. The head of the school was thrilled to hire someone with so much experience. "We don't see too many primary instructors with type ratings around here," he'd said when he offered her the job.

It was almost noon, and Tris was ready for lunch. There was a restaurant on the field, a diner whose greatest claim was its view of the runways. It was less than a mile away, but she wasn't going to walk to it in her uniform in the heat. She'd ask the van driver to take her.

She began packing up. All of a sudden, the ether around her shifted. It was barely perceptible at first, just a slight swing in wind direction and speed. As seconds passed, it grew stronger. Tris became part of it. She smiled as her shoulders relaxed under the touch of his invisible hand—sensations she knew with and by heart.

As he stood beside her, Tris closed her eyes to be with him again. In his unmistakable tone and timbre, a huge smile on his face, Bron greeted her in their common language.

"Good morning, Captain."

ACKNOWLEDGMENTS

I wrote this book at least 30 times. At the end, at the very end, when I had a finished product for publication, I realized that I'd strung together a bunch of words in a sequence that no one else had ever thought of before. And that, friends, is the only thing I take credit for.

This book's journey started over twenty years ago when I began jotting down notes about some of the stranger things I'd seen and heard as a corporate pilot. But it wasn't until I discovered the Novel Writing Certificate program at San Diego Writers, Ink. in 2015 that it became a real book.

Carol Pope was one of my first readers, and has been a fan of Tris long before that was my protagonist's name. (I'm not going to tell you what it used to be. Best left in deleted items.) Dan Trujillo, a writer and high school principal became one of my subject matter experts and helped me give context to Tris's decision to leave teaching.

Thanks to my military experts, Ed Gallagher, LTC, USAF (ret) and Corry Jeudeman Prestidge, CDR, USN (ret), both pilots. I have nothing but the highest regard for those who serve. Thanks Ed and Corry for what you selflessly gave to our country, and for helping me understand what it was truly like to be in the military flying game.

Ed and his wife Chris Gallagher, along with Mary O'Tousa, Bette Barnett, Deak Wooten, Mitchell Kardon and Martha Kardon were early readers. Authors E.P

Sery, Lois Letchford, Bruce Ashkenas, Mikel J. Wilson and Sam Ashkenas read later versions, as did Kay Collier, Barbara Shaw and Theresa Freese. All of your critique were invaluable.

Christina Munro, an Air Traffic Controller at Southern California TRACON, made sure I used correct phraseology when quoting ATC. My longtime friend Rosalind Heinemann schooled me on proper simulator procedure, and has always been my cheerleader in any endeavor I've pursued in or out of the cockpit.

I was a member of two read and critique groups through San Diego Writers, Ink. The first was a general fiction group, where I received useful insights. The second was a Master Workshop where I was truly fortunate to work with two-time author Jill G. Hall and YA novelist Dina Koutas. Their suggestions helped bring this book in for a landing. The final content edit performed by Holly Kammier made sure that landing was a 'greaser.'

Holly and Jessica Therrien, my publishers at Acorn Publishing, LLC, gave this story a home. I am so proud to be a part of what they are building. Acorn author Lois Letchford introduced me to Zan Strumfeld. Zan became an invaluable resource in so many areas I've lost count. In all respects she is my "right-hand-Zan!"

In the end, there is always one person without whom no book would exist. For this book, and for me, that person is novelist T. (Tammy) Greenwood.

Tammy taught the courses in novel writing craft that gave me the tools to finish this book. She proctored both the read and critique group and Master Workshop I was a part of, providing her thoughts and suggestions at every turn. She performed two full developmental edits of this book that helped me to understand how I could better reach my readers. If I had a question, Tammy had the answer. Thank you, Tammy, from the tip of my pen to the bottom of my heart. Nothin' without ya.

ABOUT THE AUTHOR

Studio Bijou Photography

Robin D. "R.D." Kardon is a native New Yorker, educated in the New York City Public school system. She attended New York University where she earned a B.A. in Journalism and Sociology, *magna cum laude,* and was a member of Phi Beta Kappa. Robin graduated with a J.D. from the American University, Washington College of Law.

After ten years as a litigator, Robin began her professional flying career. She holds an FAA Airline Transport Pilot certificate with three captain qualifications and has flown all over the world in everything from single-engine Cessnas to the Boeing 737.

She currently resides in San Diego where she volunteers with local animal rescue organizations and dotes on her beloved rescue pets.

Follow Robin at
rdkardonauthor.com
@rdkardonauthor